REBWAR

PLAN B

OLS SCHABER

PROLOGUE

Beckse was moving around some of the decorative plastic flowers in the large flat which overlooked Colliers Wood tube station and beyond up to London. She checked her watch and stepped up to a mirror to add some more lipstick to her already plump red lips. Adjusted her black pencil skirt and opened one more button on her blouse. A knock at the door. She took a deep breath and went over to open it. A girl with a wide smile and curly red hair greeted her.

'Mum! So glad to see you.' Behind her were three guys and a girl.

'Daisy, so good you could come—'

'Wow, what a gaff, is it yours?' Daisy walked past her with the others following in, the last presenting himself.

'James Hewitt-Thomas pleasure to meet you.'

Charlie studied him. He was tall, wore a black v-neck jumper and white shirt with grey suit trousers. 'Nice, you could make it. Please sit down.' The others were more eclectic. Daisy checked out the large flat like an excited child, picking up decorative statues and checking out the framed pictures. 'Anyone fancy a drink? I have some bubbly.'

'What are we celebrating?' Asked one of them.

'You are?'

'Sorry Mum, got carried away.' Daisy stood in front of them. 'The Filthy Five.' She smiled and turned to one of them. 'Henry Trent.' Who raised his hand; looked rugged, his jet black hair was tied into a pony tail, and a limp. 'Pinky Knight.' Who had bright pink hair with her left side being shaved back, a pretty face with a nose piercing. 'Joseph Brunje.' Ginger hair, heavy set with tattoos and by his straight stance was ex-military. 'And you've met James—'

'What's the offer?' Said Hewitt-Thomas walking up to Charlie.

'Please all sit and I'll explain.' Charlie got a bottle of Champagne from the fridge and handed over to Daisy and told her to serve it. Charlie went into one of the bedrooms and came out with a sports holdall.

'What, are we going to play tennis.' Said Trent. 'I've got a doctor's note.' And he rolled up his left jean's leg to reveal a prosthetic leg.

Charlie put the bag on the long glass coffee table and opened it up. It was filled with cash. A couple whistled and Trent laughed.

'She wasn't joking.' Hewitt-Thomas picked up one of the wads. 'And what's the catch?'

'I need your services.'

'And you are? Said Trent.

'I'm paying for you not to ask questions. I pay and I get results.'

'Oh Mum—'

'Daisy,' Charlie held up her index finger at her. 'We talked about this. This is the rules, we don't talk about this, you don't contact me, I contact you, no questions. I know all your dirty pasts and secrets, OK.' Charlie turned to Brunje. 'Ex Dutch Military and your employer fired you, been doing odd jobs here and there.' She walked passed him. 'Hewitt-Thomas bored posh boy looking for adventures, dropped out of school, uni and now an estate agent. Pinky Knight music student drop out, likes the dope, a little too much.' Stopped in front of Trent. 'And you lost your leg in a motorbike accident as a courier—'

'Prescription meds.' He rattled a plastic container at her.

'Now Daisy made all this possible...'

They looked at each other and Daisy smiled and shrugged at them.

'A bunch of misfits who like money.' Charlie took out a piece of paper from her jacket and laid on the table.

Hewitt-Thomas picked it up and read it. 'Who are these people?'

'I want you to start with Jack Hill. Convince him to find another vocation.'

'OK, and Anthony Peckworth... MP?'

Daisy got up, took the list and walked up to Charlie. 'What's all this about?'

'Money, patience and like I said, no questions.'

'Why should we trust you? I don't know you from Eve.' Said Knight.

'There door is there if anyone is in doubt.'

Daisy smiled at them, and they all stared at the money.

Charlie raised her glass. 'To a lot more of this.'

Trent laughed and raised his glass.

Hewitt-Thomas stood up. 'Fuck it, this is mad and I love it.' He raised his glass, and downed the Champagne.

'I'm going to have to leave, but here is a little something.'

Charlie put a small plastic bag with white powder on the glass table. 'Close the door on your way out.' Charlie walked over to Daisy. 'Hon have fun and we'll talk tomorrow. Love you.' And she kissed her on the lips and walked out.

ONE

Rebwar was driving his Toyota Prius on the south side of the River Thames towards the House of Commons. The roads were clogging up and his sat nav was telling him to take an alternative route. He looked into his rear-view mirror at his passenger. Jack Hill was wearing round black-rimmed glasses; and Rebwar put him as an intellectual who from his acne-scarred cheeks had only recently left university. He was shifting about, another impatient passenger that needed to be somewhere. He pulled at Rebwar's seat. 'Mate, mate, how far are we from the river?'

Rebwar noticed Hill's hand had a ring with a skull on it. He looked at his sat nav and pinched the screen to get an overview. He put on his reading glasses to get a better look. 'With this traffic... ten, twenty minutes.'

'Fuck.' Hill clenched his fist like he had a rubber ball in it. 'What do you think? Can I walk it?'

'About the same, I would say. What's the rush? Smoke?' Rebwar showed him a cigarette.

'Sorry... No, no, and it doesn't bother me...' Hill looked down at his smartphone. 'Some bloody demo... Ah, the fucking idiots!' And he shook his head, smiling. 'Can you believe it? They're throwing dead fish into the Thames.'

'Why would anybody do that?'

'Nigel.' Rebwar looked at him and Hill rolled his eyes in disappointment. 'You know... Brexit man, Nigel Farage.'

'Why would they be throwing fish? You don't waste food! It's a sin where I come from.'

'It's not clever, I agree. Just makes good headlines.'

'So you work for those fake news newspapers?' Hill's slight frame jumped in a silent laugh. 'Tell me where you want to be dropped off. I don't think we're going to get close to the water.'

'What made you come over here?'

'Job and a better life.'

'Is it?'

Rebwar nodded and slowly moved another few inches in the traffic.

'What do you think about all this Brexit?' said Rebwar.

'A Tory issue that has infected the nation like Chernobyl's radiation. Just ask anyone and you'll get another answer for what it should be.'

'Government conspiracy, richer getting richer and poorer getting poorer. At least you can say what you want in this country. Which paper do you work for? I'll look out for your articles.'

'Mate, I'm freelance. Mostly blogs, I sometimes sell a story or two. Have you got any?'

'Stories? Me? Just an Uber driver. I like the simple life.'

Two police bikes drove by with their sirens bouncing off the surrounding high-rise buildings.

'Well, I'm sure you have some. That face holds many stories. I can tell, mate. Sure, you could tell me a few. Where did you come from?'

'Iran.' Rebwar chose not to give him too much to go on, as he could tell he had desperation in his eyes. And he didn't trust the press as they all had an agenda.

'Ah, can't fool you! Something like a copper? I'm sure. You look around too much. Or *Savak*[1]?'

'*Savak!*' Rebwar laughed. 'Every rich Persian says he has worked for them, old school.' Hill smiled. 'Like you lot like to say you worked for MI6. Everybody wants to be James Bond.' Rebwar looked into his rear-view mirror. Like his son, Musa, Hill was glued to his mobile phone. '*Vaja*, they're the ones you have to lookout for.'

'Shit, it's all kicking off. I need to rush. Nice talking to you.' Hill opened his door and ran out of the car. Hill tried to run while looking at his phone and trying to keep his bag from bouncing off his shoulder. It was as if he was trying to keep a bouncing dog off him.

Rebwar confirmed the end of the cab ride, took out another cigarette and wound the window down. Traffic was crawling and drivers were starting to lose patience. Horns blared around him. He rested his arm on the window ledge and enjoyed the sun. He put on one of his CD mixes, a classic Iranian pop song filled the car – 'Do Parandeh', by Neli, and it made him smile. She had performed during the era of the Shah and was banned by Khomeini – like all women singers. He'd heard that she had moved to England and become a dentist. His wife, Hourieh, had mentioned that she was on Facebook.

Facebook was something that he had avoided; he found this social network a waste of time. Why live in another world? Make this one better. He would tell this to his son Musa when he was staring into his phone. That said, Raj, Rebwar's IT expert, had found some amazing facts and leads for his cases using social networks, Rebwar was content to leave him to it.

His phone flashed, asking him to take another fare. It took him a few moments to think about it. He was still stuck in traffic and the client was only going to moan about it. He confirmed it anyway. Ten minutes later he picked up his next client: a slim and pretty brunette in a dark blue suit. She sat down in the back.

She waved a hand at all the congestion. 'What's going on?'

'They are throwing fish into the Thames.'

'Oh, for fishing?'

'No, protesting. Brexit.'

'For fuck's sake, haven't they got better things to do? Why?'

Rebwar shrugged his shoulders.

TWO

Geraldine and Beckie walked out of the Curzon cinema on Shaftesbury Avenue in Soho. Beckie threaded her arm through Geraldine's and both were laughing, enjoying each other's company. The pavements were wet and the heavy traffic was peeling off the wet tarmac of its darkness. Both of them looked up at the dark orange night sky and ran off, trying to avoid the raindrops. Geraldine pushed open the old wooden door of the Coach & Horses, a pub just behind the cinema. Packed with tourists and locals, its small square windows had steamed up. The wooden panels and odd pictures of caricatures brought back a lost era. It felt post war, and Geraldine thought of her gran drinking her Guinness.

Beckie was leaning on the bar. 'What do you want?'

'More of you.'

Beckie smiled. 'I mean drink.'

'Something like you. Dark, sensual, smooth and filling.'

'Oh, is that what you think of me?'

'Come on, girls,' said the barman. 'Haven't got all day.'

'Guinness and a large white wine,' said Geraldine.

'Oh, yeah, fine. Just take the lead then. It's my round.'

'I can guess who's wearing the trousers,' said the barman.

'Sorry, B. Just feeling a bit thirsty.' Geraldine grabbed her closer and kissed her and whispered in her ear, 'Still not ready to be a lesbian?' Beckie looked around and took a small step back from the bar.

'Twelve fifty, please.'

Geraldine looked at the drinks and took a moment to process what the man was asking for, smiled and reached for her card. The man presented the card machine. She tapped the card on the screen which gave long beep. 'Going to have to ask for a raise.'

Beckie brushed back her hair from her face. 'Did you like the movie?'

'Bit soppy for me. Prefer action.'

'Why didn't you say so?'

Geraldine handed her the wine. 'Cheers to us.' And they clinked their glasses. That first smooth cold sip stopped time and brought a mix of fond memories of lazy Sundays drinking Guinness. She looked at Beckie's warm glowing face. Such a happy smile and that olive skin that she was eager to kiss. Her shirt buttons had been undone to show her white bra. It was a game of how many buttons she could undo till she got caught.

'You should tell me these things. I want to know all about you.'

Geraldine grabbed her waist.

'And not just that. You're a naughty monkey.'

'What's wrong?'

'Nothing.'

'Come on, tell me.'

'Stop being such a copper.'

'I'll put you in cuffs if you're not careful.' Geraldine looked around to see if there were any keen ears about.

'You scoping for criminals?'

Geraldine took a large gulp of her Guinness and then wiped the foam off her top lip with the sleeve of her black bomber jacket. She brought out a pack of cigarettes and rattled it in front of her. She spotted a moment of disappointment on Beckie's face before she left her pint, went outside and lit up. She peered around at the other smokers – all blokes hiding from the rain. Geraldine looked through the misted windows to see Beckie at the bar. They had met in a morgue when Geraldine was still going out with Zara. And since then, it had been an on and off relationship that both had given the status of *it's complicated*. Beckie was on her phone. Something was bothering her, but she wasn't giving it away. She didn't want to ask either, as she knew it would be something about Beckie's husband and Geraldine wanted some escape.

'Got some money for me?'

Beside her was a scruffy man with his hand out. His white hair had a dirty yellow tinge to it and his face was covered in a film of Soho grime. His forced smile revealed a few stray teeth. She dug in her pockets for some loose change and handed him what she had.

'What I am going to do with that?'

For a moment Geraldine didn't know what to say. 'It's money.'

'Fucking liberty.' And he walked away.

Geraldine looked back and Beckie was no longer at the bar. Her wine glass was standing empty next to her own pint of Guinness. She flicked her cigarette into the gutter, went back into the pub and scanned around for the toilets. They were on the opposite side of the pub. She took another gulp of her beer and crossed over, apologising as she squeezed through the crowds. Geraldine wondered what she would find. Had Beckie gone home? Gone back to her man? She took a deep breath and pushed the door. A thin blonde girl was in front of a mirror patching up her make-up. Opposite were two cubicles, one of which had its door closed. Beckie was wearing black suede heels, but Geraldine couldn't see the shoes under the door. The blonde girl stared at her in the mirror as she did her make-up. Geraldine knocked on the cubicle door. 'Becks, are you all right?' The girl looked over and there was a moment of silence. Geraldine knocked again. 'Who's in there?' Geraldine asked the girl, who just shrugged her shoulders. 'Becks?'

'Will you stop following me like a lost puppy,' Beckie said.

The girl left.

'I'm worried about you.' Geraldine bent down to try to look under the door. She spotted a hankie. 'You're crying.'

'Can't a girl have some peace? For fuck's sake, G, leave me alone. I... I...'

Geraldine tried to push the door to see if it would open. She searched in all her pockets until she found a two-pound coin. She used it to open the lock.

'What the fuck!'

Geraldine darted inside and locked the door again behind her. She leaned on the white tiles over Beckie, who sat with her mascara running down her cheeks and her skirt and panties around her ankles. Geraldine grabbed her soft face and kissed her. At first Beckie tried to push her away. But the longer and deeper she kissed, the tension melted like butter over a hot pan. Her body giving itself to her. Beckie's arms wrapped themselves around Geraldine's waist and legs and hugged her closer.

Someone walked in and got into the cubicle next door. They stopped kissing. They both smiled and tried not to giggle. Beckie held her hands over her ears, not wanting to hear the noises coming from the next toilet. Geraldine held her nose instead and Beckie giggled a little. A phone vibrated. Geraldine searched her jacket and took hers out. It wasn't the one that was ringing, so she slid it back. Beckie looked at her like a rabbit in the headlights. Geraldine reached down onto the floor for Beckie's phone, which was in her back pocket and took up the call.

'Hello?'

Beckie tried to take the phone off Geraldine.

'Yes... Aha, yep... No this is Geraldine...' And she hung up.

'What the fuck!' Beckie laughed. 'You're crazy... let me guess, work calling?'

Geraldine had stopped breathing for that moment.

'Oh, wait OK, G! What the fuck, babe, who was it? Really, who was it?' Beckie grabbed the phone and looked at the number.

Geraldine looked into Beckie's eyes. 'Was that him?'

'Yeah, but that's different. Not fair. Come on, babes. He...'

'Oh, fuck off!' Geraldine walked out of the cubicle. A girl washing her hands looked at the two of them. Geraldine pushed her out of the way and walked out of the toilet.

THREE

'You stink of alcohol. Good night?'

Geraldine was sitting in the back of Rebwar's cab. It was new, but already smelled of cigarettes, it made her want one. She took a deep breath to take stock. It had been a long night and not one she wanted to talk about or particularly remember. Rebwar handed her a cigarette. She hesitated for a microsecond and then took it. The smoke helped. Rebwar put on some of his music, which made her smile. This was a little weird eastern cocoon that felt warm and far away from the rest of London. And she had missed him.

He laughed.

'What's so funny?'

'You are, and your heavy heart. Got a visa for me?'

'Fuck off.'

He laughed again, a deep smoker's laugh like someone walking through gravel.

'Job. That's what I've got for you.'

He stopped laughing and took a drag on his cigarette. Geraldine thought back to the last time they had met. Reality had sunk in and there was a moment of silence. Plan

B had gone quiet, very quiet, and now there was something new. They hadn't really talked about Daisy or O'Neil. They both knew it would come back at some point, as everything does. The canal boat that had exploded and killed O'Neil had been reported as a boat fire. There had been no mention of their names, just that four people had been killed in a gang-related fight. The whole story of O'Neil going rogue and setting up an illegal immigration ring had been hushed up. Neither Geraldine nor Rebwar had found out how Plan B had been involved with O'Neil. The last contact they had with them was with the Badger who had taken custody of Daisy, who was the daughter of Sir John Merkenstand. A billionaire who had been seriously injured in a helicopter crash.

Like old friends, things clicked back as if nothing had changed. But it had been nearly a year since they had seen each other.

'Go on, tell me then? What is it?'

Geraldine shook her head. 'Something new and different.' She passed the manila envelope forward, and he took it. She leaned back on the seat and looked out of the window. Drops were running down the window to the sound of light drumming on the car roof. She could see a children's playground in a small park surrounded by blocks of council flats. The Shard towered behind them like a needle disappearing into a cloud. Going up the Shard was something she had wanted to do with Beckie but twenty-five quid each for a view. That was a bit steep, and she'd heard that the viewing area was open to the elements. What if it rained? Did you get a refund?

'Why did we meet here?' Rebwar said. 'Is someone following us?'

'Oh, long story. Read the job sheet.' Geraldine heard

the shuffling of paper and saw smoke swirling around. 'Weird, hey?'

'Different. And two jobs? Are they running out of cheap detectives?'

Geraldine watched two young kids running through the playground and couldn't work out if they were chasing each other or going somewhere. Usually by now, she would have been to a pub and been clubbing and feeling ready for sleep. It was 7 am. This stuff wasn't urgent, either, she could have sat on it, as she usually did, she liked to organise work and then some fun. But she needed a change of scene.

'So a surveillance job and check out a burgled flat,' Rebwar mused. 'Burgled? And a weird name. You know this man, Anthony Peckworth?'

'No, who's he?'

Rebwar read the brief. 'Says a politician for the Labour Party.'

'I don't like the sound of that.'

'You didn't read it?'

'Wasn't in the mood. What are they playing at?'

'And there is money. Need some?'

For a moment Geraldine wanted to grab a few notes. She was a little low on funds. 'Shit. That'll teach me not to open the envelope!'

Rebwar turned in his seat to face her. 'Go on... have some. I can tell you want to from those hungry eyes.' He left a nice chunk on her lap. As she took it, muffled voices passed by; it was two young men whose footfalls resonated off the brick walls. They were suited and booted and probably coming back from the night shift in the city. How long that was going to last with Brexit ongoing was anybody's guess. She put her hand on Rebwar's shoulder and he held it. She wanted to cry.

'You seeing someone?'

'Why are you asking? Rocky marriage?'

'Oh, the usual. No, you look tired and...'

'And?'

'Look, I need to start my shift. Want a lift somewhere?'

Geraldine let that question sit with her. She wasn't too sure what mood she was in. 'Find me a pub.'

'At this time? Oh...'

'What?'

'Job... It's Charlie... I have to tail your boss.'

Geraldine sat back down and exhaled. 'Fuck off! Really. What does it say, go on?'

Rebwar flicked through the files. 'Didn't Charlie pass this on?'

'Got it delivered by a courier.'

'It says to follow her, see what she gets up to during the day. Surveillance. Maybe you should tell her.'

'Fuck a duck sideways! What's going on?' Geraldine grabbed the envelope and looked for further clues about who had sent it. She leaned back and looked out of the window. 'You think we're being watched?' She bit into her fist.

FOUR

Rebwar was on the sofa reading last month's newspaper. It had a few stories from home: an Aseman Airlines had crashed into the Zagros Mountains killing all sixty-six passengers, with bad weather being a possible factor; a three-year-old report had been published that said forty-nine per cent of Iranians were against the compulsory veil. Rebwar skipped quickly to the back for the football news. It had been a while since he'd watched Persepolis play, and he was wondering how they were doing, from the headline they had lost to Esteghial. Hourieh walked in wearing a grey tracksuit bottom and had taken off some of her jewellery. There was still enough on her to pay four months' rent.

'Husband!'

Rebwar looked up. 'Yes, my desert flower.' He noticed she had on an old shirt with some colourful abstract patterns.

'You know that list in the kitchen?'

Rebwar nodded.

'As we discussed, you need to do some of those things.'

Rebwar put the newspaper down and took the smouldering cigarette off the edge of the ashtray. 'And take Musa. He's done his homework, so he might as well do something useful instead of playing those annoying games. Can't you take him to the football?'

Rebwar got up, adjusted his trousers and went over to kiss her forehead. 'It's called growing up. They do that.'

Hourieh tutted and went back into the bedroom. Rebwar glanced in: she was clearing out boxes. Her phone rang and she picked it up.

'Dinah! Nice to hear from you... Yes, a moment...' Hourieh went over to the door and closed it.

For a moment Rebwar wanted to listen in, but instead went into the kitchen to look at the list on the fridge. It comprised the things that annoyed them as a family. The top one was the graffiti. Back in Teheran graffiti was considered social media, each gang making their mark on their territory and proclaiming who was in and who wasn't. Here it was more vandalism – or that's how they saw it. Rebwar hadn't mentioned that they were going to paint over tags made by gangs.

———

Rebwar and Musa were outside by a wall that led down into the underground garage of the Dorney Building. This was part of the Chalcots estate in Chalk Farm, a twenty-three-storey tower block built by the council in the sixties and evacuated after the Grenfell Tower disaster because it had the same flammable cladding. It had been removed but the council still hadn't replaced it.

'Dad, can I get a cigarette?'

Rebwar shook his head and put down a tub of white

paint. Musa was holding some brushes and another container. He noticed Musa's t-shirt, which said: *If you can read this my invisibility cloak isn't working.*

'Hey, you twos!'

Rebwar looked up to see a fat lady with a pram staring at them. She was young and her blonde hair was flat and greasy. At some point in her life she must have been pretty.

'Yous not from the council, are you? It's their job, you know.'

'It's been over three months. They haven't done a thing. Have you called them?'

'Uh... Yeah. It's their bloody job and we pay all that council tax. Don't let them get away with it. Do you hear me? Leave it alone. They'll get lazy. You know what I mean.'

'Look, Mrs? I can't wait that long. You have to take care of your home. Can't expect other people to do everything, can you, Mrs?'

'Look, mate... I pay my council tax and taxes and I've got enough shit to deal with. I'm too busy, right? Don't have any time for this. I'm calling the council.'

'Sure, sure move on. Come on, Musa, open those tins and let's get going.' Rebwar took a step back and looked at the graffiti tags. Some were letters spelling some kind of acronym others were swear words. Probably describing their moods. Musa started on the far end. Rebwar looked over and saw a crescent moon with IS written underneath it. He stared at it as Musa painted over it. 'Musa!'

Musa carried on painting it and ignored him.

Rebwar went over to him and pulled off his head-phones. He took a few steps back and studied the graffiti. 'You know who did these, don't you.'

'What are you talking about?'

'The one you just covered. Was it yours?'

Musa looked up and dipped his brush in his white paint.

'Son, these are your mates, aren't they?'

'Don't know what you're talking about.'

'Son, I've got a photo of this. I know your handwriting.'

'I... I... was made to do it.'

'Who?'

'I'm not grassing.'

'Well, I am going to get them. OK?'

'Dad, please... it's going to make trouble.'

'And where is this going to stop? And then it's this and then that.'

'But it was... Dad... sorry.'

'You carry on and I'm going to talk to your friends.' Rebwar put his brush down and went looking for them. He'd seen them with Musa outside. There were four to five of them. Two of them had a scooter and they took turns to go for little joy rides. Musa hadn't really said what they got up to and Rebwar had turned a blind eye; he wanted him to learn to trust him. But now some light intervention was needed. He found them by the Bray Tower.

'Hi, guys.'

The four nodded and looked back down to their phones. Two of them had headphones. One laughed and nudged his elbow into the guy next to him.

'Hey? Need to chat.'

The taller one with short red hair and freckles took off his headphones. He had clear blue eyes and wore a black hoodie and grey tracksuit bottoms with white trainers. 'What's up?' He lifted his hand like he was going to greet him like some rapper. 'You Musa's dad, yo. Hey, brovs, this ya is Mus's old man. Legit. Yo.'

The other three turned to him and fist bumped each other. Rebwar stood there measuring them up, looking at their postures and faces.

Black Hoodie smiled. 'Man, you intense. Get me?'

'I'm here about the graffiti.'

'Business, man. That's our marketing. Yeah, brov.'

'Business,' repeated the freckled one. 'Yeah, man.'

'Well, it has to stop.'

'And let some other crew take our space?' said the taller one. 'No, brov, our cous' won't take that. And business is down.'

'OK, what are your names?'

'Travor the Terror,' said the shorter one, and lifted the bottom his hoodie to reveal a knife slipped behind his belt.

'Washington.' The tall one pressed his fist to Rebwar.

'Tommy,' said the freckled one.

Rebwar waited for the fourth one to introduce himself. He stood waiting for something. His hoodie didn't hide his weight. His round face wore a forced smile but his eyes showed it wasn't felt.

'You the boss?' said Rebwar.

Tommy laughed. It was followed by another moment of silence.

'Listen, I'm OK with your little business here. You'd just get replaced with another gang. Can't fight it. I understand. But let's have a little compromise. Can we find another wall? Or space...'

'How much?'

Rebwar looked at Washington.

'Brov, it's lost revenue, Business need to feed the family like you, brov. Otherwise my cous' will have to take... if you get my drift.'

FIVE

Rebwar arrived at Gardnor Mansions on Church Row in Hampstead. He'd decided to take on the less contentious job. He stepped back and studied the six-storey brick building. At the bottom was a lower ground floor basement and above was an attic with large windows. The front door was painted in a black gloss. He pressed the buzzer for Flat 7 and waited.

'Hello.'

'Mr Peckworth?'

'Speaking.'

'I'm from the insurance company.'

There was a moment of silence and the sound of fumbling. 'Insurance?'

'For the break-in?'

'Oh, yes, yes!'

The door buzzed and Rebwar walked in. The flat was on the third floor. He got there to see the door half open. Classical music played, some violins and piano. He knocked on the door as he pushed it open. He knocked again as the music crescendoed.

'Yes, yes! Come in!'

Rebwar walked into the hallway which had a series of paintings hanging on the walls. Between the paintings were doors that led to the other rooms. The scent of freshly cut flowers passed him. He noticed two of the paintings were of London: a street in Notting Hill, which was bright and colourful and showed a pub called the Commercial Tavern with people sitting outside it, it looked a little childish and cartoon-like and it was signed T. Cox; the other was smudged colours and cut-outs with some photographs stuck on the canvas and he couldn't see a signature.

'Yes, they left them,' Peckworth said, looking at the pictures. He was a tall man with short greying hair. His face was angular with a small chin that made him look a little meek. He wore a white shirt and a yellow silk tie. He smiled. 'Weird, I like them. They're probably worth... Oh, what would you say?'

This took Rebwar by surprise as he hadn't thought he was here to evaluate the property or what was taken. 'What did they take?'

Peckworth's gaze broke away from the painting. 'Oh, I'm miles away, where are my manners? Tony Peckworth, Labour MP for Exeter.'

They shook hands. 'Amir Begani.'

Peckworth waited for a moment for Rebwar to say more. 'What did they take?'

'Oh, Yes, yes. Oh, nothing of much value, just an old laptop, not even sure it worked. No idea what brand it was or anything. And not my work one either. Otherwise, you know...' He laughed nervously as Rebwar looked at him. He put up his hand to shield his mouth. 'A police matter and all that.' He laughed a bit more.

'I see. But did you report it?'

'Oh, do I have to? I'd rather not. Nothing of any value on it. Not of government value. Why have you come?'

Rebwar walked into the living room. It had a big cushioned sofa that matched the red and white striped chairs. The whole place had an air of grandness and reminded him of Bijan's palace. 'Is this place yours?'

'Why do you ask?' Peckworth looked at him with an air of puzzlement. Rebwar noticed that his face shone a bit. 'You see this is my uncle's pied-à-terre and he lets me have it when I'm in town from time to time. I really don't see why they sent you. It seems the excess won't cover it anyway.'

'Do you know how they got in?' Rebwar walked back into the hallway and over to the main door.

'I... don't. The door was just open.'

'Anyone else have keys. Family?' Rebwar inspected the locks. They weren't easy to pick – a deadlock and a fancy Chubb latch.

'I guess so, but why?'

'Drugs? Money?'

'Sorry?'

'Any of your family in trouble?'

'Oh... the usual, nothing that spectacular. Look Mr... Begani... there is nothing really to see. I have explained to you lot. Let's not take this matter further. It's a waste of time – and your time, too.'

'Can I get a glass of water?'

'Oh... yes, sure.' Peckworth walked off into the kitchen.

Rebwar saw a sign of two drill holes in the door that had been painted over. He could hear Peckworth running a tap and grumbling to himself. He came back with a glass of water and Rebwar gulped it down. 'When did someone drill through the door?' He pointed at the two holes.

'Oh, haven't noticed that. No idea. Must be old, don't you think? Been painted.'

'They could have made it.'

'What? And you think they tidied up after themselves?'

'Is there an alarm?'

'Oh, yes, the alarm. Here it is.' He pointed at a keypad by the door.

Rebwar looked at it. 'Can you switch it on?'

'It is.'

'Now.'

'What do you mean?'

'You don't use it, do you?'

'Now, that's not strictly true. I do.'

'When?'

'Look, like I said...' Peckworth took Rebwar's glass away. 'It's not worth taking time over this. If you need more information just call me.' He looked at his watch, which had a nice crocodile strap on it and looked antique. 'I have a meeting that I must attend. *Must.*' Peckworth held the door, looking eager to shut it again.

'I do have more questions. Were you in?'

'Now, Mr Begani, I must ask you to leave.'

'Did you see them?'

'Just call me! So sorry to be rude but you must now leave! This is private property, Mr Begani. Please leave. Otherwise–'

'Call the police? I can help.'

Peckworth held his hand up to him and breathed out. 'Please, leave. I must insist.'

Rebwar backed out and heard the door close. He stood there looking at it and for a moment wanted to ring the bell. He thought back to his notes. He'd only visited Peckworth to look around and report. He could tell that the man was hiding something. For a moment, he thought of coming back and having another go. But that wasn't the job. He turned around to see a woman walk down the stairs. She was dressed in a suit with a knee-length skirt and her hair was tied up. She looked up. Rebwar said hello and she continued to walk past. Again for a moment, he wanted to ask some questions. He shook his head and followed her downstairs. She didn't even hold the door open for him. She put her sunglasses on and walked off down the road. Rebwar took out a cigarette and looked up at the flat.

SIX

Geraldine was holding a bunch of flowers she'd taken from an office reception that she'd visited a few hours before. The receptionist had been suffering from hay fever. They looked colourful and smelled sweet but she hadn't a clue about their type. Geraldine breathed in and took the scent in again and felt Beckie swirl around her head. Her heart felt light and powerful, even if the grey overcast sky was trying to flatten the world. A glass door opened in front of her and with it reality. She was at Beckie's office. The smell of death had already hit her. How in the world did she end up going out with a forensic pathologist? She couldn't stand the sight of a morgue.

Beckie's office was empty. Just her laptop and an open drawer. She put the flowers in a large beaker that was on a shelf, then looked around. She could smell Beckie's sweet scent – she had just missed her. Her suit jacket was on the back of her office chair. She took the flowers and the glass beaker to the bathroom, filled the glass and looked at herself in the mirror. She still felt that she was punching above her weight. What had Beckie seen in her? She spotted a pair of legs slumped under the cubicle and went over to push the door. It was locked. She fumbled in her pockets looking for a coin to open the catch.

Beckie's body was sprawled in front of her. She had a needle in her arm.

'Becks! B! Wake up! Babe, hey, get up!' Geraldine slapped her – nothing. *Fuck, fuck. Think, think.* Geraldine ran back to Beckie's office, opened the medical cabinet. Her eyes scanned around frantically and on the third pass she found what she was looking for and darted back. She ripped the packaging, took out a shot of Naloxone, undid the protective sheath and plunged the needle into Beckie's shoulder. Pressed the plunger and tapped her cheeks. Beckie inhaled, and her eyes flicked around. Geraldine smiled and she too breathed in. Then took the syringe and needle from Beckie's arm and slipped it into her pocket. She lifted Beckie onto the toilet seat and closed the door. 'What is it with toilets, heh?' She felt the pulse on Beckie's neck and kissed her. She breathed deeply, her eyes still rolling around. Geraldine hugged her. 'Why? Why?'

'G...' Beckie breathed. 'Fuck, I'm–'

'Shhh... don't talk.' Geraldine kissed her and opened the cubicle. She took the flowers from the glass beaker, rinsed it and filled it with some freshwater and made Beckie drink it. 'Can you walk? We need to sort you out.' She lifted Beckie and put one of her arms over her shoulder. Geraldine scanned the hallway. It was empty. She had a story ready, one of feeling sick. Which here with all the dead bodies around was kind of plausible. They stumbled back to Beckie's office. Beckie looked white, drained. Geraldine made her a strong coffee. On the third sip she was sitting and moving.

Geraldine pulled Beckie's short hair. 'Becks, why?'

'Oh, G... I'm so sorry.' Tears dripped down her cheeks.

Geraldine squeezed her hand. It felt like a piece of cold chicken. 'How long? You should have told me.'

'Oh, please, don't. It's a... oh.' And Beckie bent over and sobbed into her hands.

Geraldine put her hand on Beckie's back. 'You have to tell me if something is wrong. I am a copper... if you had forgotten.' She scanned Beckie's desk, looking for any clues. What she really needed to see was her phone or her laptop. This wasn't in character. Beckie wasn't an addict of any sort. She took out the syringe and put it on her desk. 'You know this feels more like a cry for help.'

Beckie looked at it.

Geraldine took her arm and rolled her sleeve, looking for more marks. There were none. 'Who did this to you? Beckie, you are going to have to tell me. Otherwise, I am going to have to tell. I can't have you like this. I love you... you know that.' *There.* She had said it, and for a moment she could feel the silence hanging like a deflating balloon.

Beckie's eyes fixed on Geraldine. 'I love you too.'

SEVEN

Rebwar turned off the North Circular into a run-down industrial estate. Old units with broken and faded signs lined the rutted road. At the end was Circular Motors Ltd. He parked his Prius just outside the unit. A man with a welding helmet was cutting away a panel from a car with a blowtorch. Rebwar stepped inside the workspace. Car parts were lying around – worn tyres, rusting tools, and in the middle was a big car jack. Sparks bounced along the cracked concrete floor. Then the car's panel dropped and smoke escaped. The man flipped up the screen of the helmet and stood up. His hair had grey streaks, he had thick-lensed glasses and wore a blue grease-stained overall that stretched over his belly.

'Rebwar! Good to see you!' He stretched out his thick greasy hand.

Rebwar shook it. 'Barry–'

'Let me guess... another vandal? Wait, wait...' Barry closed his eyes. 'Keyed? Wait, no, no. Cracked lights? You got me.'

'My son needs a job.'

'Your son? Shouldn't he be at school studying?'

'You don't need to pay him. Just get him to do small jobs. Cleaning, or making tea.'

'Want one?'

'Coffee?'

Barry turned and walked to the back of the garage. 'Are you sure? I mean... really I'm no master mechanic.'

Rebwar went into the small back room which contained a couple of chairs with soiled and ripped fabrics, old car posters, a 1996 calendar showing a naked woman, a desk with oily paperwork. Barry went next door where he ran a tap. 'Take a seat. Look, I can't promise anything but you're a good customer. What's his name?'

'Musa. Fifteen and needs something to do. Plays too many computer games. Studying is not his thing. And I need to get him off the streets, you know.'

'Yeah, back in my day you could leave all the doors open. Kids would be running around the streets. Now ice cream vans deliver drugs. It's gone to pot.'

Rebwar took out a pack of cigarettes and offered one.

Barry brought out a Skol beer branded ashtray and two dull white cups. 'Must say, I need some help.'

'Where's Florian?'

Barry lit his cigarette and slouched on the chair behind his desk. 'Left. Went back home, didn't he.' His big magnified eyes looked up. 'Brexit!'

'Has it happened?'

'Happening or you'd think so. Couldn't take my jokes no more, that's what I think. Didn't feel welcome any longer, he said.'

'Hire another one?'

Barry sipped his tea. 'Can't find anyone or they all want too much money. Look, he can come... what days?'

'Any day. After school.'

'Yeah, OK. You know I thought... Oh, I don't know, mate. Thinking of jacking it all in. Not the same. Take my caravan and drive it to Europe. Florian did say I could visit. So how's business?'

'Busy. And clients always know of a better route and want to get there quicker. One even said he would pay for the traffic fine. But good car.'

'Yeah, popular with you lot. Giving the old black ones a run for their money. Soon they're going to have to change them too. Electric! Can you believe it? Too much change. That's what's wrong, Rebwar. Need to slow down. So, tell me about Musa.'

'He's a nice boy. Just needs a kick up the ass. When I was his age...' Rebwar stopped himself. 'It was a different place.'

'What, Iran?'

'Yes and you British were there.'

'Were we? Maybe I'll go and visit there too.'

Rebwar laughed.

EIGHT

Rebwar drove to his second and very questionable Plan B assignment. It had kept him up and he had tried to discuss it with Geraldine. The brief was marked 'Top Secret' and was simple: *Follow the movements of Charlie Atkins, code name the Ferret.* It was unnerving and disturbing. How was this going to be kept a secret from Charlie? She knew both of them. And he was sure they were monitoring him. Why hadn't they simply given the job to a fresh face? Rebwar had bought a shoulder-length brown wig, black-rimmed glasses and a baseball cap.

He turned into Dolphin Square, a massive 1930s bricked apartment complex with a couple of entrances, the main one being on Grosvenor Road, facing the Thames. He decided to stake out Chichester Street where the back entrance and the Spa was. Rebwar figured that the tube station was closer to the back entrance than the front one and that if she took public transport to work, that would be her preferred exit.

The file had Charlie's name, address and a picture which looked like it was taken from a social media profile.

She was smiling with a sunny beach behind her. Rebwar had done a quick search on his phone and found a few links to her LinkedIn profile. She worked for a data company called Persious in Holborn. That picture was a portrait of her with mid-length brown hair and rectangular black glasses that contrasted with her round face. He wasn't sure if it was all a front, but the Plan B operatives he had met, all had a day job.

What wasn't mentioned anywhere was that Charlie, aka the Ferret, was Geraldine's contact. She had been her contact for over a year and when they last met, she had taken Daisy Merkenstand into Plan B's custody. Rebwar wasn't sure what had happened to her and where Daisy was. Charlie had also been involved in a financial scandal, which is where Plan B had whitewashed her involvement, which had been under the understanding that she was to work for them.

Eventually, from the Rodney House exit, Charlie walked out with a tall young man. He was dressed casually, blue sports jacket, tight jeans, his long hair was tied back in a ponytail. The two kissed each other goodbye, and she kept looking back to see if anyone was looking. The young man walked off with a limp and put on his white headphones. Rebwar left his car behind and followed her. As he walked, he texted Kamal to go and pick up the car. Rebwar and Kamal still shared it and drove in shifts. Since Rebwar had lost his first car, this was the only way he could afford to run it. They shared the finance payments, but it was under Kamal's name, so technically he owned it.

Rebwar followed Charlie to Pimlico tube station. At least he had an idea that she was going to Holborn. It was 8:15 am and rush hour was in full flow. It wouldn't take much to lose her in the crowd, and so he had to risk staying close. She wore a trouser suit that was loose on the shoulders but tight around the midriff. A cheap make, he thought. Its dark fabric glistened a dull grey and he knew that particular fabric was mixed with synthetic fibres, a favourite back home.

They headed towards Green Park. Rebwar got pushed around further away from her. At Oxford Circus she got off her seat and exited. Rebwar tripped over a bag and fell on the floor, and by the time he'd managed to get out of the carriage, he'd lost sight of her. And decided to head for the Central Line and got on the westbound platform. It was full of passengers and he couldn't see her past the crowds. He didn't have much time as the next train was arriving in a few minutes and he had to get on it. He wove to the end of the platform, which was crammed with reluctant passengers guarding their own space like it was their property. A packed train arrived. People squeezed themselves off the carriages, with everyone on the platform positioning themselves to get in.

Rebwar ended up by the tiled wall too far away to get on the train. He spurned the English reserve that he had noticed around him and pushed himself to the door, but they closed in front of him with a thud. He swore as the train rushed off. A wall of faces were staring at him. He mouthed sorry at them, then watched the train's red tail light disappear into the tunnel. After taking the following train he made it to Holborn and lit up on the pavement outside. There was no point in trying to find her. He used his mobile to find Persious's address, which was on Sandland Street. He found a coffee place and planned his next move.

———

Rebwar returned to the Persious office for 5:36 pm. He was late because he had returned home to drive Musa to football practice. There was the chance he had missed her. He hadn't any evidence that she had family to rush home for. From her white pasty look, he suspected that she over-worked herself. At 6:31 pm, Charlie walked out of the office building. She had changed her trainers to high heels which made her white calves look a bit thinner. He followed her along the busy streets towards Covent Garden. She stopped in front of an All Bar One on the corner of Henrietta Street and Bedford Street, taking out a little compact and touched up her face. He walked past her and stopped across the street to watch her walk in. He finished his cigarette and followed her inside.

It was a European style bar with large shiny ornaments and tall dining tables. He walked up to the imposing zinc bar and looked around; she was alone by the window.

'What can I get for you?'

Rebwar turned around to see a smiling barman, behind a brown beard that nearly reached the bar. Rebwar looked at shelves of wine bottles. He went for the simple option. 'Small beer, please.'

'On tap or bottled?'

'Bottle, please and...' He looked at the lit fridges behind the barman. 'That yellow one.' The barman went over and showed it to him and Rebwar nodded. The man cut a slice of lime and put it in the bottle. Rebwar went with it.

'It's Mexican. Refreshing.'

Rebwar looked back to Charlie. A man was sitting opposite her. It was Jack Hill, the reporter he'd taxied a few days ago. He looked nervous and kept looking around, keeping an eye on the room. Rebwar stepped behind a pillar. By their body language they seemed to know each other. Nervous laughs, both nodding and shaking their heads in unison. But there was an air of tension as she kept touching her face. And stopped their conversation when someone wandered too close to them.

Hill finished his pint in four large gulps and then Charlie slid a bulging envelope across the table, which he immediately put in his inner jacket pocket. It wasn't subtle. He said a few harsh words and got up. Rebwar moved towards the door and as he passed by bumped into him and spilled some of his beer over him. Hill swore at Rebwar, who excused himself.

'Hey! I know you,' said Hill. 'Right?'

'No. Sorry you must be mistaken.'

'I'm Jack Hill.' He stared at Rebwar. 'I'm the guy you...' Hill looked behind him in Charlie's direction.

Rebwar hesitated to turn but didn't want to draw attention to himself or catch her stare. 'Oh, yeah... you were in my car.'

'Right...' Hill took a few hesitant steps back. 'Remember, any stories and call me. Right? I've got to go.' And Hill rushed out.

Rebwar turned around and felt his leather jacket pocket for the envelope he had just taken from Hill and headed for the toilet. Rebwar found a cubicle to go in. He took out the envelope.

He'd learned his pick pocketing skills back when he was a teenager. It was something that had been a necessity growing up as a street kid. He'd also been one of the fortunate ones. Many of his friends had been caught and punished. And you were lucky if it didn't cost you a limb.

He knew he should have left the envelope alone, but he couldn't help himself. He opened it and saw a large wad of cash. Probably about ten grand, maybe more, in used twenty-pound notes. He had to get out of there and find the man.

He strode out of the bar, stood on the street and looked around. Hill stubbed his cigarette out and crossed the road and walked straight at Rebwar, his eyes fixed on him as a target. Rebwar walked in the opposite direction, around the corner towards Covent Garden market. Once there, he turned left into the square and walked to the side of St Paul's Church into a little side alley and stopped.

Hill walked up to him. 'I didn't put you down as a thief.'

Rebwar simply looked at him.

'I know it was you. Give me it back.'

'Who were you meeting?'

'None of your business, I'm a reporter... I don't give up my sources.'

'You know who you're getting involved with?'

Hill stepped back and looked at him. 'What? You know her?'

Rebwar nodded.

'All right, who is she? You're bluffing... and how did you find me?'

'Can't say but she's not to be messed with.' Rebwar took out an envelope he had taken. 'Is she paying you?'

'Trade secrets.' Hill reached for it. 'Stop messing around. What do you want? Money? Is that it? Get me a story.'

Rebwar wanted to smack him and make him talk straight. But he needed to observe. That was his assignment. Not to apprehend Hill and make him run for cover.

'OK, sorry.' Rebwar handed over the envelope and took out a pack of cigarettes and offered him one.

Hill took one. 'So how do you know her? Or are you just bluffing?'

'Wanted to know about you. Your stories... And yeah, I might have a story. How much do you pay?'

'You know her, don't you... I can tell.' Hill drew on his cigarette. 'You got some pick pocketing skills.'

'How much?'

Hill shook his head. 'Only when I get the story and then I can shop around. Give me a headline.'

'When the other story comes out. I'll see if I like it.'

Hill laughed. 'You strike a hard bargain, my friend. I'll send you a link. Email?'

Rebwar shook his head. 'Text me.' And Rebwar turned around and walked off.

'Hey, what's your number?'

Rebwar carried on walking. He knew Hill would find him.

NINE

Geraldine had been called in by Charlie, aka the Ferret. It was odd, as she didn't have anything to report to her. And, of course, she carried the secret of Charlie being watched by Rebwar. Was this the reason she was being called in? How could she even face her? And she couldn't lie for toffee. She had been at the pub and drunk a couple of pints to calm her nerves. And Plan B knew well that she couldn't lie. What were they thinking? A test? But Charlie had been off ever since they had a little heart-to-heart on the Serpentine about eight months ago. They both had got drunk and friendly, which was strictly out of bounds. But no one was stopping them. Geraldine's friendship with Rebwar was against regulations, of course, but you couldn't stop human nature.

Now Charlie had asked her to meet at a children's playground in Belair Park, Dulwich in South London. It wasn't a place that Geraldine had been to before. It turned out to have a small lake with a Georgian manor house, which had been converted into a cafe. There were wooded areas and neatly cut lawns. The playground was a small enclosed area with a ship-like climbing frame with slides and swings. A very odd choice, and when she got there, it felt strange.

Charlie was sitting on a bench watching two children. A little blonde boy and a red-haired girl of similar ages, the boy being slightly taller.

'Geraldine, nice to see you.' Charlie stood up, gave her a kiss on her lips and hugged her. 'Come, sit next to me.'

For a moment Geraldine looked at her, wondering if she had really just kissed her on the lips. 'Charlie, are you all right?' She caught the smell of alcohol and noticed her bloodshot eyes. As if she'd been crying.

'Yeah, totally.' Charlie leaned back on the wooden bench and looked around. 'These are my children, Paul and Steph.'

Geraldine watched them climb the make-believe ship. 'Oh, Rebwar said you didn't have children...' She realised immediately that she'd put her foot in it. 'You know we had a bet... What are we doing here?'

'Not a fan of children? I didn't put you as the mothering type. Classic dyke. And you're on chatting terms with the Robin. I thought–'

'I'm not here to be analysed, all right.'

'Prickly. Is it that time of the month?' She leaned in. 'I get it bad.' She smiled.

'Charlie, are you on something? I... I'm–'

'Relax, Geraldine. It's a beautiful day.' Charlie looked up and let her head hang.

'So what are we meeting about?'

Charlie leaned in. 'Kiss me?'

Geraldine moved back. 'What?'

'Kiss me, Here. Now. I want you.'

'Charlie your kids are here. What the fuck?'

'Kiss me now.'

Charlie grabbed her towards her, and she kissed her. Initially Geraldine gave in as Charlie's soft lips smothered hers. Her tongue darted out and into her mouth. Geraldine pushed her back. 'What is this about?' Charlie tried to kiss her again. 'No, no, Charlie! I'm not interested. What the fuck?'

'Hey, kiss me now. It's an order. You fucking kiss me again.'

Geraldine looked over to the kids who had stopped playing and were staring at them. With a few passers-by rubbernecking in. Geraldine shielded her eyes with her hand. 'Oh, shit look, fuck. Oh, fuck this is so wrong.'

Charlie grabbed her jacket with both hands. 'No, this is so right. It's so right. Kiss me again. Geraldine, I want you.'

'No, no, you don't. Is this some kind of twisted game?' Geraldine stood up.

'Sit back down, now. Bitch! You can't abuse me like that. OK?'

For a moment, Geraldine stared at her. What was she on? 'OK, I get it.' Geraldine looked around for any suspicious faces around. 'This is some kind of set-up, isn't it? Or you're drunk. Or off your meds.'

'No, I need you, OK? You can't leave me like this.'

'Fuck! You need help.'

'Hey, bitch, you do what I say, OK? I am in charge. You're my subordinate.' And she stood up. 'I'll report you. Understand?' Geraldine watched her stern face. 'I own your arse.'

'Fuck off, Charlie. You do know that I'm still a police officer. I can make your life hell. Do you really want this? Heh? Really? Think about it. You've got children–'

Charlie stepped closer to her as if she was trying to grab her. It wasn't aggressive and had a tenderness to it. 'Listen,

Geraldine, you're nothing. No more than an insignificant cog in this machine. Just because you're a policewoman doesn't mean anything. You better think about which side you're on. Otherwise I am going to make your little shitty life hell. Like you wished you'd never crawled out from under that stone. Are we clear?'

Geraldine turned around and breathed in. Who the hell did this woman think she was? 'Did you work for O'Neil? Is that what this is all about?' She looked at Charlie. Her kids were still staring at them. 'I thought...' Geraldine looked up, trying to think. She so wanted to tell her that Rebwar was watching her.

'G, we need each other. I've thought about this. You think we're going to get anywhere with Plan B? They own us both. How do you think we're going to make a life for ourselves?'

Geraldine wanted to run. Run away. Away from this psychopath. What had happened to her?

'You know it makes sense, us women sticking together.' Charlie brought out a small bottle of Gordon's gin. 'Fancy some. It brings up the spirit. Great medicine.' For a moment Geraldine fancied a gulp, a hit of fire and followed by the buzz. Charlie waved the bottle in front of her. 'I can see it in your eyes.'

'What, and be thick as thieves? Is that what you're really trying to get me to do?' Geraldine rushed over to her and searched her. Charlie spread her legs and smiled. Geraldine took out Charlie's phone and tried to access it. 'You're recording this shit?'

Charlie took a mouthful of gin, and with the back of her sleeve wiped her mouth. 'Don't look a gift horse in the mouth.'

'Yeah, right!' And Geraldine laughed. She pointed at Charlie's kids. 'And what do they think? Hey?'

'I've opened up to you,' Charlie said, slurring slightly. 'I've no more secrets. I'm yours...'

And for a moment Geraldine felt sorry for her. She looked pathetic. Her children just stood there, too scared to come any closer, like lost lambs feeling rejected.

'You know...'

Geraldine waited. 'What?'

'Your dress sense... it does you no favours. Like a boy.'

Geraldine sat next to her. 'I don't need this, right? Now you finish this gin and sleep it off. Call a friend, OK?'

Charlie looked up with a smile. 'Fancy a shag?'

'Oh, fuck off. What is wrong with you?' And she took the gin bottle and emptied it on the grass. 'Charlie, go home and sober up. Your children need you.'

'I'm finished. I'm done. Like a dodo.' Charlie laughed and sniffed. 'You know they are going to retire me. And you know what that means. Like roadkill.'

'What are you saying?'

'Like I said. Finished. They don't want me any longer.'

Geraldine still felt she was being played. Charlie was playing her for attention. But it felt heartfelt and touched her somewhere. But it was also ugly, crude and mean, which made it all the more somehow truthful. She turned and walked away. Charlie laughed.

TEN

Rebwar was at the Shishawi on Edgware Road, his regular where he could find some company that mostly left him alone. He was having a coffee and a smoke outside waiting for his Uber shift. Other customers around him were having their shishas, which he'd tried and from time to time smoked one to make Berker happy. Around him was a mix of Arab nationals with a few tourists. Berker asked him if he wanted another coffee to which he nodded.

'Are those Prius things any good?'

Rebwar looked up from his newspaper. 'I thought you couldn't drive?'

'I'm thinking about it. I like cars. Thought of buying one for the family.'

'Who can drive?'

'None of us. But you have to start somewhere.'

'You're buying the cart before the horse.'

Berker shrugged his shoulders, took the empty cup off the table and returned inside the restaurant.

Rebwar returned to his newspaper. There was a series of Brexit stories and Rebwar was trying to avoid them.

46

Everyone was arguing about what kind of Brexit people wanted, soft, hard or another referendum. All of which were against the will of the people. He thought it was like a bunch of children arguing in a sweet shop. And it was between sweet or salty liquorice. There was going to be some tears and the bullies in the back were threatening violence.

'Rebwar.'

Rebwar looked up. It was Jack Hill, the journalist.

'You need a ride?' Rebwar quickly glanced to check if he was alone. Hill's clothes were creased and his courier bag dirty.

'Call me Jack. Can I join you? Not waiting for anyone?' Hill pulled a chair and Rebwar saw his rings. One of which was a skull, the one he'd noticed in the cab and wondered if there was a story behind it.

'Yes, yes. Please sit. What would you like? Coffee?' Hill nodded and Rebwar signalled to Berker for two coffees. 'Still want my story?'

Hill adjusted his smudged glasses. 'I was just walking in the area. Nice here. Like a little oasis in London. Reminds me of Kabul.'

'Yes, some call it little Cairo, or that's what I heard.'

'So, Rebwar, tell me, what's the story?'

'You're persistent. How did you find me and what do you really want from me?'

'I'm a journalist. And you look like a man about town. You must have some leads. Something you heard in your cab. Or from a friend.'

Rebwar chuckled and folded his newspaper. 'What kind of stories do you write?'

'Any really. Oh, come on, you've seen things. Sure you have. Iran, right?'

Berker arrived with the coffees and put them on the table. 'What newspaper do you write for? Berker, this is Jack Hill. Maybe he wants to do a story about this place?'

Hill smiled. 'Don't do lifestyle features.'

'This place has history,' said Berker.

'Like I said. Need something a little more substantial.'

'You should try the food. That's substantial.' He put a menu on the table and walked off.

Hill scanned the menu and pushed it away. 'Look, there's money if it's a good story. But you know that.'

Rebwar dragged on his cigarette. 'Jack, you just need to look around. There are loads of stories.'

'Yeah, but I want something deeper.' And Hill took out his phone and brought up a website. 'Look, this is my blog, see? *Conspiracy*.'

Rebwar got his glasses out and looked at some of the headlines. The one about Facebook being hacked by Russians caught his eye. He nodded. 'Oh, yeah, you British lackeys are behind all those conspiracies. All the problems of the world and you have a finger in it.'

'That's what I mean. So... any leads?'

Rebwar took another drag and looked at him. Hill was nervous and his hands couldn't keep still. 'How did you find me?'

'That's what I mean. I knew it. Spy, heh?'

'Sorry, Jack. Just a simple man from Iran.'

'Look...' Hill scanned around the restaurant and dropped his voice to a whisper. 'I did some digging. I couldn't find anything about you. Usually I can. But it's like you don't exist.'

'I'm here trying to make an honest living for my family.'

'Were you in the war?'

'Listen my friend, Jack, stop trying to make trouble. I live a peaceful life here, respected also—'

'Rebwar, listen. You're a regular here, right? How did you get here? Give me a clue. I don't have to print any names or places.' Hill leaned back into his seat and sipped his coffee. 'OK, I'm working on a piece. You can't tell anyone.' He slid forward on his chair and leaned in. 'There is this cell. Mostly drop-out students, They're called the Filthy Five. I know the government pays them to make trouble. Like intellectual thugs, yeah?'

Rebwar rolled his newspaper and said, 'Governments are always creating some alternative narrative. This is how they keep us guessing. My home country is full of those stories. Nothing new. All those marches are sponsored by someone. Hey, all over the world it works like that.'

'Well, that's what I mean. Tell me more.'

'I can't, the *VAJA* will have me killed.'

'Who?'

Rebwar laughed. 'I'm pulling your leg. It's the Iranian Secret Police. Look, Jack, I can't help you. I'm nothing more than an Uber driver. Simple man with a simple life.'

'I'm getting close. I know you know more. I can see it. I've met agents before and you have the look. How did you get that injury?'

Rebwar put his hand under the table. 'Changed a flat.'

'You got that from a fistfight?'

'OK, Jack, let's make a deal. You leave me alone with my simple life and if I find something I'll tell you.'

'Come on, give me something to chew on. Can't just let me hang here.'

Rebwar took a moment to think. He still wanted to know about Daisy Merkenstand and what had happened to her, but he knew Hill would cause more trouble than it was worth. He was like a terrier with a bone. 'If I hear of anything I'll call you, OK?'

Berker came back. 'Are you going to spend some money here? You know it's an expensive street.'

'Put it on my bill,' said Rebwar. Berker snapped his finger at Hill and went off to another table.

'OK, Rebwar. I'll be waiting for a call. Here is my number.'

ELEVEN

Rebwar was running late for his meeting with Geraldine at the Dog House in Lambeth. She had sent him a series of text messages. He had driven down, which at the time had seemed like a good idea. But he got stuck in traffic and ended having to double park, which was unusual for him. Leaving the car on Denny Crescent, just behind the pub, he rushed in and heard Geraldine instantly.

'I told you to keep away. Yeah, away. Further away.'

Geraldine was pointing her finger at a woman who was collecting some drinks at the bar. Geraldine held on to the bar but carried on swaying like a ship in a storm.

'Geraldine, hey! I'm here.'

She turned around and nearly lost her balance. For a moment, her eyes searched him. 'Drink?'

'Oh, Coke, please.'

'What? Coke and rum, then.' She hiccuped.

'No, just a Coke, please,' Rebwar asked the barmaid.

'Are you with her?' The barmaid looked at Geraldine in disgust.

'It's OK, just a little bit drunk. Can I get a coffee for her?'

'And then she's out. She's been upsetting the patrons.'

Geraldine sat down on the stool and nearly fell backwards. Rebwar grabbed her arm to steady her. 'Geraldine, what's wrong? Did something happen at work?' She waved her hand at Rebwar as if he was an annoying fly.

'Six pounds twenty. She's on her eighth pint and got some blokes to buy her chasers. She nearly drank them under the table. Is she your friend?'

'Did you let her get this drunk?'

'Hey, I just sell booze. I'm not a councillor.' She grabbed the ten-pound note from Rebwar.

He helped Geraldine over to an empty table and made her sit on a chair. 'So, what happened?'

'Everything.' Her head slumped back and she fell asleep. Rebwar looked at her and sipped his refreshing Coke. He saw a copy of the *Metro* and flicked through it. On the fifth page stopped and got his glasses. *Anthony Peckworth takes his own life*, read the headline. After a series of sexual allegations from various women, the Labour MP for Exeter committed suicide by jumping off the top floor of his apartment building.

Rebwar sat up, looked for his cigarettes and went over to the bar. He ordered a double brandy. The woman asked him if it was for him. He took it back to the table, and for a moment, wanted to wake Geraldine.

Police have said that they found a suicide note and that the MP had threatened to kill himself within the last few months. He was also responsible for opening an inquiry into Sir John Merkenstand, the tech billionaire. There is an ongoing investigation, but the police do not think the death was suspicious.

Rebwar noticed that the article was signed off by Jack Hill. Was that the link between Charlie and him? He closed the newspaper and finished his brandy.

Geraldine woke up and looked around as if the room was spinning. She leaned over to one side and threw up to a few jeers of disgust.

'Right, that's enough. Out! Get her out of this pub.'

Rebwar grabbed her arm and helped her stagger out of the door. Outside the pub were some wooden benches and he sat her down. He stayed standing and a few feet away from her so he could smoke.

'The guy I went to see has killed himself.'

'Who?'

'That politician... Anthony Peckworth. He was hiding something. But I thought it was something else.'

'What do you mean? He killed himself, of course he was hiding something. What did they say?'

'Sexual allegations.'

'What? Kiddy stuff?'

'No. Women. Why would you kill yourself over that?'

'Women!' Geraldine blew a raspberry. 'A lot of reasons.'

'Yes, but not a politician. That's what they deal with all the time. Lies and deceit. No? And I think Charlie is involved.'

'Fuck, I feel ill.' She took a few large breaths.

'So, what happened to make you drunk?' Rebwar waved the smoke away from her as if it would stop her from being sick.

'Beckie tried to take her life and Charlie is being a fucking psycho. Although work's OK.' She hunched and folded her arms.

'Beckie? The pathologist?'

'Yeah, we've been going on and off and then she goes

and tries to take a heroin overdose. Cry for help and all that. Fuck, why do I always pick the ones that are broken? Don't answer that. Drama and drama. Fuck, and Charlie is trying to get me to sleep with her. I mean, what the fuck? She's made me kiss her in front of her kids, the sick bitch.'

'Kids?' Rebwar whistled. 'Strange world you attract...' For a moment Rebwar wanted to ask her if she was the problem. 'Do you think Charlie is playing some game?'

'That's what I thought. Some kind of set-up but I couldn't work it out. She acted so strangely, like a lost child looking for salvation. Desperate to try anything.'

'Do we need to find some insurance for ourselves?' said Rebwar.

Geraldine seemed to ponder for a moment and swayed. 'We need to take precautions. That suicide was a set-up. We could very easily be used in their game – whatever it is.' Geraldine threw up again. It was time to move again before the waitress called the police.

'Need some water? I've got some in the car. If I give you a lift, you tell me before you throw up? OK?' Rebwar waited for her to nod. Which she eventually did. They walked slowly over to the car. 'Do you think it's all an act? You know... Charlie, since I'm following her.'

Geraldine sobbed, her eyes red and cheeks wet with tears. 'You know she tried to kill herself. And for what? Why? Oh it hurts so much. You know? I feel so selfish. Guilty.'

Rebwar hugged her, and she sniffed. 'Look, take a few days off and get away from this madness. Don't think about it. Get some fresh air. Go home or some safe place away. You need some peace. Time off. And look after Beckie?' Rebwar got some tissues and a bottle of water. He watched her mop her face with a paper tissue.

'You're right, Rebs. This is not me. She's back with her husband... such a mess.' Geraldine looked up into the dark sky. 'Sorry... don't know what's gotten over me. What the fuck is going on?'

'I'll tell you when I find out. Come on, let me take you home. Get in.'

TWELVE

Geraldine drove her Ford Fiesta towards Margate on the A28, the wipers furiously flicking water off the windscreen to give her fleeting moments to see the road. Next to her was Beckie, held up by her seat belt and sound asleep. Geraldine tried to brush her hair off her pasty, damp face. She was still worried about her state; it had been a rough couple of days. Behind them on the back seat, a couple of suitcases had been thrown in like rubbish. Geraldine kept fighting with the heater controls to fend off the misting windscreen. She had only just managed to grab Beckie from her flat in Southwark. Geraldine had waited for her husband to go off to work, then invited herself in and packed a suitcase. Beckie was bruised and high as a kite.

The rained eased, and the sat nav on her phone announced their arrival. A cartoon-like cottage stared back. It was wedged between modern houses and a sixties build. The roof was like a tiled pyramid, in-between the main door were two turret-like bay windows. There was a little garage and the whole front garden was a paved driveway. Geraldine drove in. Behind it was a view of the grey channel.

Geraldine switched the engine off, and Beckie stirred. 'We've made it, love. We're here.'

Beckie looked around her, puzzled.

'Broadstairs. Auntie Linda's house. She's off on a cruise for a couple of weeks. Come on. Let's make a cuppa.'

'Why are we here?' Beckie curled up on the seat and put her feet up.

'You'll see. The sea air and the change of perspective will do wonders.' Geraldine dragged herself out of the car, stretched, got the luggage out and opened the front door to a familiar smell: flowery, slightly musty, salty. She let it sink in and then went to get Beckie. She had to help her in; she was so weak and in pain. 'You can have your own room. And we'll get through this turkey.'

The house had a thick white carpet with lots of fussy furniture, all flowery and ornate but with a cheap plastic feel to it. Beckie sat down on one of the armchairs. Geraldine went into the kitchen and filled the kettle, opened the small hatch between the kitchen and the living room. 'You'll see, Beckie! You'll love it here. We can go on beach walks, talk, read you know... all these things that... girls do.'

'When are we going back?'

'Oh, when you feel better.'

'Did we talk about this?'

Geraldine filled the fridge with some shopping she had brought along and made some tea. 'Sugar right?' She looked through the hatch to see that Beckie was looking through the patio window. Between the houses was a glimpse of the sea. Geraldine came out with two mugs of tea and handed one to Beckie. She stepped as close as she dared. She wanted to hold her and kiss her, share her joy at being finally here and together. But Beckie was still not relaxed and she could feel her edge like a sharp splinter on a wooden bannister. 'Nice tea?'

Beckie sipped it and Geraldine saw her back relax. As Beckie cupped her tea, Geraldine wanted to be that cup. Warm and comforting. A little tear escaped from Beckie's eye. 'I'm sorry, G. I'm such an ungrateful bitch. You know I thought that you'd be an ungrateful...' She sipped her tea. 'First impressions, hey?'

Geraldine sipped from her mug and looked out onto the sea with its endless horizon. 'Look, I'm going to be the one to get you through this, too... The mess you're in. You realise that?'

Beckie turned to her. 'Is that why we are here?'

Geraldine looked at her deep brown eyes. 'Yes. And we'll get through this. Together.'

Beckie grabbed her hands and gave her a deep kiss. Geraldine had a job holding onto the cup of tea. Her body just giving in like a soft toy. They hugged each other. Beckie's tears rolling off her soft cheeks.

'I'm so sorry, and... I was...'

Geraldine placed her index finger softly on Beckie's mouth and hugged her as tight as she could.

THIRTEEN

The following evening, Rebwar decided to go and check out Peckworth's flat in Hampstead. He had some doubts about the story the newspapers had printed and suspected inconvenient facts had been missed out. The pavement to the right of the building was taped off. He looked up and saw that Peckworth must have jumped forward or been pushed hard as it was some distance between the basement flats and the steel railing next to the pavement. He couldn't have just dropped from the flat window as he would have fallen short. A man walked out of the front door while talking on his phone. Rebwar took the opportunity to sneak into the hallway. He walked up to the top floor. There was an emergency exit and he pushed the long bar across the door.

Behind the door was a stick to prop the door open and keep it from locking. Rebwar used it and walked onto the flat roof. There was a series of large square bricked chimneys with six pots on top of each. They ran along to the end of the building. By one of them was an ashtray. Rebwar went up to it and picked up a roach. It smelled of cannabis. It was just above Peckworth's flat. There were no signs of a struggle, no scuff marks, broken masonry, or blood – nothing. Rebwar looked around at the surrounding flats that faced the building. It was possible that a neighbour might have seen something.

Rebwar made his way to Peckworth's flat. The police tape had been cut and Rebwar rested his ear to the door and listened for any movement. He could hear muffled TV sounds from other floors. He grasped the round doorknob and turned it gently. The door opened and he pushed it very slowly. The hallway was dark, with a flickering light at the end. He wasn't sure if it was coming from a street light or a room. He made his way in and closed the door behind him. Holding his breath and listening for any sounds, he took a careful step. A man was standing in the hallway with the light flickering behind him. Rebwar couldn't see his face. He was a little taller than him, wearing jeans and a dark blue coat. His hair was cut short and he looked in good shape.

Rebwar flicked the light switch. Both stood there. Rebwar waited for his eyes to adjust. The man moved to get a better look. The man had a square jaw with deep-set eyes and his hair was tied back into a ponytail. Rebwar had expected him to make a run for it, as all thieves do, but he held his ground looking at him. Rebwar noticed that one of his white trainers looked newer than the other; there was a good chance he had a prosthetic leg. Then it clicked this was the young man with the pony tail that he had seen with Charlie.

'What are you doing here?' said Rebwar.

'Could ask you the same question.'

'I interviewed Mr Peckworth a couple of days ago. I came here to see him.'

'You could have used the doorbell or called him and got

your answer. What are you really here for? I've seen you, Rebwar.'

Rebwar took a moment to think about it. 'Plan B?'

The man shrugged.

'You've been watching him then.' Rebwar looked at the blue latex gloves. 'Come to clean up?'

'Look, mate, don't stick your nose where it doesn't belong. Turn around and leave.'

'You killed him. A robbery gone wrong? Just one thing… How did he get to the pavement?'

'Like I said, it's none of your business.' He stepped closer and Rebwar kicked his leg away from him and he dropped to the floor. His leg slammed down like a piece of scaffolding. The man grabbed Rebwar's legs. He was powerful. Rebwar used his fists to hit his ears hard. This stunned him for a moment and Rebwar punched his face. The man used his powerful arms to swing his body around. His knee hit Rebwar's stomach. He struggled for breath and his lungs burned. The man dragged himself upright and held Rebwar down with his metal foot. Rebwar's lungs slowly filled. He wheezed and felt the nausea rise.

'Word to the wise. Keep your nose to the grindstone.' His foot pressed harder.

Rebwar was still trying to regain his breath, but the man's weight stopped him.

'You feeling like Deckard? It's a moment, isn't it?'

Rebwar let out a groan.

'I guess you didn't see the movie, did you? Lost on you… Well, I don't think Peckworth jumped. Do you? But hey! I'm not here to think. Not my job, is it?'

Rebwar felt his lungs burning.

'Now tell me. I've been here before. The feeling of ending it. You know, just leaving it all behind me. Just finishing it. It's a good feeling, or is it? Then you worry. Worry that you might have left something, something.' He pressed down harder. 'Oh, sorry, is that hurting? Why do you do this?'

'Money,' said Rebwar while trying to breathe and trying to keep his nausea down.

'Really? I see something else. You're a truth seeker, aren't you? You have a moral code. Right and wrong. So what is that? Did Peckworth do the right thing? Did they do the right thing for him? What is the right thing? Why did Roy let Decker live?'

Rebwar tried to repeat the names as questions. They came out as desperate moans and groans.

'We're just foot soldiers, aren't we. Pawns on a chessboard. Ready for the next sacrificial move. What is the bigger picture? Who's calling the shots? What is the next move?' The man grabbed Rebwar's cigarettes. He lit one. 'Mmm, Jesus, I've missed these. Bloody world telling us what we can and can't do. Mate, what are you doing here? This country is going to shit. The snake's head has been lopped off and...' He laughed. 'You know the rest of the story. Fucked up, mate.'

For a moment, Rebwar wanted to wrestle him down. But he could feel the pain and realised it was his pride talking.

'We're foot soldiers. Cannon fodder.'

And he walked off, dragging his now faulty prosthetic leg.

FOURTEEN

Rebwar woke up to the sound of Hourieh swearing. He waited for it to either stop or get worse. He got up and grabbed his dressing gown to go into the kitchen. Hourieh was emptying the fridge and throwing packets of food into the bin.

'What's going on, my desert flower?'

'It has stopped doing its job. Another broken thing in this rat-infested apartment. And where is this landlord? Look at the list. It gets longer by the day.'

Rebwar went over to get his filter coffee, poured it in a mug and stirred in some sugar. He had sip and let its magic sink in.

'When did you come in last night? And that bruising? Another customer not wanting to pay?'

'Three or four.' He lit a cigarette, which he passed to Hourieh. 'You know a boy got stabbed last night.'

'Not another one. What are the police doing?'

'It was Joe.' Musa came into the kitchen with a black t-shirt saying, *I have CDO it's like OCD*, and in small letters underneath, *but the letters are in alphabetical order, as they should be.*

'You knew the boy?' Rebwar took a drag of his cigarette. 'Was he in your class?'

'Na, year above. Drug dealer. Family business.'

'Doesn't mean he had to follow that path,' Hourieh said. 'Like you, Musa... you're not going into the police like your father. You study hard and get a respectable job. Like a lawyer or an engineer and make your mother proud. Have you been to work at that garage?'

'Mum, will you stop and dad is a taxi driver. And no, not yet.'

Hourieh looked at Rebwar, who shrugged his shoulders and turned around to refill his cup.

'Do you know why he got stabbed?'

'Dad, I'm not a copper. How am I supposed to know?' He got up and opened the fridge. 'It's empty.'

'Lucky for us,' said Rebwar.

'Broken, my sweet son. Here is some money. You can go out for breakfast.'

Musa looked at the ten-pound note. 'Cool.'

'Did you break it on purpose?'

'Dad, everything is broken in this flat. Sure you can get your Mario suit and fix it.'

'Who?'

Musa pocketed the note and shuffled his way out of the kitchen.

'You going to Starbucks? Get me an Americano if you do.'

Without turning, Musa stretched out his palm. Rebwar found another ten-pound note and put it into his hand. 'I want some change from that.'

Hourieh handed Rebwar the phone and with her eyes

pointed out a number scribbled on the piece of paper. He knew who it was and dialled the number. It rang till a recorded voice answered. Rebwar spoke after the beep. 'Hello. This is Mr Ghorbani from Apartment Twelve in the Dorney Building. Our fridge has broken down and needs fixing. Could you please call me back on this number.' And he hung up.

'Now, husband, you go and use your detective skills and find out where this man lives.' Rebwar drank some more coffee and took a drag of his cigarette. 'Or call the council they own this building or I'll do it myself.'

'You know what happened to the Guptas... They called and...' He pointed to the window. 'Or have you forgotten?'

Hourieh stubbed out her cigarette and got herself some more coffee. 'So what do you propose? And what are we going to eat tonight? Now that it's all in the bin – which you can take out. And not fried chicken.'

Rebwar checked his phone, which had been charging on the counter. It had three messages: the first one was just a click, second was Jack Hill telling him that he had found some interesting information and that he had to tell him face to face – he wanted to meet; third one was Geraldine saying she was fine and staying at her auntie's house in Kent for a couple of days. Rebwar called back Jack Hill and it rang until diverting to voicemail. Rebwar dropped the call and thought of sending a text but decided otherwise. He didn't want to leave too much of a trail if anyone was on to him.

'Have you taken the rubbish out?' said Hourieh from the living room. 'I don't want it to stink out this place. And that bruising? I haven't forgotten!' Rebwar took the bag and walked out in his dressing gown. On the way down the stairs he met Chris. He was part NWK of the Chilcot estate gang.

'Hi, man, nice outfit.'

'Hey, did you hear about Joe?'

'County lines man – fucking up our business. You hear me, bro? All change in this world. Going back home, man. To the motherland.'

For a moment, Rebwar wanted to quiz him further but Chris ran up the stairs. His phone was ringing; it was Jack Hill.

'Hey, Rebwar, we need to talk ASAP. Where can you meet?'

'In town. My local?'

'Sure, in an hour.'

Rebwar was at the Shishawi, his unofficial office, and told Berker to be on the lookout for Hill, to which Berker grumbled and told him he was going to charge him rent as Hill hadn't spent any money on his last visit. It was busy, but Berker had made a little corner at the back of the restaurant by the fish tank. Rebwar kept fidgeting with a cigarette, rolling it around his fingers. The surrounding guests kept staring over, wondering if he was going to smoke it there or go. He looked at his watch and it was 9:06 pm. His coffee cup was empty, and he checked his phone for any messages. From the conversation with Hill, he had expected him to be there in a matter of moments; he was now an hour late.

Rebwar got up and went outside onto the busy street. With an eye on the bustling bodies passing him, he lit up, inhaled deeply but still felt anxious as he remembered the chat he'd had with Hill. He hadn't sounded worried, just excited by something he'd found out and wanted to share. Something that he needed to say in person. Rebwar should have pressed him for a clue. He dialled Hill's number, and it rang a couple of times before going to voicemail.

Rebwar lit another cigarette and looked across the street and around him. People were going from one place to another. After a few puffs, he went back in to look for Hill. Maybe he had missed him. He looked at the diners: a few families, couples and a business meeting with suited men speaking a foreign language that he guessed was Russian.

'Your friend is late,' said Berker.

'Have you seen him?'

'No, but from the look on your face, he should be here. Drink?'

'Get me a Coke.' Rebwar went back to sit down, picking a newspaper from the bar. He scanned the headlines: *Leaked Brexit Report Says We Will Be Worse Off* followed by *Stephen Hawkins visionary physicist dies at 76*.

Rebwar folded the paper and called the number again; this time it didn't even ring and went straight to his voice-mail. He stopped himself from texting as he didn't want to leave a trail for someone to find. He rechecked his watch: 9:54 pm. Hill would have contacted him to say he was late. Rebwar didn't have a good feeling about Hill not turning up. He called Raj and asked him if he was around. To which Raj asked if Tamar was there. To which Rebwar told him to get his big ass over. Raj was his go to IT guru and he had helped his father back in Iran.

The murmur and laughter had quietened down in the restaurant. The occasional shout was coming from the busi-nessmen. Two of them were asleep and the others drunk. Rebwar spotted Raj. His big frame filled the yellow and red criss-crossed patterned t-shirt hid a few stains. The camo hoodie clashed with it, but it fitted with the restaurant's decor. He smiled, sat down and looked around.

'She's not around tonight.'

Raj shrugged his shoulders. 'So, what I am doing here, then? You know I could be—'

'I need you to find out something about a journalist called Jack Hill. I think he's gone missing.' Raj was reading the menu which he had taken from the table next to him. 'Are you listening?'

'That mezze and a few fig leaves.' Raj turned around and waved to Berker.

'Ahh, it's the incredible eating machine,' said Berker and put his hand out. 'Don't tell me... Mezze and fig leaves and pitta bread. Oh, yes, and beer?'

Raj just giggled and nodded.

'Another Coke? For your friend?' said Berker as he went to put the order in.

'Look him up on your phone,' Rebwar said. 'I need to find where he lives.'

'OK, OK, keep your hair on,' Raj said. 'Why the panic?'

'I think he's gotten himself with the wrong crowd.'

Raj's fat fingers scrolled the smartphone. 'Isn't that what journalists do? And from his website, he likes his conspiracy theories. Is this guy legit? Just missing some UFOs and zombies. How did you guys meet?'

Rebwar grabbed the phone and put on his glasses. He flicked through the website: how the Russians had armies of hackers; Trump and his Facebook campaign; Wikileaks – but nothing that Rebwar could link to what happened in the last few days. 'Can we find where he lives? I need to go there.'

'I need my computer and some luck. Should I get this as takeaway?'

Rebwar got up and gave Berker a couple of notes. 'I'll be outside.'

A trail of IP addresses, cloud servers and cookies had led Rebwar and Raj to Jack Hill's derelict house. Rebwar had no idea how Raj had done it and what all that meant or that such things existed. Hill was paranoid – and probably for a good reason. Their search had taken them a couple of days. Rebwar's gut feeling had been right, and he hated seeing a trail going cold. It was like watching ice melt away and evaporate. Out of frustration, they drove to those pinpoints that Raj had found on a map – about ten of them all clustered in the east of London around Docklands.

It was dusk before Rebwar arrived at Grenadier Street just by London City Airport. There was a series of identical small houses tightly packed together, each with enough space for two bedrooms and a little garden. The intermittent roar of jet engines rumbled the quiet street. Raj pointed at the one without a number; its once white front was now a dirty grey. A ripped black rubbish bag was in front of the entrance. Rebwar opened it up. There were remnants of food, McDonald's wrappers, KFC and Domino's boxes. Any fox or stray pet could have ripped the bag and snacked on the leftovers. Under the boxes was some finely shredded paper, crosscut and impossible to piece together. It fitted with Jack Hill's paranoia – although leaving the rubbish in front of his entrance didn't.

The house had most of its windows boarded up and weeds grew out of the brickwork. You would pass it as an empty shell. To Rebwar, this all fitted with Jack Hill's underground profile. The other rubbish bags didn't look like they had been there long. There wasn't a film of grime on them, as with some other rubbish bags down the road.

Rebwar went up to the door as Raj looked on. 'This is your bag.' Said Raj.

Rebwar saw that the two locks were shiny and new. They had been recently replaced. The door frame was cracked with marks of filler around the lock. Rebwar got out his little wallet of tools for picking locks. 'Raj, check the street to see if anyone's being too nosy. And check the windows for any movement.' Rebwar started on the locks. He got one open, but the lower one wasn't giving in. He swore.

'Hey!' Raj came closer to him. 'Top window is open.'

Rebwar stepped back and saw that the window above them was slightly ajar. He looked at Raj. He was going to have to go up there; as the only thing Raj had ever climbed was a cupboard in the kitchen while foraging for some food.

'All right, give me a hand. Come on.'

He looked at Raj's confused face.

'Bend down and I'll climb on your back. What kind of childhood did you have? Don't answer that. I know. In a dark room.'

After some groans and puffs that were masked by a departing aircraft, Rebwar managed to reach the ledge. And squeezed himself under the window, he fell into the dark room, exhausted and filling his lungs as if he had gone for a run. The wooden floor was wet and dirty. He dusted himself off and used the phone's torch to make his search. There was a mess of boxes and papers. He made his way downstairs to the main door which he unlocked to let Raj in.

'Right, don't switch any lights on, OK?'

The wallpaper was peeling off, and the place hadn't been cleaned in years. Raj sneezed and got his inhaler out. Rebwar shone his torch into the front living room. The couch was covered with plaster that had come down from the ceiling. No one had been in there for a while. Dust covered every surface. He went to the kitchen, which was at the back and beyond the stairs that led upstairs.

'Rebwar... We're not going to find a body, are we?' In the kitchen was a pile of dirty plates and half-eaten microwave meals. Raj checked them out and smelled them. 'Asda's own. I get them, too.'

A collection of empty Coke bottles lay on a counter. Rebwar went upstairs to the room he had come into. The wall facing the street was a collage of articles, notes and pictures. It was like looking into Hill's mind.

'Wow, dude had issues,' Raj said. 'Shit man. You can't make these stories up. Look.'

Rebwar snapped some pictures with his phone and carried on taking photos of the floor, which had more scraps and notes.

'Who are they?' Raj pointed at a collection of pictures.

Rebwar looked closer. 'Kids, students? Activists?'

'Terrorists?' Raj pointed at the words *Filthy Five* that were written around them.

Rebwar looked at one of the girls. She had curly red hair. Her face was freckled, and she had stunning blue eyes.

He took a few photos of the team and stepped back and pointed at the picture of the redhead. 'Daisy... Daisy Merkenstand... What's she doing?'

Raj looked at her picture.

'We found her with O'Neil,' Rebwar explained. 'And Charlie took her. I wondered what happened to her.'

'O'Neil? That racist cop? Didn't you break his arm, and he ended up running that human trafficking ring. Cute, she is.' Raj took her picture and carried on searching.

'What in the world has she got herself into?' Rebwar stepped back and looked at the pictures and arrows. '*Madar Ghabah*.[1] That's Charlie's guy. The one from the flat.' Rebwar read out his name. Henry Trent, aka Hooly. He read the other names. Pinky Knight who had short bright pink hair, James Hewitt-Thomas who was tall, dark with a side parting and was their leader, and Joseph Brunje, aka Docker, who had bright red hair and had the build of an athlete. Rebwar wondered if this was some Plan B cell that Charlie was running.

Raj whistled and brought out a laptop from under some newspapers.

'Does it work?'

'Don't know... Looks a little old and broken.' The plastic case had a crack running along the side.

Rebwar looked at the sagging desk where he had found the laptop. He shone his torch over the surface, looking for other traces. There were some Coke cans and two mugs. He got a plastic bag from his pocket and put them in it and sealed the ziplock. He went to the back room that faced an overgrown garden. The room had an old mattress in it with a sleeping bag and a notepad next to it. A rucksack was on the floor next to a window. He went over and searched it. It contained a t-shirt, jumpers and a collection of cables. Raj took a closer look at the cables.

'Yep, another computer and an Android phone, I think,' Raj said. He showed Rebwar the cables. Rebwar nodded and smiled. A knock at the door made them freeze. A second later it was a bang, as if a hammer had hit it. Rebwar waited for a third knock – which came. After telling Raj to stay put, he went to the door and opened it. A tall man stood in front of him. His face shielded by the hoodie.

'You're late.' Rebwar held out a ten-pound note.

The man stepped back and looked left and right. 'Where's Jack?'

'Where's the pizza?'

'Jack Hill?' The man took a few more steps back.

Rebwar approached him. 'Yes.'

'Is he in?'

'And you are?'

'A friend. And you are?' He put his hands in the hoodie's pocket.

'A friend.'

Rebwar took another step forward and thought of grabbing him but spotted a curtain move in one of the neighbouring houses.

'No.' The man turned and walked off.

For a moment, Rebwar wanted to stop him, but the man would easily outrun him. He took out his phone and searched the pictures he had just taken of the Filthy Five. It was Joseph Brunje.

SEVENTEEN

Geraldine and Beckie were walking around the little side streets of Margate. A storm had just moved in and was blowing them from one side of the street to the other. The little alleys tunnelled the wind so hard that Beckie let herself be carried into Geraldine and they spun together like tops till they were too dizzy to stand straight. They laughed, giggled and kissed then carried on going from street to street, sometimes catching each other's reflections in shop windows. Geraldine felt like a teenager again, carefree and bursting with happiness. But she knew Beckie could swing like a pendulum and lose it all to the darkness that was still inside her. The last few days had been a mix of euphoria and anger. She carried the bruises that were like the sunsets, dark and moody.

Suddenly, a wall of rain hit Margate as if someone had switched on a shower. Beckie ran off for shelter and Geraldine followed, running down the steps to Marina Drive. Beckie rushed into the Marina Cafe. Geraldine dived in after her. It was cramped, with just a few tables. They sat down close to the window. Five faces stared at them, old ladies with a range of coloured hair. It made Geraldine giggle. The waitress came over wearing a stained apron and a perm. She waited with her pad in hand. Geraldine grabbed Beckie's hand. She wanted her warmth.

'What can I get you ladies?'

'Honey, what do you feel like having?' said Beckie. 'Something hot?'

'Latte would lovely and do you have cakes?'

'Yes, we've got some Victoria sponge, chocolate gateau and cheesecake.'

'Uh, love some Victoria. Is she moist? Sorry... bad joke.' Geraldine giggled.

'A cream tea for me,' said Beckie. She grabbed Geraldine's hand and was about to kiss it. Embarrassed by the audience, Geraldine pulled it back and tried to tap her. Beckie smiled.

'OK... so a cream tea, latte, Vic sponge, and yes it is...'

Beckie winked at her and as she walked off said, 'Mmm, cute arse.'

'Will you stop it?' said Geraldine. The waitress looked back and smiled, and Beckie shivered. 'Lucky I'm not jealous.' Geraldine grabbed Beckie's cheeks. 'Will you behave? So, what about this holiday?'

'Oh, was miles away. Soorrry.' Beckie rolled her eyes and hid her smile with her hand like a naughty schoolgirl. 'Yes, somewhere hot... Never been to Florida or San Fran.'

'America? Mmm, what about Asia? Thailand is amazing, but you know not in the seedy places. Or Sri Lanka.'

'Aren't they Muslim?'

Geraldine looked at the old ladies who had leaned in to talk to each other while monitoring them. She could feel her ears burning and for some reason felt self-conscious. 'No idea, but it's hot there?'

'Yeah, but homophobic. Maybe not Thailand – anything goes there. Ping-pong!'

'What?'

'You know...' Beckie leaned in. 'It's a show – and they put all kind of things up their snatches.'

'Becks!'

'That as well.'

Geraldine laughed. She grabbed Beckie's hand and squeezed it.

'Go on then.'

'What?'

'Kiss me, who cares.' Beckie turned to her audience. 'Yes, we're lesbians, ladies. Watch out.' And they turned away and carried on talking. Beckie grabbed Geraldine and snogged her, making sure it went on a little longer. It was stopped by the waitress bringing over the tea and coffee.

'Oh sorry,' said Geraldine.

'Oh, don't be. They'll be gossiping for the next week. Sure one or two of them wished they were free as you.'

Geraldine's pocket buzzed, and she took her phone. It was Rebwar. She stood up. 'I've got to take this. Sorry, love. Hi.' She walked outside. The wind had blown the shower away. 'So what's so urgent?'

'Are you in a wind tunnel?'

'Still in Margate.'

'Oh, I guess somewhere outside London. I've got Charlie wanting to meet me.'

'Yeah, I guess she knows I'm away. Did she find out from work? Why hasn't she called me? I'm your handler.'

'That's why I'm calling.'

'She is a devious bitch and up to something. I wouldn't trust her. Meet her anyway and see what she wants.' Geraldine checked her reflection and pulled on her jacket and t-shirt to straighten it out.

'Should I hold off telling her what I've found out about Jack Hill?'

'Who? Oh, you're breaking up there...' Geraldine spotted that Beckie was on the phone. Her expression had changed and Geraldine could see that some darkness had moved in. Rebwar's call had dropped out.

EIGHTEEN

Rebwar stood in front of St Giles-in-the-Fields, a church just off Covent Garden, and wondered if he was in the right place. He had imagined something else. This looked a little bland for a Christian temple. But Rebwar wasn't too interested in religion; he had seen all the trouble it had caused. He saw it as a series of guidelines rather than facts and evidence. He looked at the angular grey building that more resembled an old official government building than a place of worship. Only the tall spire gave it away as a church.

He went under an imposing stone arch to get to the entrance on the north side of the building. He felt nervous, as if he wasn't sure of its rules and customs. At the entrance, he stopped and was about to take his shoes off. But couldn't see that anyone else had done that. He felt odd going in and bringing in London's grime. Once inside, he was impressed by the colourful stained glass windows. He looked up to see paintings depicting scenes he didn't quite understand. Simple gold decorations ran along the walls and ceilings.

He'd never been in a church. He hadn't dared to. He knew there was a god and his son, which he guessed was represented in the pictures. He'd heard of that. The main hall was filled with rows of benches with a few people either looking down or just sitting there taking in the tranquillity. So far, no one had asked him what he was doing there or demanded any ID. It did feel welcoming and there wasn't any obvious set order to anything. He guessed there wasn't a sermon going on. He spotted Charlie sitting on one of the benches at the front of the church. She was as Geraldine had described her and was looking at the stained glass windows. She seemed mesmerised by their colours and religious depictions.

'Hi, Charlie?' said Rebwar, and she looked at him as if he was in the way.

With a hushed voice she said, 'Code names only, Robin. Sit, please.' And she waved him to a seat.

'Sorry... Ferret. You wanted to see me?'

'Yes, I did. You like this place?'

Rebwar looked at the altar. 'It's a peaceful place. Can I smoke?' He expected a reaction.

Charlie pursed her lips. 'Strictly forbidden. Kidding me, right? You don't smoke in your mosques. Are you religious?'

'No, I'm not.'

'Does this place bother you?'

'I don't understand it. It has a purpose for some people.'

'So why...' She waited for a moment. 'But you know the story?'

'Of your prophet. Yeah, he was crucified by the Romans.'

Charlie looked around her and raised one of her legs so she could turn and face Rebwar. 'OK, enough of theology. I need to know that you are with me.'

Rebwar nodded.

'A nod will not suffice here. I need loyalty and a

hundred per cent dedication. Actually, a hundred and ten per cent.'

'What about Geraldine?'

Charlie looked around her and then into his eyes and said, 'You mean the Field Mouse.' She sighed and shuffled. 'I can't talk about other agents. I need you to be committed to the cause. Otherwise you'll be on a plane back to where you came from. If you're lucky. Understand me? On your file, it says you have problems with your superiors. You know the classic subordinate issues. I'm a woman and I'm in charge.' Charlie stopped as if a stone had dropped in a pond and she waited for a reaction as if expecting it to float. She took a breath. Rebwar noticed her nervous energy. Her face had a slight greasy shine to it. He took a moment to reply, keeping her hanging.

'I am getting a visa. And I am getting paid.'

'Look, you don't dictate or ask for anything in this organisation. Understand me?'

Rebwar sat back and stretched out his hands over the bench. 'What do you want me to do?'

Charlie stood up, walked past him and sat back down. 'You're going to have to frame Geraldine.' Rebwar stared at Charlie, looking for any signs that this was some kind of test or a joke. 'She's gone off the rails and we need to deal with her. She's trying to compromise the organisation and we can't let that happen. I'm not letting that bitch take me down.'

Rebwar leaned forward and held on to his knees. 'Are you sure about this?'

'Christ.' She looked up. 'Sorry, sorry. Fuck's sake, of course I am! We don't need to make a case out of this. Remember what I just told you. Now you are going to put this bag in her flat. Don't bother looking into it. It'll be more trouble than you want. Once you've done it, text me at this number.' She handed him a piece of paper. 'If she calls you, just go along with what she says. I don't want to arouse any suspicions. You can do that?'

'Am I getting paid?'

For a moment Charlie looked surprised and tried to say something. 'This is for the organisation, you understand? Our survival, not some job. We are in danger here.'

Rebwar glanced around. 'Are we being followed?'

'You have a job to do. Now go and do it. Understand?'

Rebwar got up and picked up the bag which was lighter than he expected. He looked at her and took out a cigarette in front of her. 'Do you believe in him up there?'

'Go, and stop wasting my time.'

Rebwar walked off, his footsteps echoing on the black and white stone floor.

NINETEEN

Rebwar had just picked the lock to a ground-floor flat on Freemantle Street in Southwark and walked in with the bag that Charlie had given him. He heard some snoring coming from the front room. He walked past it and went into the kitchen, which doubled up as a living room. Cans and empty wine bottles littered the flat surfaces. There was a pile of mail which Rebwar checked, most of it was addressed to Geraldine Smith and he put the envelopes back and walked back to the closed door he had passed on his way in. He stopped for a moment, took a deep breath and opened the door. Geraldine was naked on her back, snoring. Rebwar looked down in embarrassment as he picked the crumpled up duvet off the floor to cover her, he knocked an empty can. It clonked and rolled across the wooden floor.

Geraldine stirred and her eyes flashed open. She squealed. 'Motherfuck... Who the fuck?' She grabbed her pillow.

'It's me! Rebwar. I... I'm sorry.' And he turned away and passed her the duvet.

She took the duvet and wrapped it around herself. 'Why? Why? Oh, man, you've given me a fright. What the fuck are you doing here?' She slid up onto the headboard and reached for the light switch.

Rebwar stopped her. 'We are being watched.'

'Rebs, shit! Couldn't you have called? This is a little dramatic. And you saw me naked...'

Rebwar thought about it for a moment and didn't have anything to say back. 'We need to talk about Charlie. And you don't like men, anyway.'

'That's not the point. I was, was...' She held her heart and sighed.

Rebwar looked down to see some more crushed up cans. 'There's a young man, Henry Trent or Hooly. He's working for Charlie and he's out there waiting for me to get out. I've brought this to leave with you.' He lifted the black bag to show her.

'Can't we put a light on? I can't see.'

Rebwar sat on the side of the bed. 'I'm going to leave it and you should only have a look once I am out of here. It's drugs, fake money and a phone. Charlie wants me to leave it here so the police can find it. She wants to take you down.'

'What? She's insane! Is this Plan B's doing?'

'No, I don't think so. That's why she wanted to meet me alone and had me tailed.'

Geraldine shrugged her shoulders.

'And get this... She's fucking him, he could be her son... She's up to something but I don't know what. He was in that MP's apartment.'

'That fucking bitch. She's lost her marbles. So what are we going to do with this bag? And she's going to call the cops on me?'

'We need to move this bag to a safe location. We could

use it later.' Rebwar handed a cigarette to Geraldine and lit up.

She giggled. 'Oh, if only.'

'What?'

'Oh, nothing.'

'What? You're thinking about the last time you smoked a cigarette in bed?'

Geraldine stared at him and winked. 'Yes, cheeky. When was the last time you did that?'

'Too long!' He laughed with her.

'OK, it's getting embarrassing. I'm still naked here! Can I get a tea or something? Feel like it's a booty call.'

'Booty what?'

'Oh... Let's move on, please.' Geraldine swung out and missed. 'What are we going to do?'

'I need to let that idiot see me leave here. Where can we hide this?'

'Under the bed.'

'OK. After I've left, take the battery and chip out of the mobile. Wrap the mobile in aluminium foil and put it in another plastic bag. That will stop the phone from being tracked or hacked. Then once I've lost my tail, I'll come back for the bag. They will still presume that the bag will be here.'

Geraldine dragged on her cigarette and watched Rebwar stand up. 'Oh, I need your help.'

'Yes.'

'Sit again.' And she took a deep breath. 'Need to find Beckie. We fell out. She somehow found out that I am, or was working for Plan B.' She shook her head and looked down. 'Fuck knows how she knows.'

'How? Is she involved?'

'I think her husband had something to do with it. We

need to spy on them. Something odd is going on. Don't you think?'

'So she's back with him?'

'Yeah, hashtag FML.'

'And there's Jack Hill.'

'I didn't manage to tell you what I found out.' She grabbed his hand and looked at his watch. In her reaching, Rebwar caught the sight of her breast. For a moment it aroused him and she caught him out. She smiled and for a couple of seconds they stared at each other. 'Come on... I think I'm still drunk. Get going, you old fool. It's two in the morning. What's your wife going to think? And it would never...'

'You do talk nonsense.' Rebwar got up and walked towards the door. 'I'll knock on the window four times and then you can hand me the bag. Remember, wrap the mobile in foil.' He watched her yawn. 'Set an alarm. I don't want to break in again.'

Geraldine smiled, blew a kiss to him and wrapped herself in the duvet. Rebwar closed the door behind him and went out onto the street. It was quiet and cars were parked on either side all the way along. He looked around, trying to spot Trent who had been wearing a white baseball cap the last time he'd seen him. Rebwar walked into the middle of the street, making sure he would be photographed or recorded. He spotted some movement in a car. It was too dark to make out who it was. He walked up to it.

'Hi, Henry, checking on me?'

Trent lowered the window. 'Arsehole. Think you're clever. Hey. If it was up to me, I would have put a bullet in your head.'

'You can tell Charlie that I've left the bag under her bed.'

'Watch your back, mate. The reckoning is coming.'

'Yeah, about that. You two trying to take over Plan B? I don't really see you as a crime lord.'

Trent started the engine and pulled away, nearly taking Rebwar with him.

TWENTY

Rebwar returned to Geraldine's flat to find her ready to go back out. She had showered and dressed in a blue denim jacket and white jeans. She'd tidied up the empty cans and the pizza boxes. It was like she'd slapped herself into shape as if it was a beautiful sunny morning.

'You coming along?'

'Aren't we going to find Beckie?'

'Can't it wait? We should investigate Charlie. Remember, she's after you.'

'Can't we do that in the morning? And I need to go into the office to find out who she really is... OK, at least get some dirt on the bitch.'

Rebwar grabbed the bag with the drugs and opened the front door. It was 3:30 am and in the bright street lights birds sang to each other from some randomly planted trees. 'We are going to have to use your car.'

———

They were parked outside a white-brick, two-storey house on Gatonby Street, which was in a new housing estate with flats and semi-detached houses just off Peckham Road.

'You've been here before?'

'Yeah... They've lived there for four years and have a £1,123 a month mortgage on it. Her husband is Kurtis Webster, who works in the accounting department of Starbucks and was born in Southwark. He's a cunt. Excuse my French but he has a history of beating women. His last girlfriend nearly took him to court, but then she went back to France.'

'Are they both there? We could just go in. Nothing like middle of the night to get people at their most vulnerable.'

Geraldine turned in her seat to face Rebwar. 'Did you plan to break in while I was asleep?'

'I thought you'd be out. I had to do it ASAP otherwise Charlie would suspect that I was going to warn you.'

'Is she tracking you?'

'Raj checked and I haven't got a phone on me or anything registered to me. I wasn't going to make it easy.'

'Look! There's someone at the front door.' Both sank into their seats and peeked out. Two silhouettes moved behind the frosted glass. Kurtis Webster opened the door and looked out. He was wearing a grey suit, white shirt and no tie. His black skin glistened in the morning sun like he'd just showered. He turned around and kissed a woman.

'Is that Beckie?' said Rebwar.

Geraldine shook her head.

Hands grabbed Webster's buttocks and squeezed them.

'Fuck, fucking hell! Is that Charlie? That fucking bitch and... they're snogging.'

Webster moved out of the way and let Charlie walk out.

'What the fuck... and Beckie?' Geraldine took out her phone.

'Wait! Wait and switch it off.' Rebwar lit his cigarette. 'It makes sense now. That's how Kurtis found out that you work for Plan B and then it all kicked off with Beckie? Right?' Geraldine nodded. 'Charlie is playing us. Are we sure Plan B is not involved in this?'

Charlie, in a blue skirt and matching jacket, walked off down the road. Webster closed the door.

'It doesn't add up. This all feels personal. I mean really... That bitch!' Geraldine shook her head. 'And what! Conspiracy? Me... Us?'

Charlie opened a blue convertible Mini and got in.

'I'll follow the bitch or you go and I'll sort out Kurtis that cheating piece of shit.'

Rebwar held her hand. 'Calm, calm. Let's think. We can't just charge in. Do we know anyone else in Plan B? Who's her boss? Someone must be in control.'

'Checks and balances; that's what we have in the service.'

'We need to dig around.'

Geraldine looked at the house and took out her phone to place a call.

Rebwar started the car. 'I'll drive you home.'

TWENTY-ONE

Geraldine had come back the next morning and was sitting in her car, watching the low sun break through the dark clouds. It competed with the street lights and created a criss-cross of shadows. A man wearing white headphones crossed the street with his head down. He had a briefcase in hand. Geraldine opened the window and for a moment hesitated on lighting up, but thought about how Beckie hated the taste and smell of cigarettes. Parked on a side street with a view of Kurtis and Beckie's house, she checked her phone and scrolled through her text messages for a reply to the four she'd sent to Beckie. She typed a few words and deleted them again and put the phone away. It was 6:20 am and she couldn't remember when she had arrived. She had been in such a rage that she had walked up to the door, triggering the security light which had stopped her from battering the main door.

A movement caught her eye, and she looked up and saw Kurtis leaving the house. Her instinct was to go and confront him. She let go of the car's door lever and looked on. He was wearing a dark suit and white shirt with no tie.

He slung his rucksack over his shoulder and passed the car. Geraldine was kind of hoping he would spot her, but he carried on walking down the road. She got out of her car and crossed the street to the house. She could smell Kurtis's aftershave. It made her feel sick as she pressed the doorbell. It was a cute little synthetic tune, and it seemed to go on forever. Geraldine turned to face the street and waited till some locks clinked open. She faced the the door and saw Beckie's eyes.

'Christ, what are you doing here? Go away!'

'I need to talk. Talk about Kurtis.'

'No! Geraldine. No, we don't. Please go away... No! Piss off!'

Beckie's face was red. 'He's beaten you, hasn't he?'

'What do you expect? He's right.' Beckie pushed the door but Geraldine had put her Doc Martens shoe in the gap. 'Fuck sake. I'll call the cops. And the real ones.'

'Kurtis is sleeping with Charlie right under your roof.'

'What? Who?'

'My Plan B contact. You know the people you hate so much.'

'Stop lying to me.' Beckie pushed the door with all her weight.

Geraldine got her phone out and showed her a picture. 'Look, last night. Snogging in front of your house.'

Beckie squinted at the picture. 'That could be anyone. Charlie, you say... a bloke?'

'No, a she, a dangerous and manipulative she. And she's trying to mess us up. And where were you last night? I was worried sick.'

'Why? Why would they do that? I was at a convention, OK?'

'Couldn't you smell her? Go on, smell his clothes.'

Geraldine showed her the picture again. 'Wearing a light blue suit. Go on and smell it. Sure it'll smell of Chanel. That's what she wears. Left it on me, too. And that bitch tried to have it off with me. I wouldn't. You're in my heart, Beckie. Listen to yours.'

Beckie stepped back a bit, and the door opened slightly. Geraldine could see that her left cheek was red and swollen. She was wearing a dressing gown with a tank top underneath it. 'Cuppa?'

Beckie stepped back, exhausted. She hit the wall with her back and slid down. Hiding her face with her hands, she started sobbing. Geraldine closed the front door. She could smell Kurtis, which made her nervous and anxious. She crouched down to help Beckie off the floor, put her left arm around her and with her right held her elbow. As soon as she took it Beckie flinched. Geraldine knew it was a bruise. Instead, she moved her hand on her ribs, feeling her loose breast. Beckie's head fell into her shoulder and Geraldine held her for a moment, smelling her and hearing her heart thumping into her ear. She was being soothed and not a word was said. Just a few sniffs and sighs.

'Come on, let's have some tea, my love.' And Geraldine helped her slowly off the floor and led her to the kitchen. There were leftovers of a fight. Smashed cups and plates with a knife implanted into the wooden cutting board. 'Have you got any cups left?'

Beckie sat on a bar stool and pointed at a cupboard. Geraldine went over to it and found one that said *Little Miss Trouble*, to which Beckie smiled. She found another one that said *Mr Good* and Beckie asked for it. Geraldine handed it over to her and Beckie threw at the wall. It smashed and pieces bounced and skidded across the wooden floor. They both laughed.

'Is there any other one you'd like?'

'Tea is in the jug under the cupboard. What have I done? I always believed him. Why?'

'I did too. I mean my husband. He was always right, always never wrong. Till one day he was.'

Rebwar was driving his car up Edgware Road with Geraldine in the back seat, watching the traffic pass by and listening to the radio. *David Davis and the EU's chief Brexit negotiator Michel Barnier have agreed on a backstop solution to the Irish border. This is seen as a significant step forward to—*

'Tunes please! Can't bear all this Brexshit.'

Rebwar put on a CD and it was the King of Iranian Pop, Viguen with his hit song *'Bordi Az Yadam'*. Rebwar indicated to turn left and his wipers flicked across the windscreen to chase some raindrops.

'There's someone waving on the right,' Geraldine said. 'Big fat lad.'

'That's Raj.' Rebwar drove past him and made a turn across the road.

Geraldine turned around. 'Raj! That's him? I had imagined him... different. You know, like someone who hasn't seen daylight and with glasses. He's jolly!'

The car behind Rebwar didn't bother waiting and overtook him. Rebwar reversed, and the car honked him. Geraldine wound the window down and flicked her cigarette stub at the car. Rebwar drove up to Raj, who opened the front passenger door and got in. The car dropped a couple of inches as Raj fist bumped Rebwar.

'Who's the passenger?'

'Raj, this is DC Smith, a friend of mine. You know... Geraldine.'

Raj turned around, his mass swivelling like a rolling barrel, and smiled. 'Are you carrying a piece?'

'No.'

'Can we go to a diner?'

'You should take up smoking,' Rebwar said. 'Cuts the appetite. We need to stay in the car.'

'Oh, like hush-hush spy stuff. Wink, wink, tickle my nose stuff.' Raj giggled. 'But, dude, I insist on different tunes. None of this grandpa music.' And Raj searched for a radio station.

'Yeah.'

'There's a McDonald's with a drive through in Islington.' Rebwar handed over his mobile to Raj and a few seconds later it was guiding him to the restaurant.

Geraldine leaned forward and asked Raj, 'So what have you found?'

'He'll need food before he can fully brief us,' said Rebwar.

'Uncle! You make me sound like an ogre.' And for a moment croaked on his next comment. 'OK. Yeah, no denying you're right. What can I say? I like food. It's my passion.'

'Uncle?' said Geraldine.

'Long story. Just an easy metaphor or something like that,' said Rebwar. 'I met his dad on a burglary case back home. He was the victim, and we became friends.'

'Top man, he is,' said Raj. 'Still owe him.'

They arrived at the McDonald's just off the A501 on Wharf Road. It was behind a Texaco petrol station and wedged between new glass high rises, building sites and a council estate. The restaurant was a little square box with a slanted roof and would have looked more at home in Middle America than in a sprawling metropolis.

'Reminds me of Sim City. Shall I order something for everybody?'

Rebwar smiled.

'Can I get a salad?'

'Got to try the Signature menu.' And Raj shouted over to the microphone, which was on Rebwar's side. Rebwar thought he was just reading out the menu but soon realised that this was the order, so he waited until he was done before moving the car forward.

It took a few moments for the order to be processed and boxes and wrappers filled the car. Geraldine had to create a larder on the empty seat next to her. Rebwar drove off and found a parking space a few streets away, close to the many building sites around but away from the bustling streets. Raj had already eaten his first burger and was working on the second one, the classic Big Mac.

'Can't beat it. Yeah... So...' Raj said with a mouthful of burger. 'This Jack Hill guy... I managed to get into his cloud storage.' A rain shower moved in and drummed on the car's roof. 'The cloud is remote storage in an undefined place. Bit like those clouds but these servers are dotted around the world. With spinning disks.' Rebwar motioned his hand for Raj to move on. 'OK, OK, I got into it and, man, it's got some weird stuff. Not weird as in porno, but conspiracies. Get my drift? Yeah? So...' Raj took out his laptop out and flipped it open. 'There is this cell of activists. They have quite a few names... The Antichrists... Movement of Freedom... the Reckoning of the Youth, etc... etc... It pretty much comes to five. And yes, they used *Five Go on a Riot*.' Raj giggled.

'Kids' books by Enid Blyton,' said Geraldine.

'Jack was following them for what I guess was going to be an article, as that is what he does. Like political conspiracies. He was finding parallels to what Putin and his thugs are doing. Like funding opposition parties, shape shifting, keeping people guessing what you're doing and all that good stuff. And these five are hired chaos.' Raj flicked through some pictures and finished his cheeseburger. Geraldine passed another box from the pile. 'Thanks, how's the salad?'

'Green.' Geraldine was flicking through some printouts that Raj had left in a folder. 'Is that who I think it is?'

'Funny you should ask,' Raj said. 'Rebwar mentioned her and get this... it's weird. That girl, Daisy, you asked about... She's called Daisy Merkenstand and her father was Sir John Merkenstand. You two look like you know this... Am I repeating myself?'

'Was?' said Geraldine.

Raj took another bite of his burger, and he moved his head from side to side in enjoyment. 'Coming, coming.' He took another bite. 'He died in a helicopter crash and had a data company. And this is interesting—'

'Hold on... So that Sir John character is dead? I read he was alive.'

'Well...' Raj burped. 'Sorry. Everyone thinks he's dead but, look here... my kind of techie stuff.' Raj showed them some code. 'Yeah, yeah, I know, but it has clues.' And he highlighted some names and characters. 'Tracking/data mining software. It goes around the internet looking for information about user habits. They can look at what you do on Facebook or other social networks. All for scientific research, of course. Loads of data companies do this and his is still at it. That's what Jack Hill had found out. Boom. Hey?' Raj looked at them like he had won a gold medal.

'And what about the Filthy Five?'

Raj sucked the straw of his Coke till it slurped empty. 'A mixed bunch and I think sort of uni mates.' He flicked through some of his printouts. 'Pinky Knight, the one with the crazy hairdo, she was at school with Daisy. Got into Cambridge at seventeen. Dropped out and got into drugs. Yeah, bored toffs. James Hewitt-Thomas was also at Cambridge, rich dad, and is their sort of leader. Works as an estate agent and seems like the one normal one...' Raj grabbed a few fries. 'Henry Trent that's shacking up with Charlie as Uncle said, well he's more working-class stock. Was a cycle courier and lost his leg in an accident. Hence the prosthetic one.'

Rebwar stretched out his neck, still feeling the beating he got from Trent.

'And then we have Joseph Brunje. Sniper with the Dutch forces, got discharged for mental problems. Became a drug runner and a dealer. Man, he's the nutter.'

Geraldine leaned in. 'Is this Charlie's creation? Or Plan B? What a bunch of misfits.'

'Cover, maybe, as they sound like a bunch of hippies. What does Hill think of them?' asked Rebwar.

Raj shrugged his shoulders.

'I'm going to ask Charlie what is going on.' Said Geraldine.

'Don't, we have to keep the advantage. Lets see where all this leads us.' Said Rebwar.

TWENTY-THREE

Rebwar was standing in front of the Marlin Apartments on Long Lane in Southwark. It was a concrete high rise with glass balconies. The blue-tiled entrance still had some missing fittings. Large posters and signs hung in and out of the building with promising slogans of spectacular views and luxury. Geraldine had accessed Hill's phone records and found that he had called a number from this location. Rebwar had called the estate agent that was handling the property. From their website, there were four apartments for rent.

A girl with short dark hair approached him in a tight-fitting grey skirt that started just above her knees and a white shirt with a golden chain that disappeared into her small cleavage, which was squeezed in together by a tight bra. Her smile was as wide as her dark eyes which captured all your attention.

'Hi.' She looked down at her file. 'Mr Ghorbani, I'm Samantha Morgan from Foxtons. You'd like to see four apartments?'

'Yes, Samantha.' Rebwar shook her soft hand. 'Yes, my sons are coming over to study and I can't decide whether to buy or rent.'

'Lucky sons.' She smiled and posed as if there was a camera on her.

'I only want the best for them. I have worked hard.'

Samantha opened her file and flicked through some pages. 'We'll start with flat thirty on the eighth floor.' She walked off with her sharp, black stiletto heels tapping on the square polished granite tiles. Rebwar followed her into the lobby which had a long desk with a security guard behind it. He was on the phone and wore a dark uniform with a cap. Samantha swiped at her phone as they waited for the elevator. The corridor didn't have any natural light and Rebwar spotted a couple of cameras in the corners.

She opened the door to flat thirty.

'This is furnished, two bed with two en suite bathrooms. Perfect for two sons. What are they studying?'

Rebwar looked at the large open-plan living room which had a couch, dining table and a kitchen running the length of the wall. Beside it were full-length windows with a balcony and a view onto the Thames. 'One is studying law and the other medicine. Their mother wished it. I would have told them to find a job. You learn more about business by doing it than from a book. Did you study, Samantha?'

She opened the two doors to the bedrooms. Rebwar had a quick look at them. The beds were made and ready to be used. 'Has anyone been here before?'

Samantha looked at her file. 'No, this is new. Actually, they're all new. They've been built to the highest specifications. All the mod cons, as you can see. Exceptional.'

'Can I see the next one?'

'Sure. Follow me.'

The other flat had a similar layout but had a south-facing view and different furniture. This time Rebwar opened a few of the cupboards, which were empty. There were no signs of anyone having been there. He asked if any of them had been refurnished, to which she said no.

Number 26 was on the tenth floor. Its door had a scratch on it, which Samantha didn't notice.

'Will they'll fix that?'

'Just niggles. Clumsy builders.' She struggled to find the right key. None of the keys turned freely inside the lock.

'Can I try?' She handed the keys to Rebwar, he selected one, pulled the door hard towards him and the lock turned easily. He swung the door open.

'Strong man... I'll make a note to fix it.'

Rebwar walked in first as she wrote on the file. He could immediately smell something different: a musty smell, not the fresh smell of paint or glue. There were some scuffs marks on the wall and the place looked unfurnished.

'Oh! They haven't finished it, have they? So sorry about this.'

Rebwar walked into the large open-plan room, which was a similar set-up to the last two. The kitchen was a mess and had leftover ready meals lying around on the counter-tops. There were a pair of black jeans, a dirty white t-shirt, socks and a puffer jacket spread over the couches. He opened one of the two bedrooms and saw a couple of cut cable ties. He picked them up and surreptitiously checked if they fitted around his wrist. They didn't but would certainly fit someone smaller.

'I'm so sorry, Mr Ghorbani. I think this unit hasn't been cleaned. Very odd but as you can imagine this is very similar to the others. Just with a better view. Let's go and see the final one and I'll report this to the management. So sorry again.'

'I'm sure the other one is the same. Thank you for the tour. I have a few others to see today. But I am interested. How is the security?' They both walked out, and she tried to close the door.

'There is CCTV and twenty-four-hour security guard downstairs and there is a garage under the building. All we need is a six-month deposit, bank statements and utility bills.'

Both walked out of the building and they said their goodbyes. Rebwar lit up in front of the building and looked up at it. After a few puffs, he went back in and up to the security desk.

'Hi.' Rebwar read the man's badge. 'Mr J. Jamestown. Just saw some flats with Miss Morgan from Foxtons.'

The man nodded.

'I was taking photos. I'm looking for a flat for my sons and very stupidly left my phone up in flat number twenty-six.'

Jamestown looked at him, took a moment to think and nodded. A few curly strands of greying hair escaped from his cap.

'I know... I forgot... Just need a minute and go in and get my phone... Five minutes.'

'Man, I need management to authorise it. D'you have some ID?'

'I was just in, you saw me with Miss Morgan. Call her. She'll confirm. And I need the phone to call my wife. Sure you can understand. If I don't...' Rebwar looked at his watch. 'I'll be in trouble.'

He nodded his head. 'Mister?'

'Ghorbani... I'll leave my wallet. I'll come back.'

Jamestown looked around and leaned in. 'OK, but you be quick about it. No want trouble from you, all right?'

———

Rebwar opened the broken door of Flat 26 and went in carefully studying every inch of the flat as if he was hunting for a pin. He took out his phone and photographed the scuff marks. They looked like they might have been made by shoes. Possibly Hill's shoes, kicking out and struggling against his assailants. In the bedroom were little brown marks on the mattress which Rebwar guessed must have been dried blood. He looked underneath the bed and found a ring. It had a skull on it which he recognised from meeting him at the Shishawi. Hill had also been wearing it in the cab when he drove him to that demonstration on the Thames. He put it into his pocket and went into the bathroom where he found a blue latex glove floating in the toilet. He fished it out with his pen and put it into his handkerchief.

He looked at the large bathroom mirror. It had a few marks. He exhaled on to it. Two letters appeared: *H* and *c*. He carried on until he could make out a message: *Help Jac*. It was partial but clear enough. In the corner was an empty roll of gaffer tape with a few more cable ties. Rebwar photographed other pieces of rubbish and discarded clothing in the flat. There wasn't anything else that gave a clue to where they could have gone. From the food and beer cans, he guessed there couldn't have been more than three of them there. He closed the flat and went downstairs where he asked Jamestown, 'Where is that name from?'

'Caribbean. Yeah, I know. I'm nearly white. Long story.'

Rebwar showed him his phone. 'You like your job?'

'Yes, it pays. Why you ask?'

'A few nights ago, did anyone go in that flat?'

'Why?'

'Someone's been in there and left a mess.'

'Man, you putting your nose where it don't belong... not my job to–'

'You just let me in. Someone's been in there and been squatting.'

'You say what? Squatting?'

'Check your camera. You can go back?'

'Squatting? Man, you sure it's no tenant.'

'It's a mess in there. Look it up.'

Jamestown moved his cap and scratched his hair. He tapped his keyboard and Rebwar came around the desk to look at his monitor. He was rewinding video images and people flashed by like ghosts. Then there was someone being dragged along by two men.

'Shit man, who in the hell...' He zoomed in and they watched Jack Hill being dragged out towards the lift. He looked at Rebwar, who nodded.

'Look... I'm a private investigator. No need to worry, I just need some pictures of the video and when they came in and out. Then you can either ignore this and let someone else find out, or call it in. Your choice. I'm not going to tell.'

'What? You say, private investigator. Trouble, you say? I like this job, I need this job. Understand me?'

'Say nothing and let someone else deal with it. They might fire the security company. If you own up, they might use you as a scapegoat. Happens all the time. Easier for one underpaid, nice person like you to get dismissed than the boss going and losing the contract. And you have any problems you can call me.'

Jamestown swallowed and looked out into the distance. Then he tapped his keyboard. Rebwar took snaps of all the locations they had been. They hadn't been there for more than a day and had left a day ago in a car. He now had the registration and their fuzzy faces. He recognised them, Hewitt-Thomas and Brunje. He called Geraldine to hear if she had heard anything from Charlie.

TWENTY-FOUR

Rebwar was having his coffee sitting outside the Al Arez Cafe on Edgware Road. It wasn't in his repertoire of hangouts, but he needed a new perspective. He needed to go through his options. His initial brief was to follow Charlie, which had led him to Hill and the Filthy Five. Did Charlie know she was being followed? Is that why she was trying to frame Geraldine? Rebwar sipped his coffee and added another spoon of sugar. He felt like he was being played but just wasn't sure to what end. He also suspected that Hill had written Peckworth's obituary for Charlie. Was that why she was paying him? So far he hadn't found any evidence. Geraldine had been trawling the CCTV footage for any clues on the Filthy Five's movements, but they only appeared for brief moments here and there.

Another strong Turkish coffee arrived and was put down in front of him without any presentation or fuss. Rebwar thanked the man, but he was already on his way back inside. Rebwar went back to his thoughts on who he could find who worked for Plan B. A text from Raj appeared on his phone but as soon as he swiped to read it the phone rang.

'Where are you?' said Raj.

'At the Al Arez Cafe.'

'I'll be there in five.'

He dropped the call. Rebwar took out a cigarette and lit it. Some other guests next to him stared at him. He continued to rack his brain about how he could contact someone further up the Plan B chain. He wanted to know what was going on up there. Since the last two jobs, things had changed and it wasn't just a PI jobs with a hidden racist agenda. Mr Peckworth MP had been being blackmailed, and it had either backfired or they'd ended up having to contain it. There was more to it than a simple suicide, and Rebwar would have loved to have seen that letter he'd left behind. But they had neatly closed it not to be pried open again. What they needed was an inside man, someone who knew Plan B, but no such luck had come their way.

A black cab pulled up in front of the cafe and out of the door stepped Raj. He was breathing heavily and covered with a sheen of sweat. He paid the cab driver and went over to sit in front of Rebwar.

'Black cab?'

Raj got out his laptop, opened it and typed his pass-word. He flicked it round for Rebwar to see it. There was a picture of Jack Hill and some text. *We have taken Jack Hill. His release will cost you 200 bitcoins click here.*

'And if you click there?'

'Haven't tried it and don't!'

'Bitcoins?'

'Cryptocurrency and digital money that can't be traced, and it's about a million pounds depending on when you take the exchange rate. Goes up and down like a bloody Yo-

Yo. And if you look, it's on this website. They hijacked his URL and took it offshore.'

'Russians?'

'I couldn't find any obvious traces that it was them.' Raj closed the laptop as the waiter arrived. 'Coke, please, no ice.' The waiter left. 'Did you fall out with the Shishawi?' Rebwar motioned his hand for him to carry on. 'The low-down is that I can't find them.'

'Filthy Five?'

'Oh, yeah. Who else? Are you thinking of some other organisation? It also looks like he didn't have many other friends. Well... that have money.' Raj opened the laptop and typed away. 'Look, a petition set up by some friends. Not many but some... I thought of an idea. You're probably not going to like it. Amir... we could revive him and see what kind of attention he gets. You know, get him to sign up on this petition and make a noise on social networks. Might draw out something.'

Amir Begani was an identity that Rebwar had used to infiltrate Richard O'Neil's gang and he had worked for them as a delivery driver.

'You know, Raj, sometimes you surprise me. Great idea! What do I need to do?'

'Not much really, I'm just going to make you exist on the internet. You'll be like some ghosts. Hey, you know this petition could be a lie as well. Fishing to get people's information.'

Rebwar sipped his coffee. It wasn't as good as his local.

TWENTY-FIVE

Rebwar was on a morning run, stuck in traffic in Camden and heading to Holmes Road in Kentish Town. His passengers were a mother and a daughter who looked alike. He could see that her daughter looked up to her. Both had similar haircuts, a short bob that revealed the neckline, and both wore gold necklaces. The mum's being the more expensive as it had five large rings on it. Both had thick-rimmed glasses that gave them an artistic air. The daughter had dark red rims while the mother wore yellow ones, which was the only difference between them. Both wore a wavy black and white stripy top. They smiled and chatted to each other.

'Sorry about the traffic.'

The woman looked at her watch and carried on chatting. Rebwar had checked her profile and her name was Christine L., but he found it rude to just call out someone's Christian name without being introduced. Also, he couldn't understand what they were saying; they were speaking in a language that he guessed was French. In front of him were some signs for roadworks, which was probably the cause for delay.

'Sorry to ask, but what language is that you are speaking?'

'French.'

'It sounds musical.'

'You never heard it before? You're not from the UK?'

'No, I am from Iran. I know people emigrated to France after the Shah. And his two wives lived in Paris. One loved him very much. Sad story really.'

'Who was the Shah?' asked the little girl.

'He was the King of Iran,' said the mother.

'He had two queens?'

'Three,' said Rebwar. 'One after the other. The second one couldn't have children and so he married again.'

'Why couldn't she have children?'

'Oh, not everybody is blessed in this world. She loved him very much but couldn't give him a prince. Sad story.'

The little girl looked at her mother wanting to know more and the mother looked at Rebwar. 'It's something you will one day learn at school, OK? It's–'

'How come I don't know any princes or princesses?'

For a moment, Rebwar was going to pitch in, but he didn't want to put his foot in it again. Instead, he honked at some slow traffic next to him. As he passed the loud road-works, he took a left along a little residential street and two scooters overtook him. Both of them had pillion passengers which dismounted just in front of him. A black ponytail trailed out from a white helmet. Before Rebwar could find reverse, the left side window burst into little diamond frag-ments. A man reached into the front passenger door and grabbed the inside door handle and opened it. The action unlocked the central locking and another helmeted man stepped into the back seat next to the little girl and mother.

Through the full-faced helmet the man spoke loudly. 'Not a scream! Drive on!' He showed a pump-action shotgun that had been hidden in his large black sports jacket. The two scooters drove off. 'Take a left and then a right. Go! Go!'

Rebwar saw the two frightened faces in the back. The little girl's white fingers were digging into her mother's arms. 'You want my money?' Rebwar got his wallet out.

'Stay off our patch. Are you listening, you foreign fuck? Understand that we are going to fuck with you bread and butter. Get it, motherfucker?'

Rebwar looked into the man's black piercing eyes. James Hewitt-Thomas, Filthy Five's leader.

'Stop following us, OK? And it's not a request. My tall friend in the back. Well, he's an angry little shit, and he likes violence. Can't control him – get my drift, shitface? Now stop the car! Look forward not at me.'

Joseph Brunje was in the back, and Rebwar could smell his heavy aftershave mixed with sweat. He kept twitching like he had some itch, drugs probably, or some kind of high. His eyes kept darting around, searching for someone.

'Where's Jack Hill?' said Rebwar and felt a punch land on his jaw. His head bouncing off the headrest.

'Wallets and jewellery now!' The man in the front had a Tesco's bag. 'Rip it off! Come on!'

The mother looked through her handbag and took out her wallet. The man in the back ripped the necklaces off their necks. A couple of the rings fell on the floor. 'You dickhead.' And they both stepped out and got on the back of the two scooters that had followed them. 'Don't even report this.

Otherwise you're fucking dead and your children. Understand.' And they drove off on the back of the scooters.

The little girl's eyes streamed with tears and panicked little hiccups came in little stuttered waves. Rebwar's phone had been taken and his wallet. Luckily they hadn't opened the glove box as they would have found his pistol in there. And that would have escalated the whole situation. He looked at his two shocked passengers.

'What are you involved in? Mr?'

Rebwar tried to find something to tell her but couldn't.

The woman grabbed the seat and pulled herself forward. 'Are you going to call the police? I... I never thought it would happen to me. Never, I am so angry. My friends have been mugged...'

Rebwar hit the steering wheel. 'Sorry, sorry. If you want to call them, do. I can't... you heard them. I'm in danger.'

'But you must! This is London, not Iran or Algeria or Africa. *London.*'

'I'll drive you. Where do you need to go? Then call your insurance.'

'But I need a police statement of something.'

'You can call and report.'

She looked at her daughter, cuddling her and sniffing. She said something in French, opened the door, got her daughter out and slammed the door as hard as she could. Rebwar drove off. The Filthy Five had made their point and he must have rattled them. His lip was swelling up and starting to sting.

TWENTY-SIX

Geraldine was in her car, crawling along in London's morning traffic, and Beckie was in the passenger seat, drumming her fingers on her leg. She turned in her seat, rolled her sleeves up and made some popping sounds with her lips.

'Becks, will you stop, please? We'll get there.' Geraldine stared at her left arm, which had little marks like it was acne. Beckie rolled down her sleeve and pointed ahead. Geraldine inched the car along. 'You'll be free, free of that demon.'

Beckie propped her head with her right arm, which was now resting on the door. 'You know that's a lie. You're just conveniently putting me away. I... I...' Tears snaked down her face and she sniffed. 'Sorry, babe. Shit, I'm a bloody basket case, aren't I? You'll check on Kurtis?'

What the fuck! Geraldine held her breath and gripped the steering wheel as if it was his neck.

'Like you said... I know, I know. He's... but I love him!'

What the fuck! Geraldine counted to ten like her mother

had told her. *You'll see the sun will shine again as soon as that dark cloud has passed. Three, four, five.*

'Sorry, sorry... I love you and you know... You can feed me chicken soup.'

Raindrops hit the windscreen and Geraldine used the wipers to flick them off. At that moment she wished it was as easy to deal with Beckie's erratic emotions. She understood that she was not logical and lost in that dark cloud of addiction. Geraldine grabbed her hand and held it. Beckie's bloodshot eyes looked out onto the road ahead. The green digital clock read 8:42, and they had just passed the Westway and were into North Kensington. Just a few more streets and... For a moment, she too wanted to turn back.

'Dr Phelman sounded nice, didn't she? I'm sure you'll be like... the Beckie I fell in love with. Remember?'

'It'll be torture. They'll hurt me. Please don't let them do that. Oh, the shame! I can't... I can't.'

Geraldine stopped the car. They had arrived at the Gladstone Clinic. It looked like a large residential house. It had a white facade that stopped at the first floor, a central entrance with two little columns and above were two more sand-bricked floors. Identical houses lined the street apart from a boring rectangular block of flats a few doors down. World War Two bomb damage, no doubt. 'I'll get the bag and help you in there. Is that OK?'

Beckie's head was hanging down as if it was being held up by a wire. Dangling and bobbing to the sound of sniffing. Her hands rubbing a handkerchief.

'Come on, babe, it's like a hotel and looks like a five star one. Wish I could stay with you.' Geraldine held the door open, waiting for Beckie to come out. By the front gate were two men in white coats waiting for her to come in. They were smiling, but it looked like the smiles were painted on.

'Please, let's go home. Look at them! No! Please, G, don't let them take me.'

'Can we help?'

The two men were by the car. 'She's... she's got an appointment. Sorry we're late. Beckie.'

'Hi, Beckie.' One of the men leaned into the car. 'We're here to help. I'm Duncan and my colleague here is Mo. We are here to make you better. I hear you need help. It's a lovely clinic. We have loving people to help you.'

Beckie crossed her arms and looked at Geraldine like a child that was looking for her mummy. Her big black eyes staring up at her with welling eyes. That image seared itself into Geraldine's consciousness. Duncan's hand grabbed Beckie's arm and tugged twice till she gave in like a weed being pulled from a rock. Both men helped her across the road. Geraldine watched her walk, crouched and weak, and followed with her bag.

TWENTY-SEVEN

Rebwar was in the garage, gaffer taping plastic sheets over the car's broken windows. He had been here before, and it had also been a scooter gang. Even the London police were having problems dealing with them. The only way the police had managed to stop them was to ram them off their bikes. How had they found out that he was onto them? Hill's house and that man. He heard Musa's voice echo off the concrete walls, followed by another set of footsteps. They were the quick sharp taps of stilettos. The woman's voice was unfamiliar but had a Persian accent to it and sounded older than Musa. Rebwar looked over and saw Musa and a shorter woman with him. She had long wavy black hair, a dark pencil skirt, a cream shirt and jangly jewellery. He called out to Musa.

'Dad, what are you doing here?' Musa eyed the roll of duct tape. 'Oh, not again. Oh, sorry, this is Auntie Dinah. Mum's friend.'

Rebwar watched her flick the long fake eyelashes. They studied each other as if they were two predators that had stepped on each other's patch. Dinah stepped forward, her flowery musky perfume floating over him like a net. 'I've heard so much about you.' She smiled with her red lips, shook his hand firmly and put her hands on her hips, a stance that rooted her. It reminded Rebwar of the TV series, *Charlie's Angels*.

'Dad, she's offered me a job.'

'Oh, don't you like the one you have?'

'It's only if he wants to. It's marketing in a boutique.'

'In a what?'

'Shop on King's Street. Good rich clients, I think being so handsome he'll do well. Hourieh is very excited for him to start.'

'Oh, and you're going today? I've...'

Dinah looked at the car. 'It's not a great area. Should tell the council to up the security. And that poor boy getting stabbed in front of his house.'

Rebwar looked at his watch. 'Musa get in the car.'

'I've got a lift.'

'I'm going to Barry's.'

'Look, I'll leave you two to chat,' said Dinah. 'Lovely to meet you.' She offered her hand to Rebwar, and he shook it out of courtesy. She turned to Musa and kissed him on the cheek. 'Now, tomorrow... I'll be there tomorrow.' She looked at her watch. 'How time flies! I have a hair appointment.' She smiled and walked off, swinging her hips and stopped. She turned and said, 'Oh, I forgot to say, you have a new fridge. I had one spare from my divorce and offered. Also...' Dinah delved in her Chanel handbag and walked forward and took out a card. 'I told Hourieh that I have a good friend who is looking for a discreet driver. As you can see, he is an important man. Give him a call. I've said that you were a policeman and come from a respectable family.' She turned again and headed off.

Rebwar waited for her to walk out of earshot. He watched her turn for a last look at them before stepping into the lift. Rebwar waved.

'Are you swearing at her?'

'No.' And he finally noticed his son's t-shirt: *I'm so broke I can't even pay attention.*

'Mum said it was OK. She wants me to do that job. And isn't that cool, who is it?'

Rebwar ripped the card up before Musa could read it. 'I'll be talking to your mum. Who is that woman? And why did you wear that t-shirt?' Rebwar held the rest in as he could tell it would fall on deaf ears.

Musa shrugged. 'Dad! What about the job! It's good money, hey? And then I could get a scooter and–'

'Son, I'm not going to listen to some rich man brag about himself and tell me how much he earns while I get the minimum wage from him. I prefer to listen to my passengers talk about Brexit.'

Two scooters drove down into the garage. Their whining engines filling the bare space. They stopped in front of them. Rebwar glanced back at his car. One of the riders took off his helmet.

'What's up, bro?'

Musa fist bumped the rider. The other took his helmet off too. Both were teenagers. One was black with bleached hair. The other had red dyed hair and looked Indian.

'This is my dad... Vin and Dobbo.'

'Nice to meet you,' said Vin with the bleached hair. 'Heard a lot about you. Had some trouble?'

'They're taking me to Barry's, Dad. They work there.'

Rebwar took out a pack of cigarettes, which he then quickly put back in his pocket. 'OK, tell Barry I'll be there soon and to make sure he's ordered the parts. Be safe.' The boys revved their engines. Musa grabbed the spare helmet from Vin's bike and jumped on the back. 'And, no, you can't get a bike.' But Rebwar was drowned out by the accelerating scooters. Rebwar walked off towards the lift but stopped. He looked down at his hand, which was shaking again. Taking out his cigarettes, he lit up, glanced at the no smoking sign in front of him and walked back to the car.

TWENTY-EIGHT

Back in the London traffic, Geraldine wiped the tears that kept coming as she remembered her emotional goodbye to Beckie. She tried and tried to focus. There was work to do, and she had to keep it together. Beckie was in a safe place and she could visit her soon. It still felt like she'd left her in an emotional prison. Geraldine focused on the task ahead, which was to go and inspect a demonstration in Trafalgar Square. It was about Brexit and austerity, and the Filthy Five were going to be there. She got the tip-off from Raj and some other police colleagues that she had chatted to in her break.

Having parked the car as close as she could, Geraldine walked the rest of the way. She had packed a rucksack like it was going to be a day out. It had two bottles of water, in case CS gas was going to be deployed, a mask, a short baseball bat, a camera and a spare pair of clothes. It really did look like she was supporting the cause, but she knew it could get out of hand, especially if she was going to follow the Filthy Five.

From what Raj had said, the Filthy Five were a crew for

hire. If you needed some shouting, intimidation, vandalising or any other nasty anti-social behaviour, these were the guys and gals you'd call on. Of course, there were many other groups with actual political ambitions and goals. But their lack of conviction made the Filthy Five special. And of course the fact that Charlie was sleeping with Henry Trent made them guilty of some kind of conspiracy.

Geraldine walked along Piccadilly with the crowds growing in number. Police presence was also getting more visible. Early on in her career, she had been called to a few demos. The biggest and most violent one being the one in 2010, with the students demonstrating against the introduction of student fees. A bunch of them had managed to escape the cordon and smash the Conservative headquarters. There she could see what mob rule could do.

This one was quite different, with lots of families and couples who had blue and yellow stars painted on their faces and were waving EU flags. She followed the growing crowd to Trafalgar Square, where the sounds of drums and football whistles were intensifying. Geraldine would have liked to share this with Beckie. It had a carnival feel to it. Music, speeches and painted signs. They had both discussed Brexit. Beckie had voted Remain and herself Leave. A Remoaner or snowflake, they called the pro-EU camp. Geraldine just saw it as an almighty divided mess with no winner in sight. *Bollocks to Brexit* read one sign, others *Brexit, is it worth it?* and *Cancel Brexit.* People around were chanting the slogans. Dogs were dressed up with EU flags. A Schnauzer had a slogan saying *Brexit is Barking mad.*

Geraldine pulled out her phone and flicked through the images of the Filthy Five that Raj had sent her. It wasn't going to be easy as they probably would have their faces covered. But she really wanted to talk to Daisy Merken-stand who, yes, was a spoiled bitch but somewhere inside Geraldine believed there was a sweet innocent girl – she had just taken the wrong path and was now an angry and lost soul. It wasn't even guaranteed that the Filthy Five would be here. It was a hunch from Raj. He had discovered some chatter on the internet. The police filmed all these events and any violence always made good headlines. Police horses had been deployed around the major chokepoints. The march was being herded. A helicopter hovered above them. Geraldine stayed at the edge of the flow as she wanted to explore the side streets.

She turned into a street just off St Martin-in-the-Fields towards Charing Cross tube station. She found it a little surreal how people continued with the day-to-day shopping and sightseeing while people demonstrated on the next street. The noise of high-pitched whistles and chanting spilled over. A smoke canister landed close to her. Red smoke spilled out of it and filled the street. Geraldine found it odd, as the demonstrators' colours were yellow and blue. Some police officers walked down the street, looking around them. The can rolled towards her, so had been thrown from down the road, not where the march was being held. She looked around her for anything suspicious. As she made her way towards Charing Cross Road, she spotted more red smoke spreading.

She heard some shouting. Loud swearing. A girl dressed in camouflage and with a black mask covering her face ran past her, three men in blue shirts chasing. Geraldine made some attempt to keep up with them, but they were too fast. She stopped and got her camera out. More red smoke floated down St Martin's Lane, and she went over to investi-gate. Two guys in black hoodies and reflective sunglasses were standing in front of the Duke of York's Theatre. One covered his face with a scarf as he saw her film. The longer it went on, the stupider she felt. She zoomed in. One was tall and muscular, and the other had a ponytail. Henry Trent and Joseph Brunje. A girl ran up to them, a shaven head and wearing mirrored sunglasses. It was Pinky Knight, who had now changed her hairstyle. Geraldine stepped back towards the wall.

Trent pointed at her. They chatted and Brunje ran for her. Geraldine ran down Mays Court and came out onto Bedfordbury at the back of St Martin's Lane Hotel. She went straight on into Bedford Court. He was catching up and his heavy footsteps thudded ever closer. She could hear his breathing. A police car turned into the street. She was about to stop him, but he switched his siren on and sped off. She looked behind her. Brunje had fled. She carried on running. It looked like a dead end. There was a pedestrian passage in front of her that led to Bedford Street. She knew that the Charing Cross police station was on the next parallel street, on Chandos Place. Pinky Knight was in front of her. Blocking her exit. Brunje was behind her at the other end of the street. Geraldine took out her bottle of Mace and calmly walked over to the girl.

'Hey, Pinky Knight. How's it going?'

'What?'

'Been looking for you, Pinky.'

'Why were you filming us? You with the pigs?'

'No, I'm on your side. Wanted to meet.' Geraldine looked behind her. Brunje was getting closer to her. 'Where's James and Daisy?'

'Who?'

'You know... the rest of you. The boss and the prettier girl.'

'No one's my boss. Right? Not falling for your shit.' Knight stepped closer.

Geraldine could see Brunje's reflection in Knight's mirrored glasses. He was going to grab her. She stepped back towards the opposite wall and faced both of them. 'And Jack Hill, you got him?'

'Hey? Pinky, who's this?' Brunje's voice was deep and had a foreign accent to it.

'Not too sure. Who *are* you?'

'Like I said, I'm working for your side. We need to talk.'

Brunje raised his fist. Geraldine showed him her Mace canister. 'Any closer and I'll...'

He laughed. 'So? Who the fuck are you? Police, I'd say.'

People walked by the alleyway, and as soon as they saw them, looked down and rushed away. A can rolled in.

'Fuck, get her!' said Knight.

Geraldine sprayed. Red smoke filled the small enclosed space.

'Bitch got me!'

Geraldine ran into Bedford Street. James Hewitt-Thomas was in front of her. He grabbed her neck and squeezed. He was tall, handsome and clean shaven, with a perfect smile. Geraldine tried to breathe. She stamped on his foot but he was obviously wearing steel toe caps. He didn't move, just carried on smiling and squeezing. Red smoke swirled around them. The other two coughed and spat and swore.

'Who are you?'

He let go a little. 'Fuck off, James. You're just a bunch of filthy–'

He tightened his grip on her throat. 'Careful, I'm not here to negotiate.' He leaned in. 'So? Who are you? Ever been raped?'

Geraldine kneed him in the balls but hit a plastic cricket box.

He smiled again. 'Public school. You learn certain things.'

'Hey, what is going here?'

Geraldine tried to see who it was but Hewitt-Thomas's grip was too tight for her to move. Her peripheral vision was going.

'Mind your own fucking business. Nosy little man.' Still holding Geraldine, Hewitt-Thomas picked up the Mace bottle she had dropped and he sprayed the man's face. He screamed and walked off.

'Frisk her.'

Knight went through her pockets. They found her warrant card. 'Fuck! Knew it. The bitch... fucking bitch. You lying pig!' And jumping up and she screamed into Geraldine's ear. 'YEAH, FUCK YEAH.' Then she giggled.

'Fucking pig!' said Brunje.

Sirens blared down the Strand, which was at the end of the road.

'Go on, kill her. The police are too busy for us. One less pig.' Knight punched Geraldine in the gut and she gave out some more precious air that she couldn't get back. Her lungs were on fire.

'Tell them to pay up. Otherwise, we'll kill Jack. Understand. Nod with your head.'

Geraldine tried to but couldn't find the energy. Her head dropped down and she tried to lift it. Normally such a simple and automatic gesture. But now, she just couldn't. Her energy was ebbing like a river.

'No, no!' yelled Knight. 'The message is by killing her.'

'Come on, guys, we need to go,' said Brunje.

Geraldine felt her hands give way.

'Pinky, no it's not. No. We need to get the message out there!'

'James, I'll fucking do it then... Yeah.'

Geraldine could only pick out the odd word. She felt herself losing control and convulsing.

TWENTY-NINE

It was past midnight in Shoreditch and Rebwar was outside Old Street tube station with its two massive metal arches which had a large cube suspended underneath with LCD screens lighting the area with their multicoloured ads. The pavements were busy with people either trying to catch the last tubes home or finding a bar that would still be open. Rebwar had received a text from an unknown number. It said: *have important information. Meet midnight 21 curtain road car park.* He'd tried to call it back but only got a disconnected tone. He didn't have a good feeling about it either. Too vague, mysterious and out of the blue. But someone had reached out, and he had to follow it up. His hunch was that it was the Filthy Five and he was probably walking into some trap. He'd left a message with Geraldine and hoped she would be on her way. He walked down Great Eastern Street and left another message.

It became quieter as he turned onto Curtain Road. Except for one small lone building with a pub, it was all office buildings. The Horse & Groom backed onto a huge building site. Opposite was 21 Curtain Road, an angular three-storey office block. It looked like it had been slotted together. The pub lights switched off behind him. The main entrance to the building was dark and closed. Rebwar stepped back and saw that on the left of the building was an open entrance, leading to some parking bays behind. A security light switched on as he walked to the back. He looked behind him and all was deserted, with just a few lit windows above him. At the far end of the car park, a door burst open and banged against the wall. Rebwar stopped and watched as someone stumbled out.

Drunk, he thought as the man's feet slammed on the metal platform with the steadiness of a toddler, his upper body swaying like an unsteady crane. He was holding his stomach as if he was going to throw up. Rebwar looked around him. Parked cars and bins. The man carried on stumbling down the metal stairs, tripping another security light above him. The light caught a metal object that reflected in his hands. A large knife stuck out from his belly. His jeans had a large dark wet patch that ran to his knees. Stooped over, his face was hidden by a baseball cap.

Rebwar rushed over to him. His breathing was short and shallow and he spat blood. The man's head dropped back and the baseball cap fell on the ground. He'd met him before and recognised his staring, piercing blue eyes. He'd been with Charlie when they handed over Daisy to them when they had rescued her from O'Neil. Rebwar tried to grab him, but he slid to the ground like a sheet slipping off a bed. Rebwar was left with a large bloodied knife in his hand. The man had taken it out and handed it to him. His bloodied mouth moved as if he was trying to say something. Only blood gurgled out. Rebwar crouched down and went up to his face.

'The Medusa is dead... Plan B is dead.' And the man

carried on repeating it. 'Snakes... snakes, everywhere... everywhere.'

Rebwar stayed there trying to make out what else he was saying, but the man's mouth filled up with blood. It ran down his cheeks and covered his chin and neck. Rebwar turned him on his side, hoping this would help, but the man convulsed a couple of times and stopped breathing. With his red sticky hands, Rebwar dialled 999 and gave his location. He studied the bloodied knife; its blade was a dull black, the back edge serrated, and the main cutting blade had an S shape. Most likely a Chinese model pretending to be an army issue. He put it back down next to the man and looked at his face, now still and lifeless. Above the door from which the man had walked out was a camera. They were on CCTV.

Rebwar checked the man's pockets, but they were empty. He went up the metal staircase to the open fire exit and followed the blood trail. It led up the stairs to the third floor, where he found another set of bloody footprints leading down a hallway. He took a picture of them with his phone; they had a circular worn tread.

One of the walls had a big blue logo reading *Data Vault*. Beside it was a big glass door with a reception desk behind it. The hallway was glassed off and he could see a large open-plan office with a series of desks with computers. The odd screen and desk light were still on. But no one was there, and all was silent – just a low electrical humming noise. Beside the office door was a discarded wallet. Rebwar picked it up and opened it. Apart from the odd copper coin, it had been emptied. Was this meant to look like a mugging? Rebwar hadn't got much out of the dying man. And likely he hadn't seen his murderer as he would have probably mentioned him.

The red tread marks stopped in front of a lift. He called it, got inside and pressed the button for the ground floor. The lift went down and the doors opened; the main reception to the building was in front of him. It was barely lit with a few lights shining up the tall walls and a series of logos. A chair lay fallen next to the security desk where the man must have been sitting. Rebwar went behind the desk where there was a computer. It was all smashed up. Sirens whizzed by the glass front door – an ambulance. He looked around for any information about the man, but the place had been cleared. He went over to the door, which was closed. By the wall was a green button. He pressed on it and it was followed by a magnetic click. He pushed the big glass door and left.

THIRTY

Geraldine was standing in front of an office building on 21 Curtain Road. She wore a scarf which covered her bruising. She still had headaches and had been lucky to have survived. They must have decided she was more use alive than dead. Rebwar had called her in the middle of the night and explained to her what had happened. It had added another twist to their case. She too remembered the man, and what he said in his dying breaths gave her the chills. She was there to try to get the CCTV recording and see who had killed him. She stepped into the large reception and went up to the desk. A woman sat dressed in a white shirt with a lanyard around her neck. She looked up from her computer. No hello or smile, just a dead stare. Geraldine flashed her warrant card.

'Your colleagues are out back,' the receptionist said. 'Dreadful business. This town is going to pot—'

'Did you know him?' Geraldine croaked hoarsely.

'Got a cold?'

Geraldine shook her head.

'Who, the night guard? Na, sorry, a different group, you

see. That's a security company. They deal with that. I work for all those companies.' She pointed at a long list of names behind her. 'A sort of collective, I think.' The woman chewed gum. Her nails were long and multicoloured. 'Get my drift?' She moved left to right on her rolling office chair. 'So, who was it? Some gang? I tell you... around here you hear about so many muggings. I carry Mace with me. My fella gave it to me.' She looked down at her handbag next to her on the desk.

'Where are they?'

She pointed behind her. 'Take the fire exit.'

'How did he get in?'

She shrugged her shoulders.

'Can I see the CCTV?'

'They took it, the handsome one. Had to get a new PC. Was all smashed up, like.'

'What's your name?'

'Stacey Kilmour.'

Geraldine walked over to the emergency exit. She followed the sound of men talking down a hall. Police tape blocked the stairwells and doors. At the back exit, she spotted three men, one uniformed and two suited. She took a breath and went over to them, badge in hand. As she approached them, they all turned to face her. She nodded, they nodded back. She showed her badge. 'DS Smith.'

The short, stocky man replied, 'You're here...' He looked down at her badge.

'I wanted to know if this related to my case. Do you know the victim?'

'Sure, shouldn't you be in bed?'

She didn't reply.

'And you're from?'

'Homicide. Can't really say much more. But you can

call DCI Mark Conelly.' He was an old mate of Geraldine and would lie for her. But she hadn't talked to him in a while. She was counting on their egos; in general, they loved showing off what they had found and especially what they thought happened. They looked a little tired, their clothes were ruffled, and both suited men hadn't shaved. There was a smell of cheap aftershave, Old Spice seemed a favourite.

They looked at each other. The one in uniform looked down at his notes. His large Adam's apple twitched before saying, 'His name is Edward Monkton and works for Night Sure. He was stabbed by a large hunting knife of Chinese make.'

Geraldine looked behind them where a mid-sized white tent had been erected beside the metal stairs. It seemed to be empty apart from some numbered markers that were dotted around. 'Got any CCTV?'

'Some,' the suited man said. 'The camera in the back was broken. Bloody typical. Two men were here.' He turned around and pointed with his pen. 'And we're not sure if they are connected. Although the second was on his tail.' He got his phone out and flicked through some grainy black and white pictures.

Geraldine could tell that the second man was Rebwar. 'Robbery?'

'Could be. His wallet was emptied. Opportunist maybe, as the man came into the entrance and looks like they chatted for a while.' He flicked through some more pictures.

'And the victim?'

'Ex-forces, we think, was working for the security company as a night guard.'

'And nothing from forensics?'

The two detectives shook their heads. Either they were keeping some of the details for themselves or there really wasn't anything. What was certain from Geraldine's point of view was that Plan B had been involved. And these two monkeys could also be involved. 'What was the other man doing?'

'Other? Only two.'

'Who called it in? And why didn't this Monkton trigger the alarm?'

All three looked at each other, and the uniformed man said, 'Maybe Monkton was in on it too. Inside man.'

Geraldine looked up at the office building. It was three storeys high. 'What's worth robbing in here? Just plain offices.'

'PCs, petty cash, data, loads of stuff,' said the uniformed man.

Geraldine shook her head. 'And why did he kill the man? Bit extreme. Kick him around and tie him would have done the job.'

'You're welcome to have the case. Got enough on my plate with all those scooter gangs and knifings.'

'You can send me the video and the forensics.'

'Sure, it'll be in a couple of weeks. Smoke?'

Geraldine looked at the detective and realised he could probably smell the nicotine off her clothes. She got a pack out of her pocket.

'Trying to give up.' He took out a lighter. 'Where you from?'

'Kent, yous?'

'Essex boy, but brought up in Landan.'

Geraldine inhaled the smoke.

THIRTY-ONE

Rebwar had picked up two passengers from Browns on St Martin's Lane just off Covent Garden and they were going to an address in Barnes.

'That was a damn good spread,' the older man said. 'Going to have to undo a notch on my belt.' He filled the back seat, had neatly combed greying hair, a large red nose, a wrinkled face and a tweed jacket. 'Nice to see the boys, too.'

Rebwar followed the traffic down towards Trafalgar Square. The radio had just announced the hour. Facebook's share price had dropped sharply on the news that Cambridge Analytica might have influenced the referendum's outcome. It was believed that it had access to over fifty million users' accounts. Rebwar switched to another station.

'Could you leave the news on,' said the older man.

'Dad, let it go. Can't bear it.'

'Marc, you're just a damn Remoaner. You lost fair and square and listen to them now. Trying to find any pathetic excuse to annul it. They should bloody get on with it. Leave is Leave. What do you think?'

Rebwar looked into his mirror to see the old man smiling back. 'Me? Oh, I don't get involved. Would you like the news?'

Marc leaned forward. 'No. Some classical station, please. Dad, can't you give it a rest? Had an earful at the luncheon. All talking about the empire, duty, even the bloody Great War. What the hell has that got to do with it?'

'Should have gone in a black cab! He would have joined the discussion.' The older man snorted. 'Ahh! Major Jackson had me in stitches. Snowflakes!' And his laugher built up till he was coughing. 'Damn it!' He coughed into his handkerchief.

Marc shook his head and looked out of the window. Rebwar followed the traffic along the River Thames passing Tate Britain art gallery.

'And you know all this nonsense about Facebook and people being duped into voting for something they didn't know. I'm not even on Facebook! Bunch of bloody sore losers that is what you all are. Far better off being out. All those unelected Eurocrats telling us what to do.'

'Dad, give it a rest.'

'Driver, driver! Put that damn radio on again.'

Rebwar was about to change the station again.

'Where you from? Pakistan.'

'Iran.'

'Oh, right. Sunny place, right. And lots of religion. Heh!'

'Many problems. All the world's problems.'

'Dad, what did Scott say to you?'

'Who?'

'Scott Morgan.'

'Damn idiot. Money problems. Always money problems.' And the old man grumbled. 'He's a snowflake.' And his large chest heaved to his laughter. 'On his third wife and he was lecturing me on your mother.'

Rebwar crossed Putney Bridge. He could feel the old man angling for an argument. He kept moving like he had an itch.

'Eyes on the road, driver! Have you got a license? I'm sure that where you come from you can buy them–'

'Sorry, he's a little tipsy. Dad will you–'

'Marc, I'm totally–' He burped. 'Son, it's not my fault. You decided to marry her and you made your bed, son.'

'Should never have agreed to take you to that damn reunion. Is that what you were telling them?'

Rebwar pulled up by a house on Rocks Lane in Barnes opposite a park. The two struggled out and carried on their argument. Rebwar didn't even get a thank you or a goodbye. He didn't bother to rate them. His phone rang and Bijan's name flashed on the screen.

———

After driving up to Bijan's house, Rebwar ended up having to drive his Rolls-Royce. Bijan had fired his driver a few days ago and hadn't found anyone else. So he'd asked for Rebwar to take him to his dentist in Harley Street. Rebwar had never driven such a large and luxurious car. Bijan was in the back with his cane, giving out direction on where to go. Bijan didn't let him use his sat nav and he wanted to guide him.

'Sir, are you warm enough?' Bijan's face looked pasty white and his sunken eyes made him look like a corpse.

'Yes, yes, drive along this road till the end. Damn idiot.'

'Sorry, sir?'

'Oh, Charles leaving me like that. Miserable bastard...'

Rebwar had a hard time driving the truck-sized car and was terrified of damaging it. 'I thought you fired him?'

'Yes, yes, damn man. He was having it off with the maid! Only thought with his cock that man.'

Rebwar lit a cigarette. It helped. Cars around him cut in front of him. Vans honked.

'How's Hourieh?'

Rebwar could feel drops of sweat slide down his back. Each turn and road seemed to be too tight or too narrow. 'She has a new friend called Dinah...' Rebwar indicated and honked the car in front.

'Left, down that street. It's quicker...'

Bijan managed to choose the smallest roads he could find. The car's wheel mounted the kerb and he had to drive on the pavement. Pedestrians around tried to get out of the way.

'Dinah Sasani?'

Rebwar nodded.

Bijan giggled. 'That bitch, on her second or is it third divorce. Bad news, my friend. Need to keep her out of your circle. Lock your jewellery away. That one has light fingers.' He banged the window with his stick. 'Right, down there.'

Rebwar crossed two lanes of traffic and went down another little one-way street. 'What do you think she wants?'

'New husband... What is she doing with Hourieh?'

Rebwar shrugged.

'She's as bad as the English and Americans put together. Always scheming something up. So, my friend, what do you say about being my driver? Better than having to take the public around and listening to their day-to-day problems.' Bijan tapped his stick again and shouted, 'Left.'

The big Rolls-Royce bounced over some speed bumps and again Bijan shouted some instruction on where the clinic was. Rebwar stopped in front and stepped out to open the door. He tried helping Bijan out of the car but he hushed him away, told him to wait till he was finished. Rebwar stepped back into the car, found an Iranian newspaper, the *Ettela'at* and thought about how he could let Bijan down on his generous offer. He felt sorry for him, but it was the company that he was really looking for, and Rebwar could only give him so much of that. He also mulled over what Bijan had said about Dinah.

THIRTY-TWO

Rebwar had found the estate agents where Hewitt-Thomas worked. It was on the corner of Grange Road and The Grange in Bermondsey. He and Geraldine had agreed that he was going to try to approach him when he was out of the office, either around lunchtime or just after a visit. Raj had managed to crack his work email, and he had three appointments that day, two at the same location: a flat on the corner of Abbey Street and Tower Bridge Road. It was a new glass cube shaped building that overlooked St Mary Magdalene Church. Rebwar was going to meet him there after the second appointment and Geraldine was going to check the back entrances. He entered the lobby which was unguarded. He buzzed a few random flats, waited till someone answered and then told them he had a delivery for a neighbouring apartment.

The flat was on the fifth floor, No 203. He arrived, and a man was waiting for the lift. They passed each other and Rebwar went over to the flat and rang the bell. He heard heavy footfalls walk towards the door. The door opened with a force that sucked air as if the room had been sealed.

Hewitt-Thomas was tall and looked down at Rebwar. His eyes were fixed on him like a spy camera studying a foreign object.

'I've come to see the flat.'

Hewitt-Thomas pulled a phone from his grey suit. As he looked at it he said in a high-pitched voice, 'What the fuck?'

'Well, I'm here.' Rebwar walked in.

'Hey?'

'Rebwar. How much is it?'

'Who sent you? Didn't we–'

The door shut behind Rebwar, and he carried on walking into the flat. It was a two bed with a large window overlooking the park. 'Does the sun come in?'

'If you're looking for a place to grow weed, this isn't it.'

'Sorry?'

'I mean if you'd like to have plants, I'd recommend the plastic ones. It's £2,100 a month and you get a parking space.' He opened the bathroom door and switched the light on. It was a little box with a shower in one corner.

'How long have you been working as an estate agent?'

Hewitt-Thomas looked at Rebwar with his head slanted. 'Long enough, did Charlie send you?'

'You should be suspicious as I hear your one of the Filthy Five.' Rebwar had placed himself in front of the door.

Hewitt-Thomas stepped back, holding his phone. 'What did you just say?'

Rebwar threw a sharp, fast punch just below his ribcage. Hewitt-Thomas doubled up and let out a constricted groan. Rebwar grabbed the phone out of his hand and tried to access it, but it was locked. 'Open it.'

'Twatt off. Never.' And he tried to breathe.

Rebwar grabbed his left hand and pressed his thumb on

the phone and then other digits. Hewitt-Thomas wheezed like he was trying to laugh.

'Open it.' And Rebwar twisted his hand until Hewitt-Thomas was lying face down on the floor, groaning. 'Where is he?'

'Money–'

Rebwar pushed Hewitt-Thomas flat with his foot and pulled his hand. 'Where is Jack Hill?'

'Are you dumb or some–'

Rebwar pulled his hand further back. 'Game is up. Understand?' Hewitt-Thomas tried to laugh with his face on the wooden floor. 'Pinky Knight, Henry Trent, Joseph Brunje, Daisy Merkenstand. Yes, we know all about you.'

'So why haven't you found him, Heh?'

'Only a matter of time, which you haven't got much of.'

Hewitt-Thomas tried to swing out with his free arm and sweep away Rebwar's feet. Rebwar got a black zip tie out of his jacket pocket. With both knees, he landed on Hewitt-Thomas's back. The man gave out a deep gargled breath like an air mattress being deflated. Rebwar zipped the plastic ties tight, and as he got up he ignored the stream of swearwords coming from Hewitt-Thomas who rolled away from him and tried to stand. Rebwar just pushed him over till he ran out of energy. Hewitt-Thomas laughed and breathed heavily, trying to catch his breath.

'Where are they?' said Rebwar. 'Hey? Did you hear me?'

'Fuck you and your mother.'

Rebwar kicked him, to which he laughed.

'Hey, Siri, call Henry.' Hewitt-Thomas's watch replied, and he confirmed. 'Run, I've been compromised. Sorry. Run!'

Rebwar grabbed his wrist to see that he had made a call

with his watch. He undid it and looked at it. But the action made it lock itself. Rebwar swore in Iranian.

'You MI6 or something? You're a bit amateurish, aren't you.' Hewitt-Thomas got up and ran into the window to an almighty bang that resonated into the building. He bounced off and tried another three times. Rebwar waited until he'd knocked himself out. But on the fourth attempt the window gave in and Hewitt-Thomas fell onto the balcony. He ran over to the neighbouring balcony and tried to climb over it with his hands tied behind his back. He lost his balance. Rebwar watched him topple over the railing. A few seconds later a dull thud and some screams came from below. Rebwar didn't need to go and see. He looked around the flat and made his way to the front door. His phone rang. It was Geraldine.

THIRTY-THREE

Geraldine had let Rebwar go and see Hewitt-Thomas on his own as agreed. She went to look around the building for the others. From what she had seen and read, they were inseparable – like a family unit. She found a floor plan of the fire exits, which gave her an idea of the layout of the building apartment block. The place still smelled of paint and bleach. A removal van was outside unloading. She spotted the odd piece of gaffer tape that hadn't been removed from some of the windows and corners. She walked into the lift and pushed the button for the parking level, which was two storeys below. It was well lit with bright colours making the space seem bigger than it was.

There were about thirty or so cars of various makes and ages. Apart from a few small sports cars, nothing stood out of the norm. She checked her phone for Jack Hill's car registration, which Raj had found in his computer. None of them matched it. There were more empty spaces than taken ones, which probably meant that the building still had plenty of apartments for rent, even though she had seen a sign saying there were only a few three-bedroom ones left.

Geraldine dreamt of having a house with a garden, something she could tend to and nurture. She found these apartment buildings soulless, at best a temporary placement on the way to somewhere else – like hotels.

She went back to the lift and hit the button for the sixth floor. The bell rang, and the doors opened to reveal a striped brown carpeted hallway. Hidden LED lights lit the series of doors and there was a window at the end of the corridor. The grey sky tried its best to shed some light into the building. There were numbered heavy brown doors with peepholes. She walked past them, listening for any unusual sounds. It was 11:23 pm, and they were probably all at work. It wasn't really a family-friendly building, more for professional singles or couples. How could anyone afford these rents? She had to apply for affordable housing as all her colleagues and friends had to.

She found the emergency exit at the end of the corridor, opened it and was hit by a cool breeze. Inside the bare concrete walls was a set of steel stairs led to the roof. Geraldine took the stairs down to the fifth floor. It was much the same, characterless doors with numbers. She passed the lift. The digital display above showed the floor numbers. It passed the fifth floor. She approached the metal door and heard some people get in it. There were quite a few of them and they had rushed in and banged the sides of the lift. A girl shouted something and then a man. Geraldine ran over to the emergency exit and ran downstairs. Her feet trying hard to keep up with the rhythm of the stairs. She held on to the bannisters and bumped into the walls. She opened the door to the garage. They were there. Four, she recognised, and the fifth was hooded and his limp feet dragged on the tarmac.

Geraldine shouted at them, which made them run a

little faster. Trent and Brunje confronted Geraldine. This time she didn't have her Mace spray or any other weapon. They had knives. The two girls, Pinky Knight and Daisy Merkenstand, were shoving the hooded man into the boot of a VW Golf.

'Should have bloody killed you!' said Brunje. 'Henry, you're not going to pussy out this time.' Trent looked over at Brunje.

'Daisy, stop. It's Geraldine! Remember me?' Geraldine brought out her warrant card.

The car started up and reversed. The car stopped and honked. Trent hesitated.

'Hey, Daisy, we need to talk!' Geraldine shouted as she tried to get closer to the car. 'We're working for the same side!'

Brunje pushed Trent towards Geraldine. 'Fucking do it, you pussy. Or I'll do both of you.'

The car revved and honked.

Trent pulled a knife and launched himself at Geraldine, swiped as if he was trying to smash a piñata. She avoided his awkward lunges. One slashed her bomber jacket. The large metal garage door clicked opened, and a car entered. Trent and Brunje looked behind them at car that had just driven in and they ran off into the golf. Its front wheels screeched as if they were being squeezed to death. Geraldine hesitated, she wanted to jump in front of the car to stop them. She watched it drive off and realised that it was Hill's car; they had simply changed the registration. She ran after them. As she turned the corner there, they were waiting for the metal shutters to roll back up. The reversing lights came on and the car whined towards her. Geraldine hid behind one of the pillars. They just missed her, its side scraping the concrete.

Daisy was driving, and she was clearly desperate to find first gear. The car crunched, jerked and bounced forward. Geraldine took her phone out and called. They drove out.

'Rebwar, I found them! They have Jack Hill in the boot of a car. They've just gotten away. Bloody idiot, fuck... just been fooled by the oldest trick in the book. Stolen reg and it was in front of me... Oh! Where?' The car's engine faded away and it was replaced by some screaming. 'He's fallen off what?'

Musa had told Rebwar where the local Chilcots gang hung out and he'd found them on the corner of Eton Avenue and Crossfield Road, a leafy, well-to-do area of Swiss Cottage and it was only a few streets away from the estate. They had recently rebranded and called themselves NWK in the hope of getting more business. The name used part of the local postcode and he'd been told that the K stood for knifes. It also apparently was a reference to a famous American rap group called NWA. But the whole county lines phenomena was hurting their revenue.

'Brov.' Rebwar fist bumped Tommy, the freckled boy and only white member of the gang. The other three nodded in acknowledgement. 'Doing good, man. Taxi business bringing the dollars?' He rubbed his thumb and index finger.

'Boys, I need a favour.'

Their faces poked out of their hoodies, and one of them took off his headphones.

'I've got some heat on me. Men looking for me and need an ear on the ground.'

'Yo, that sounds dangerous, man and your dirty business,' said Tommy.

'Yeah, bro, got enough on our corner. What's in it for us?' said Washington.

Rebwar waited for a moment. He wasn't flush and was hoping to barter. 'How about a ride or two?'

'Disrespecting us.' Tommy spat on the floor. 'Wasting time, brov.'

Chucka, who filled his large hoodie, got off the brick wall and stood in front of Rebwar with his hood down. 'Got business to run. This gear cost. Get my drift, bro? Got to look the part, man.'

'What's your price?'

The three of them looked at one another, each one doing some kind of coded message with their hands and faces as if they were posing for some Instagram picture.

'A grand.'

Rebwar shook his head and got out a pack of cigarettes. He offered it around. Tommy and Washington took one and Travor stepped in and took two, putting the second one behind his ear.

'Brov, as you're family... five hundred,' said Chucka. 'What do you say?'

'Look, I don't want to disrespect you. So let's just say, if you are about and you see something, just give me fair warning. And I'll do the same.'

'What?' Travor said. 'Like some kind of pact? I scratch your back and you mine. Brov? Times are tough. Got to feed the family. Get me?'

'I can only do deferred. Times are tough for me too.'

'Get out of my face.' Travor pushed Rebwar. 'Wasting my time like some homeless dude. All I can say... and this for free, man. Your wife has been spending some time with that MILF. She's got something going on...'

Rebwar took a step back, taking it in. Was this a provocation? Seeing how far they can take him? Rebwar grabbed Travor's hoodie and pushed him over the short bricked wall. The other three brought out their knives.

'Hey, easy, easy! I'm not dissing your wife!' said Travor. 'I get that... Calm. Calm. I was just giving a little bit of friendly advice. Musa's a good kid and—' Rebwar tightened his grip. 'I get it, brov. Let's just say this was just a big misunderstanding. Easy.'

Rebwar let go of Travor and stepped back, not breaking his gaze with him.

———

Rebwar wiped his feet on the welcome mat outside his apartment. As he took out his key, he heard Hourieh chatting. He slowly unlocked the door, sneaked in and listened to the conversation. He could make out Dinah and another woman's voice followed by the rattling of some teacups. Hourieh was on a rant about how filthy the area was, and it wasn't good for their son. She was worrying that he might get asthma. The other woman added that her daughter had asthma and was blaming it on the terrible London pollution. Then Dinah took over the conversation and told her how Hourieh should take control of her life. Rebwar tensed and slammed the front door shut. The chatter stopped.

'Husband?'

'Wife, we have some guests?'

Hourieh rushed to the corridor. 'Yes, a little tea party with my friends. Dinah and Minu.'

Rebwar went over to the door and looked in. He could

see the fine silver tea set he'd bought her a couple years before with the samovar bubbling away on top of the small glass-fronted cupboard.

'And some nice delights.'

'Oh, yes. Minu made them. See... gaz, koloocheh and ghotab.'

'Thank you, Minu,' said Rebwar. She smiled and looked away. She wore a scarf over her hair, a yellow and black flowery, long dress that hid her large figure. She had red lipstick and matching fingernails. Her dark eyes were striking and sucked you in.

Dinah caught his stare and said, 'Still taxiing customers around?'

Rebwar stepped close to the delicacies. The gaz looked especially tempting; it was a nougat with pistachio. But he wavered between the koloocheh, a cookie stuffed with cinnamon, sugar, and crushed walnuts, and the ghotab, a doughnut-shaped cookie. Minu passed the plate with the gaz.

And with a mouthful of gaz he said, 'Hello, Dinah.' The nougat being especially chewy, Rebwar struggled to talk while trying to keep his mouth closed. 'Actually just came to.... to refresh myself and... going to start a shift... How's the shop?'

'Very well. Just sold this season's stock and–'

'Minu very kindly brought some extra delicacies there in the kitchen.' Hourieh pointed over to it.

'So kind of you, Minu, how do you fit in this gaggle?' Rebwar tried to un-lodge a pistachio with his tongue and was regretting the choice.

'She works for me.' Dinah turned to face Rebwar, her white top unbuttoned enough to show off her expensive jewellery. 'And a good friend. Born here in London and

Persian born parents. The Heimanns are sure you remember them.'

Rebwar looked up. 'Sure, I arrested a Heimann...'

'He's joking.' Hourieh picked up Minu's cup. 'Thinking of the goo... I mean the old times when he was a street cop. Thank God that's behind us.' She brought the cup over to the samovar on the dresser. 'More tea?'

'Did you contact that friend?'

'Who?'

Hourieh poured some tea for Minu. 'Oh yes... No, haven't got round to it. Husband, before you go, could you pick up Musa from the boutique?'

'He's working where? And I thought...'

'Yes, he needs a respectable job and Dinah very kindly offered him one. It's a step up, you know.'

'Dinah, thank you for that fridge but really... I don't think my son should be selling women's clothes. He's a teenager with the fashion sense of a court jester. Not too—'

'Sir, he's doing amazingly well, has a great sense of manners and respect with the clients. I think he has a great career ahead of him.'

Rebwar took out a box of cigarettes and he took one for himself before offering them out. All three declined and Hourieh had crossed her arms. Rebwar lit up. Minu waved her hand in front of her nose.

'Husband, we have guests. You could have asked before smoking us out.'

'I did!' He puffed out a few drags and turned around.

'And call about that job! It's rude to our guest and a step up. Then you could buy me some nice clothes from Musa.'

Rebwar grabbed a koloocheh and bit into it. The flavours were disrupted by Dinah's voice as he left the room.

'Look...' There was a collective giggle. 'Yes, he gave me a

ring. He's so dashing, and I got a ride in his Ferrari. Ahh, he's such a generous man. Look, I have a picture. He's got a very respectable job at a bank and richer than my ex-husband – that pig just announced he has a girlfriend – sorry, I mean a whore.' More laughs.

Rebwar closed the bathroom door and ran the cold tap. He swore silently at the mirror in front of him.

THIRTY-FIVE

Rebwar parked his car opposite the Premier Inn in Tottenham Hale, close to a row of closed shops that bordered the car park. He spotted the white VW Golf that Geraldine had tracked down through CCTV. They had again changed number plates, which had made it a challenge to track it down. But she had an axe to grind and stayed the night at the office, trawling through hours of footage. They had also decided that if they managed to rescue Hill and disrupt the Filthy Five, they could confront Charlie with some facts and evidence.

Rebwar looked up at the modern brick building, visually it appeared to have four tall storeys, but there were actually eight. He wondered if it was done to fool people and make it look smaller. Surrounded by industrial buildings, car parks and the odd house, it was non-descript and was lost in the urban sprawl. The reception was a series of screens that welcomed you in. Apart from the humming of a few lit food and drink dispensers, the place was deserted.

Rebwar walked back outside and tried to spot any movement from the windows above. Three of them had their lights on and coloured, flashing lights bounced off the white walls, a sure sign the guests were watching some TV show. If there had been someone at the reception, Rebwar could have tried to probe them for some information, but there was only a telephone. Rebwar couldn't believe what the world was coming to a series of pre-recorded messages and cameras looking down at you.

He went over to look at the car and to his great surprise, found the driver's doors open. Immediately a strong smell hit his nose like food that had been left to rot. He looked around and found some discarded Burger King wrappers, cigarette butts and a few *Evening Standard* newspapers. Rebwar checked their dates, and they were from the last few days. Some of the pages had been ripped out. A light from the hotel caught his attention. A series of shadows moved around one of the rooms. He wasn't sure if it was television or bodies making the movements – or both.

He walked over to the boot and opened it. He swore, stepped back and put his arm over his nose. Jack Hill's face was scrunched up against the lip of the boot. It was devoid of colour, eyes closed like he was sleeping. Rebwar rang Geraldine.

'Found him... Yes, dead... No, we can't call them... I know... but we are going to close them. OK, OK.' Rebwar shut the boot, took a breath and walked over to his car. He was about to dial 999, when four people rushed out of the reception. Rebwar crouched down between his car and the one next to it. A series of boots and trainers rushed over to the Golf. He had found them. The two girls rushed into the car and the two boys opened the boot.

'Boys! Fucking hell?' said Daisy.

Trent and Brunje dragged the body out of the boot.

'No, we can't just leave him here,' said Knight getting out of the car.

'Yes, we fucking can,' said Brunje. 'He's dead weight.'

'Fuck me! You're off the scale. No, no and no! This is a human being we are dealing with, not one of your fucking cows. We're doing the right thing. It's gone too far.'

Hill's body was half hanging out of the car's boot.

Rebwar sensing an opportunity opened the boot of his own car and reached for the baseball bat.

Brunje walked right up to Daisy's face. 'Look, posh bitch... since when did you call the shots? I'm in charge now. We agreed on this. Didn't we?' He looked around and spotted Rebwar.

'I think it's game over.' Rebwar held the baseball bat with both hands. 'Daisy—'

'Come again?' said Trent.

'I've called the police.'

'Come on, let's get going,' said Daisy, looking away.

'Oh, yeah? And so what? And how come he knows you? Like that copper bitch from yesterday.' Brunje walked over, inviting Rebwar to swing his bat at him. Arms stretched out. 'Four against one, mate. Have you thought this through?'

Trent ran at Rebwar. The two girls shouted over for them to stop. Rebwar swung at Brunje. He missed. He swung again, missed again. Trent threw a punch that hit Rebwar's arm. Brunje kicked Rebwar's leg. Rebwar swung and hit Trent's thigh. Brunje and Trent laughed. Rebwar hobbled back, feeling the pain. He ducked Brunje's punch and swung the bat to smash his knee cap. Brunje screamed in pain. Trent threw a punch and hit Rebwar's jaw, which made him stumble backwards. Trent kicked high with his boot and hit Rebwar's arm, which made him drop the bat. Rebwar's vision was going. Trent's punch had nearly knocked him out. The girls were now trying to drag them back to the car.

Daisy slapped Brunje. 'You're losing the plot. Let's go...' She looked over at Rebwar. 'I know him.'

'We can't just leave him, can we?'

Knight rolled Hill's body back into the boot.

Trent stopped Brunje from hitting Rebwar who was on the floor trying to regain his breath.

'Hey, Daisy? Is he a copper?' said Knight.

'What's the story?' Trent held on to his damaged knee. 'Go on, let us know? I think you're a mole. How did they just find us? And you know I think they killed Thomas.'

Daisy stared while Rebwar, who was now crawling towards his car, struggled to find the energy to open the door.

'He's getting away. Come on then, boss, what's the order? He's compromised us.'

Knight went up to Daisy. 'We need to go!'

Rebwar had managed to open the passenger door and was crawling in.

'Kill him!' said Trent.

'You do it,' said Brunje. 'It's an order.'

'Double bluff.' Trent handed over the baseball bat to Daisy who pushed it back to him. 'Enough killing... This isn't what I joined, and he's with Charlie.'

'Call her then, ask her what she wants done.'

Rebwar heard her footsteps approaching him. He turned to face Brunje.

A car headlights lit the scene in the car park and pulled in. It stopped and two men stepped out. Rebwar couldn't make them out. The Filthy Five ran to their Golf. The two men shouted for them to stop. Rebwar tried to get up, but his body kept giving way. After a few tries he managed to crawl into the car and started it. The two men went over to him.

'Mate, are you OK?'

Rebwar nodded and took a few deep breaths.

'I'm calling the police. What happened?'

Rebwar pulled away but the two men kept up with the car.

'Mate, stop, you need help. Hey!'

Rebwar drove off, pain travelling around his body.

THIRTY-SIX

Rebwar struggled to keep his right hand on the steering wheel. The pain was thumping as if someone was tenderising it like steak. He was trying to keep up with the white Golf, which was speeding down the bus lanes. He slammed on his breaks and swerved to avoid a fallen cyclist. The Golf darted in and out of the traffic.

He caught up with them at a traffic light where they were boxed in. His hand hesitated on the door latch. The light turned green, and they honked and swore out of their windows and screamed. He followed them. The two boys were back-slapping each other like it was some kind of game.

Rebwar mounted the kerb and pulled up next to them again. Daisy swung the wheel and hit his car. They were like two tin cans bouncing off each other. Sparks and rubber squealed. Brunje reached out of his rear passenger door and punched Rebwar's Prius. His eyes wide with anger. Drugs fuelled their madness. They pulled away and turned into a one-way street.

Rebwar followed them. People jumped out of the way. Both cars swerved onto pavements. Wing mirrors from parked cars littered the road. Rebwar followed. They were making their way towards the City of London, but it was an erratic way. They took another sharp left and drove through a series of red lights. The back streets were quiet, offices and shops closed. The Golf raced down the streets, its little engine giving every horse it had. Rebwar struggled to keep up. Tyres screeched and took a sharp turn left. He followed them down a narrow alley, but they were nowhere to be seen. He scanned garages, side alleys and loading bays until he reached the end. In his rear-view mirror, he saw the Golf reverse out of a garage. It turned and went in the other direction. Rebwar mounted the kerb and hit a bollard. The alley was too tight to turn around. He reversed out. The gearbox whined as if it was warning him of its demise.

Rebwar rejoined the chase. He found them at another busy junction waiting for the light. What was their next move? Had they another hide-away? With Hewitt-Thomas out of the picture, where would they go? The car swerved from side to side. Another argument. And it stopped.

Rebwar slammed on his breaks. Tyres screeched, and he slammed into the back of the Golf. The tailgate flipped up and Hill's arm flopped out. The car accelerated. Hill's limp hand waved over the lip of the boot. Past rigor mortis, Rebwar thought. How long was it since they had moved him from the flat? Trent tried to grab the tailgate. As the car veered around cars and corners Hill's body swung out. Brunje held on to the dead man's torso. Rebwar could imagine he was thinking about tossing him overboard.

Traffic built up as they got closer to the Tower of London. There wasn't time to take in the sights as the tourists were doing. Brunje threw out the parcel shelf which flew into the air and rotated as if it was a propeller. It hit a passing pedestrian. The car slowed down. Brunje finally managed to close the tailgate. They pulled up and waited for a traffic light. Sirens sounded. Rebwar looked for them. An ambulance passed him.

Lights turned, and they drove on towards Tower Bridge. Its impressive light blue ironwork was lit for everyone to admire, the two stone towers standing high over the Thames as if they were castles protecting passage. Traffic was moving along in two single lanes towards the bridge. Large concrete blocks lined the pavements. For a moment, Rebwar thought about making a scene. It could work. Flush them out. Traffic crawled along. He was six cars behind them. He could see that they were agitated. The car bounced on its suspension.

The traffic light turned red. They were now third in line. He spotted on the pavement two Police officers in-between tourists who were asking for selfies. Rebwar debated with himself: let them drive off and possibly lose them or get them all arrested, including himself. Ahead, on the bridge, two light blue gates closed slowly. A large boat was about to pass under the bridge. This was a test of nerves. Rebwar opened the door and stepped out. Everyone was staring at the bridge, going through its transformation. Phones pointed at the impressive sight. Brunje spotted Rebwar and shouted over to to the rest of the gang.

The Golf revved forward, hitting the car in front. Then reversed. Gears grinding against each other. The car moved out onto the free incoming lane. For a moment, Rebwar thought they were going to make a U-turn. He returned to his car. The Golf's passenger door opened and three of them rushed out and ran in different directions.

Brunje was behind the wheel and he revved the car's engine and accelerated towards the closed gate. The deck of the bridge was quickly rising. Everyone watched in amazement and then horror, wondering if this was really happening.

The Golf picked up speed, smashing through the gates and carried on going through its gears over the flat first section of the bridge. It carried on picking up speed while and people cheered and screamed. The Golf passed under the first tower and drove up the ramp, which was now as steep as a set of stairs and ever increasing. The car's engine began to struggle as the bridge carried on rising.

The driver's door opened, and Brunje rolled out of the speeding car. His body rolling down the bridge's decks. The Golf carried on and cleared the end of the deck as Rebwar saw the tail lights drop. A wave of gasping and screaming erupted. And then came a distant splash. Brunje slowly got up and steadied himself, holding on to a railing. He walked over to a set of stairs. Sirens and alarms erupted. Everyone rushed over to see what had happened. Rebwar joined in. It was hopeless. They had split up.

He knew the car would sink like a stone. Windows exploding. Water gushing in. Hill was already dead. The Thames was too unforgiving, its strong tides would sweep anything down to its muddy bottom. What had they been thinking? Rebwar wasn't going to get out of the scene anytime soon; emergency services were rushing in and blocking every street. He could only watch. People were calling, taking pictures, videos. It was hot news. And he was probably the only one to be part of the story. What were they going to find? Then, for a moment, he breathed in. Trying to take it all in, he took out a cigarette and watched how the helicopter searchlights lit up the water. Divers were throwing themselves off inflatable boats.

People around were asking every question imaginable.

A woman shouted, 'Was that Tom Cruise?'

A man said, 'A robbery. They were masked.'

'Terrorists,' said another man.

THIRTY-SEVEN

The scene became more and more chaotic as the emergency services arrived, and they moved the crowds away from the incident. And Rebwar was now stuck there too, as he had hesitated from getting into the car and driving away. Like spiders, the police had weaved tape in front of every building in the area. Rebwar felt as if he was a trapped insect. He decided to walk down towards the river, to where all the crowds were being herded. The glass facades reflected the red and blue flashing lights while the sirens echoed down the little alleys that lined the embankment. Police officers tried politely to move the masses away. Rebwar looked around for a gap or alley in which to hide.

Behind him was a huge concrete hotel that towered above him. It looked more like a government security building than somewhere that welcomed guests for a sleep-over. But it did have a prime view over the Thames and Tower Bridge. He pushed his way through, pointing at the hotel as if people would understand that he was a guest there. He passed a police officer who glanced over but his attention was soon taken by a protesting cyclist. In his bright Lycra, he tried to pedal his way past the crowds as if they had to give way to him.

Rebwar walked into the lobby and saw a large staircase leading to the next floor. He walked upstairs over the thick brown carpet into a bar that overlooked the river. Everybody's attention was on the chaos outside and a few of them asked what had happened and if anyone had been hurt. The bar was a wooden island in the middle of an angular room of white-painted concrete. Large windows faced the mass of blue and red flashing lights. A helicopter's searchlight dug into the dark river and a couple of little ribs circling the site. The bar guests were glued to the windows, drinks in hand, watching every move.

Rebwar watched as they searched for the car. People around him chatted to each other, asking if they had seen what happened. One of them said it was a stunt for a film, another a police chase, and all of them were holding a phone while they listened. A man next to Rebwar was posting a picture on Instagram #newtomcruisefilm #stuntgonewrong and a few other tags that he couldn't read.

'Did you see it?'

Rebwar shook his head.

'Wow, you should have seen it. Amazing! Not sure for what film but I'm going to see it. Just plopped off that bridge like it was stone. Sure it was meant to jump over it and carry on. Something must have gone very wrong. Very!'

'Did the car sink?'

'Oh yeah, hit the water, splashed.' With his hands, he tried to make a reenactment. 'Then it bobbed up and down like a cork.'

'Man! It was sick. They are so dead. It was like that band that died.'

'Dude, it's for a movie. No way was it was a real car chase,' said the man behind him.

'Where are the cameras?' said another man.

'Everywhere, GoPros that's what they use you can put them everywhere. Sure they are now trying to get them back.'

'What about all the police. No way, man. This is a crime scene. Look!' And he pointed with both hands. 'This is not a movie... this is real!'

'Tom Cruise is in town shooting. Look... his Twitter feed says so.'

'You bunch of fucking idiots. Don't you know real from fake?'

Rebwar stepped away from the men who were now getting into a heated discussion about what they had just seen. He tried to call Geraldine but the call went straight to voicemail. He left a message saying where he was and what had just happened.

'Amir?' Rebwar turned to see two men dressed in black suits. 'Can we buy you a drink?'

'What's this about?'

'Oh, just a chat about some friends. Nothing to worry about. Beer?' And the taller man with a scar on his hand ordered three beers from the barman. 'Amir, do you know Jack Hill?'

For a moment, Rebwar thought about this. Raj had created a social media profile of Amir, and he did support his online campaign. But he had never met him. 'No.'

'But this is you?'

And the other thinner man with a goatee showed him Amir's Twitter feed which Rebwar had never seen but had been told about by Raj. 'Yes, I heard about him and liked his articles. Never met him.' The other man passed the beers and they cheered like it was some social meeting. Rebwar sipped his beer.

168

At 7:14 am, Geraldine arrived at The Tower Hotel where Rebwar had left his last message. She had texted, called and left voice messages. But there had been no word from him since last evening. Police tape and a few emergency vehicles were still in the area but the mayhem had died down. A couple of news crews were still reporting on the incident. Geraldine had missed it all as she had been with Beckie at the rehab clinic. She had drunk a couple of cans and felt a little hungover. It had been emotional with Beckie as her husband was still on the scene and she had forgiven him. Geraldine just couldn't understand and suspected the medication. She had asked to see the religious adviser but he wasn't around. Her mother had all been about forgiveness but this wasn't going to fix anything.

Geraldine went into the hotel reception. It was filled by a leaving coach party. Suitcases were piled up just in front of the desk. Geraldine picked out a curly blonde girl and went over to her. Her badge had three flags (UK, French, German) above her name: Lucy Caper. She caught her staring.

In a mousy voice she said, '*Sind sie auf der reise nach Stratford?*'

Geraldine looked at the clear brown eyes. Her smiled fixed, either waiting for an applause or a response, she said, 'Yes, can you help me?'

'*Ja? Sie sind?*'

'I'm looking for the manager.'

'Oh, I'm sorry I thought you were with the other party. I'm also the acting manager. Complaints can be sent to the manager. I have her email.' She took out her business card and handed it over.

Geraldine took a quick look at it. Ms Caper had lost her attention and was about to go over to the German group. 'Lucy Caper? I'm a police officer and–'

She rolled her eyes and clenched her teeth. 'Is this about last night? No, I'm sorry, but haven't you guys done enough? My colleague is in hospital. She's going to press charges. Now, I've done as much as I can. You understand?'

'Sorry, but I'm not here for that.'

'Oh! So?'

'I'm looking for a man who was here last night.' Geraldine brought out her phone and showed her a picture. She shook her head. 'I need to see your CCTV.'

Ms Caper flicked her hair back. 'Have you got a warrant and permission? I will need to ask management, you understand. With what was going on last night... And your colleagues have taken it.'

It was a good point. For sure, they would have taken it. 'OK, can you call your manager and sort it?' Again Geraldine flicked her warrant card.

'I will. Thank you.' She brusquely went over to the group.

Geraldine was about to shout at her and caution her for

wasting police time but she took a step back and saw the sign for the bar pointing upstairs.

At the bar was a big man in a blue polo shirt sitting having a pint. Geraldine went over to order as she needed one to take the edge off her hangover. The barman went up to her.

'One for the lady,' said the man in the polo shirt.

'Oh, I...'

'I insist. I'm Jim from Ontario.' He walked over, he was wearing khaki shorts and had light thinning hair. His face looked weathered like he had worked out in the elements.

She gave in and ordered a Stella.

'Didn't put you down as a Stella drinker.'

The barman pulled the pint. He was wearing an ill-fitting black waistcoat and white shirt. Geraldine flashed her warrant card.

'Oh, lady, you arresting me?' He smiled. 'Got some handcuffs?'

Geraldine showed Rebwar's picture. 'Seen him?'

Jim slammed his hand on the bar. 'Damn, I told you. Yeah, man. Terrorist. What you limeys say, felt it in my water. And they went in like a rock. Found anything?'

'He was here having a drink?' said Geraldine putting her warrant card on the bar. She sipped the beer.

'Not my shift, you'd have to ask the other guys,' said the barman.

'So was he the mastermind?' Jim said. 'Al Islam guy. You'd think the place would be crawling with suits.'

'Look, Jim, it's not related. He's a person of interest. Were you here last night?'

'Just landed this morning. Missed the show.' He looked at his watch: 8:45 pm.

'What's your name?' she said to the barman.

'Guido Ramirez.'

'Who's in charge of security?'

'Usually, it is Frank. But I think Lucy is in charge of that.'

'Lucy Caper?'

'Yeah, why?'

'You sure? She's the acting manager.'

'Same thing, isn't it?'

'You know where it is? You know the server room for the cameras?'

Ramirez shrugged. Geraldine gulped the rest of her pint.

'Thanks for the drink,' she said to Canadian Jim and then walked off.

———

Geraldine had decided to have a little wander in the hotel and see what she could find out. Someone must have seen something. It was odd that Rebwar had just disappeared or gone off the grid, especially after asking for her to come over. His last message was that he'd found the Filthy Five and that was about it. That crazy accident had sent the area into a frenzy so maybe mobile coverage had been shut down. She hadn't dared to call his home as that would have sent alarm bells. And there would be a simple answer coming. She was sure of that.

She found a stairwell that led downstairs. The basement was busy with cleaners, kitchen staff, large laundry bins, stacked trolleys with dirty plates. No one questioned her presence. It was as if she was invisible. Everyone doing their routine job in a mix of languages. Only urgent orders were spoken in English.

She passed cupboards and little storage rooms till one caught her eye. It had a rack with flashing lights, monitors, and fans whirred. The door was ajar and she pushed it open. No one was in, although a black jacket was hanging on the back of a swivel chair. The cup of tea was still warm. As she suspected... the security room. It wasn't state of the art – far from it. Raj could easily tap into it, she thought.

'Hey! What u want?'

Geraldine turned around to see a black man, his white shirt covering his bulk. He had an earpiece connected to a radio that attached to his utility belt.

'This private room. No guest allowed here.' He held the door open.

'I'm...' She looked for her warrant card and realised she had left it on the bar. Like a rookie. Tits. 'I'm a police officer.'

'Show me ID.'

'Yeah, I thought you might say that. You see... Can you call the bar?'

Geraldine walked out and returned to the bar where she got her warrant card back and picked up two bottled beers. Jim asked her to cuff him to which she just said that she didn't like cocks and left the bar.

She put the two beers down and showed the security man the warrant card.

'My supervisor—'

'Relax. What's your name?'

'Nelson Dufrais.' His smile was skewed and she noticed that his face was too. Like he'd had a stroke at some point.

'Nelson, I need a favour. My friend is missing and I need to see yesterday's CCTV.'

'But you guys came yesterday and...'

'You still have it?'

'Oh yes.' Dufrais smiled. 'Always make copies. You never know. You see, I studied computer engineering. I have a diploma.' He pointed to a frame beside him.

'Drink?' She handed him a bottle.

He pushed the door closed and took it. 'Who you want to find?'

It didn't take much time to find Rebwar. He was approached by two men. She couldn't make out what they were saying. For that she would need a lip reader. But it was clear that they had spiked his drink. They had helped him out of the bar. He behaved like he was drunk. And when he had left his voicemail, it was clear as a bell. The video followed the men, who weren't really trying to escape the cameras, until they reached the lifts where she saw the two men without Rebwar. They went to get a suitcase each from their room and vanished again. Geraldine drummed her fingers. Had they deleted the footage? Or avoided a couple of cameras.

She asked to find all the exits and play them in sync on one screen. It was mayhem, people had all rushed out to see the accident. Emergency vehicles everywhere.

'What about the ambulance? Find me one.' She finished her beer and wanted another one and a cigarette. They found that there had been two ambulances that had used the back exit. The first one had taken the manager who'd had some kind the nervous breakdown and the second one received a patient in a wheelchair and had an oxygen mask over his face. They worked backwards to find where the emergency had originated from. They could see the manager being taken ill but the no sign of the second incident. The wheelchair had just suddenly appeared on the second floor. She asked where the camera was located and she ran up to the spot. There was utility cupboard under the camera. The door was unlocked so she opened it and switched the light on. There were Rebwar's clothes and two suits. They had made a switch.

THIRTY-NINE

When Rebwar woke up, his face felt like wood: stiff, grainy and cold. It took him a moment to make some movement. His eyes struggled to find focus. There was a jingling, which came over as a musical accompaniment, metallic and heavy. His eyes locked onto a chain in front of him. He lifted his head and could see dark shapes. His hands were bound behind his back. He slid himself into a sitting position. Faces stared back at him. They too, were chained up. The smell of sweat and faeces, stung him. It triggered an old memory. He was back in a sandy trench with his unit, waiting for rescue at night. They had been overrun by the Iraqi Army. There was no moon to help, only darkness and your own senses. He could feel his breath speed up. Lungs trying to gasp oxygen. Bodies, screams, and the stench of death and suffering.

'Mister, mister?'

Rebwar turned and saw a black man. Thin, with an arm missing. He blinked, hoping for it to go away. He tried to hold his breath to stop the cycle. His brain told him that he'd been here before. But his heart kept thumping like it was trying to escape out of his body.

'Are you OK?'

'What?' He felt sick. He convulsed and retched at the smell and the memories. His eyes saw stars, and he shivered. A child's voice squeaked. He couldn't understand it, but there was someone who was reassuring the unknown voice.

'I... Mamoud. Friend, together?'

Rebwar looked around as feeling came back to him. He was in a metal box, probably a container. Three metal poles rang along the middle of the box, each anchored by chains. Each pole had six or seven people attached to it. Rebwar was tied to the third one. He noticed that he couldn't reach the plastic wall. Each group couldn't reach the other.

'Where are we?'

'Metal box. Prisoner.'

Rebwar tried to think back. How had he ended up here? Flashes of the Filthy Five came back to him. Tower Bridge. The Golf driving along the bridge. Police helicopters. Flashes. He held his head as if it was going to drop into a river. The beer. And his head thumped like he had been punched. The realisation of the two men buying him a beer. They had asked for Amir.

'Mister... escape. Know how?'

The man showed him the chain. 'Where are we?' There was no telltale scent or movement. 'Who are the others?'

'Prisoners.'

'And what happened to your arm?'

'Accident in work site. White man dropped metal from crane.'

The container moved. Metal chains slid and bodies fell. He could feel the box being hoisted and swung to a destination.

The exterior was muffled. People cried and screamed. Rebwar held on to his chain, trying not to be thrown around. There was a metal clang, and the container bounced and rested. Nausea rose up and Rebwar threw up. The poison was still in his system. What had they given him? His brain still pieced together the events. He tried to search his pockets. What about his family? Geraldine? Was she involved? Nothing made sense.

'Any ideas?' said an old man with a white beard. He looked Asian.

Rebwar shook his head.

On the first pole by the doors were two young girls. One appeared to be pregnant and her wide eyes were red and tearful. These were damaged goods, Rebwar thought, quite different from the cargo he had taken on his last covert job with O'Neil, where he'd had to drive human traffic up to London. He didn't think this was going to end well. They had to get out.

'Cigarette?' said Rebwar.

Mamoud looked at him as if he had gone mad.

'Helps me think.'

There was a deep rumble, and the container jerked forward. They were on the move.

Rebwar held on to the metal bar at the centre of the metal prison. It had been welded in. The chains were padlocked. 'Hair pin? Pin. Ask. I can pick this.' Rebwar showed them the lock. They all stared back. 'Look around, anything. Nail?' Rebwar searched the wooden floor for something to have fallen between the joins. The wood was old and worn, had seen a lot of cargo. You had to feel with your hands.

'This?'

The old man showed him a rusting nail. Rebwar took it and grasped the old padlock. He bent the sharp end and inserted, felt the movement. The container bounced and swayed. There was a bigger bump, and the nail broke. It had rusted and was too frail. 'Another one?'

The girls sobbed and frequently cried out for help. But behind that metal wall was some kind of insulation. This had been some kind of refrigerated container. So far they had been lucky it hadn't been switched on. An easy death peaceful, he'd heard from his forensic colleagues. But it was the opposite in here. The heat was rising. There was no fresh air. Suffocation was a possibility. Rebwar could feel sweat running into his eyes. His t-shirt was sticking to him. At first, he thought it might have been the poison working its way through his body.

FORTY

Geraldine yawned as the sat nav announced her arrival at the port of Felixstowe. Her Costa coffee cup had gone cold, her nervous energy hadn't left her and she could feel it in her tense arms. She moved her stiff fingers after holding the steering wheel like it had been O'Neil's throat. That man was still tormenting her memory. She went around a big roundabout a couple of times until she calmed down and took the exit towards a barrier with a lit building. She had hoped for a quieter entrance. There were lots of signs for freight businesses and large areas with warehouses or stacked containers.

From the pictures that Raj had found on social media sites, it felt like there was a shipment going out of Felixstowe. Raj had trawled the internet for chatter and found an Instagram post with a series of pictures of a truck being loaded and driving off. After some research, he'd found that it was going to Felixstowe. From their hashtags, they were obviously trying to send a public message. Plan B in action was one of them, and making England great was another, with a series of emojis that could be seen as racist.

No faces, but it was a lead and Geraldine had jumped on it.

Plan B was stepping out of the shadows.

Now she had to get into the port to search for that shipment, and she drove up to the well-lit gate. It was 10:11pm when a man came up to the car. He was in his mid-fifties, broad face with white hair and wearing a navy woollen jacket with a hi-vis waistcoat.

'Can I help you?'

'Good evening, I need to get in there.' Geraldine searched for her badge.

'Are you coming to visit someone?'

She showed him her warrant card. 'There is a container with people inside it.'

He looked at the card. 'Right... DS Smith, I need some authorisation to let you in. This isn't enough... and we get this all the time. Reporter?'

'Look, Mr?'

'Mathews.'

'There is a container full of people and they are in danger. They are going to die.' She showed him her phone with the picture.

He squinted his eyes, trying to see it. 'Look... call for backup and some relevant paperwork and you can fill your boots. Look, love... It's not in my pay grade. And I'm not losing my job and it could be a fake ID.'

Jobsworth was her first thought. A car pulled up behind and inside was a man in a hard hat. Mathews went up to him and looked at his ID. He waved into the building behind him and the barrier raised. Geraldine put the car into gear. In front of her was another man dressed in identical clothes but he had dark hair and was smaller. He was looking at her registration.

'Can you get him out of the way?' she said.

'DS Smith, I can't let you in,' said Mathews.

'I'm going to start arresting people. Obstructing the course of justice, you understand that?' The car passed her. She followed the car and drove on into the floodlit port. The two men shouted after her. She wondered what they were going to do. If they called the police, they would be doing her favour. She really wanted to find Rebwar before they did. She passed another roundabout and some railway tracks. Just before some huge metal cranes that looked like scaffolded robots, she turned right. Rows and rows of stacked up containers were all neatly lined up. She felt her stomach drop at the daunting task; there were containers as far as she could see. This could take days or weeks. Trucks and other specialised vehicles were swirling around carrying containers. She wound the window down in the hope of hearing something.

At the next gap, a forklift truck stopped in front of her. She got out and went up to the driver. He had dark skin, dreadlocks and a broad, friendly smile.

'Can you help me?'

He smiled. 'You lookin' for a box?'

She showed him her phone. 'I'm looking for this container.'

'Have you got a CI?' He waited for her answer. 'The ID number of the container. BIC code or anything else. See... on this picture they haven't got any of that information. See, lady, that is not a shipping container.' And he pointed at some that were next to them. 'See on them doors, you have all these numbers and information tells us all about it. This is not one you would find here.'

'But I'm sure it's here. Look at the background. Must be here.'

With his thick fingers which nearly filled the screen, he clumsily zoomed in and clicked with his tongue. 'Aye, lady, this is not the done thing. Na, na. You'll have to check this with HQ. The boss needs to know about this.' And he scratched under his hard hat.

'Can you call him?'

He looked at his watch and got his walkie-talkie out. 'Boris over to Bossman. I've got something that needs your attention. Over.'

'Boris, what now? Have you delivered it? Over.'

'I've got a...'

'DS Smith.'

For a moment, he hesitated. 'A policewoman here and she's looking for a shipment and it's highly irregular. Over.'

'Fu... I mean, really? Bloody security. Can she... can DS Smith come to HQ and we can deal with her request. Over.'

'Boris, you want me to send her over to you? Over.'

'Yes, over and out.' And the walkie-talkie signed off with a little melodic series of beeps.

'Bossman is in the building on the far east end. You follow this road till you get to the robots and then you'll see a big red-bricked building.' And he pointed behind her from where she had come.

'Robots?'

'Yeah, weird things. Gives me the willies. I go out onto the main road and come back in the east entrance. They have these trucks with no one in them... Just keep the water on your right and you will find it.' He shivered.

Geraldine got back into the car, turned it around and drove off, wondering what she would find there. For a moment she thought of taking Boris's route but she couldn't pass security again. And they were probably now looking for her. She thought of Rebwar and what he was going through. What were these people doing? Was it part of the Filthy Five crew? For a moment, she wanted to call anyone that would bring some company and comfort. In her distraction, a vehicle braked hard on the right and screeched to a halt. All she could see was a container. She looked for a driver or cab. Under the metal box was some kind of trailer with four wheels. She stared at it. This was what Boris meant by 'robots'. All around the stacked containers were more of these robots driving around. It made her shiver.

She put the car into reverse and then into first and did this a few times as if her brain had reached an impasse. She noticed that she was copying what the trailer was doing as if they were doing some kind of dance. She slammed into first and accelerated hard, making her tyres screech. She headed for the large building. Not caring what was marked on the smooth tarmac. Other driverless trailers screeched to halt as she cut them up.

She parked the car in front of a door and walked up to it. Having tried to push it open, she then looked for an intercom. After pressing a series of buttons, a voice spoke out.

'Can I help you?'

'DS Smith. Open up, please.'

'Have you an appointment?'

'I've come to see...' And she tried to remember what Boris had called him. 'Bossman.'

'Sorry who?'

'Open up otherwise you're going to have an appointment with me down at the station.'

There was a moment of silence before the door buzzed and Geraldine pushed the door open. The lights flickered as she walked down a corridor to a lift. She pressed the third floor; a sign said it housed the control room – no doubt where the Bossman was to be found. She was right.

In a room full of monitors were three men. Two of them looked like they were operating some joysticks at a desk with a wall of screens. The third man was sitting on a swivel chair which had an armrest and a headrest. He was holding a cup of tea with 'boss' written on it. His beer belly strained under his white shirt, and his red face showed years of stress. His eyes locked onto Geraldine. The other two men glanced over and quickly returned to their monitors as if they weren't allowed to stray off their jobs.

'DS Smith!' He pushed himself off the chair and his short little legs hit the ground. Geraldine was a head taller than him. 'Who invited you here and can't you read?' He smiled and walked over to her, continuing to stare into her eyes like she was some kind of sore he wanted to pick.

'I'm looking for a container full of kidnapped people and it's in your backyard, Mr?' She looked at his badge on his left shirt pocket. 'Mr Scott.'

'Call me Joe or Bossman. Most people call me Bossman. Look, if we let anyone come up with such fantastical stories Britain would come to a halt. You know we deal with over twenty-seven million tonnes a year and I am responsible for all this to go like clockwork. Now you can't just walk in and tell me to drop everything on a hunch.'

Geraldine took out her phone and showed him some pictures.

'It's a container on a truck. There are fucking millions of them and I've seen them all. I'd say that one is not here. It doesn't have any shipping information. Wouldn't even get in here. Which brings me to the other question... How the fuck did you get in here?'

The two operators glanced up from their screens to look at Geraldine. 'I am a police officer and I would like these two to find me this truck and container. It came here in the last few hours. Where is your CCTV?'

'Can I see your prosecution papers, please? Otherwise, come back with the right paperwork. Like I said... I run a tight ship here and have no time for your nosing around this site. You've caused enough delays driving in front of those bogeys. We are going to have to reset them.' He pointed at the digital clock that was behind him. 'Now I have no more time for you. Call those idiots in security and get them to escort DS Smith off the premises.'

'Mr Scott, if you're not going to be forthcoming with information I am going to proceed and search this place.' Geraldine stood in front him, looking down onto his thinning hair and red face. They stood for a moment. Geraldine waited for him to say something. His mouth masticated as if he was chewing a gum. She thought he had smoked before and looked for her pack of cigarettes, which she took out and slowly put a cigarette between her lips. His face froze with an expression of anger and need.

'While you make up your mind I am going smoke this outside.' She walked over to the younger man operating the screens. She could see some acne spots on his cheeks and his thick jet black hair kept falling over his eyes. Dandruff sprinkled his collar. 'Did you see a truck like this come in?' He looked at her screen and shook his head, at which point more hair covered his eyes. 'Can you see anything? Where do those cameras look onto?'

'DS Smith, can you leave my operative to do his job, please?'

The phone rang and Mr Scott's little legs went over to the desk with the ringing phone. 'Can you slow down... yeah, OK. Are you sure?... Again... Did you check... Where? No.' Bossman took a breath and patted his pockets like he was looking for something. 'Yeah... Boris, take a breath I can't make it out... Right, and where is it? OK, stay put... Don't fucking move from there.' Bossman clicked his fingers at Geraldine. 'Hey, copper, I think there is something. Where are your colleagues?' He grabbed his jacket from the back of his empty chair.

———

They arrived at the last row of containers on the far side of the dock. Boris was standing next to a forklift truck and looking up at a stack of containers and pointing at the top one. Geraldine opened the door of the moving car. She stepped out and looked up. It was the same colour as the one she had in the picture.

'It looks off!'

'Who the hell brought it in?' Scott used his flashlight to light up the metal box. 'Can't see any details. Get me those security goons – now.'

'We need to get it down,' Geraldine said.

'Need an operator, boss.'

'Who is?'

'Fuck, I'm going to have to wake someone up! Fuck's sake! Which shithead did this? There is going to be hell to pay.' Scott spoke into his radio and called up security and asked for a crane operator. A man arrived yawning and swearing. He inched the large crane over the stack, and manoeuvred a caddy over it and lifted it. The container clonked and moved around like there was something alive inside it.

'Where did this come from? And on my watch. Never had this on my patch. Never.' Scott shook his head.

The container came down slowly and hit the tarmac

with a heavy metallic thud. Boris rushed over to the doors, pulled the chain and banged on the door. The metal container sounded hollow as a drum. A man came with a bolt cutter and cut the lock. Boris pulled the levers to open the container doors. Geraldine rushed over. It was empty. She stepped in to look for some secret compartment. But there was nothing. She stepped out and swore.

Geraldine jumped at the sound of a snap and deep thud that travelled through her. Another container had been brought down from the stack. One of the corner fittings had given way. And was still being held up by three wires at an angle. The bottom corner had pierced into the tarmac. The container twisted around banging into another container. Two more fittings gave way and the metal box fell onto its side with a cloud of red dust engulfing it. It creaked and groaned.

'Cutters!' shouted Boris, running towards the bent container.

Scott grabbed them off the man and ran best as he could over to the doors. As soon he had cut through the chain, the door popped open. Inside was a mess of white insulating panels and bodies. Geraldine couldn't breathe. She scanned the contents, trying to work out what was in there.

FORTY-ONE

Rebwar had located his car in the police pound after a few phone calls. It was south of the river, close to the Blackwall Tunnel, just by Westcombe Park train station. After paying £150 removal charge and three days' storage, it came to £210, and he was going to claim it off someone. Charlie came to mind, as she had not paid for the last job. There had also been a lack of new jobs from Plan B and, as Monkton had said in his last breaths, the snake was dead. For Rebwar this was a clear reference that there had been a leadership change high above. Such things never went smoothly and were charged with consequences. Back in Iran, they ended up with purges and sometimes heads literary came rolling off.

His car was dirty and dented – a bit like himself. Geraldine had found him just in time. He'd been lucky to survive as they had been close to suffocating. There had been a few broken bones as the container had fallen. Luckily he'd escaped with some bruises. He had to get his car back on the road. But first, he was going to go home and tidy himself up. And he was looking forward to returning to Hourieh and Musa. Of course, he was going to have to explain and make up some kind of story, the truth would freak them out. Spending the night in a police cell was an acceptable story, as she knew he had some undercover security work and sometimes they would take him in.

By the time he got to Chalk Farm, it was past midday, and the sun was up in the blue sky with not a cloud around. He could feel spring coming. After he'd parked the car in the underground car park he went upstairs. He arrived at the door which had a strip of tape across it and a sign with an eviction notice.

He took out his phone and dialled. 'Hourieh—'

'Husband, where have you been? I have tried and tried to call you.'

'What's going on? What is this notice?'

'The council they... Dinah said, and we called.'

'You did what?'

'Dinah called them. We had no water.'

Rebwar swore and clenched his teeth, stopping himself from shouting down the phone. 'And?'

'She asked for a contractor... and they asked to talk to the tenant. They said... Like you said... no sub-letting.'

'Where are you?'

Silence. Then Hourieh said, 'At the neighbours two floors up.'

Rebwar headed up the stairs and knocked on the Jones's door. A frail white-haired old lady opened it. 'Mrs Jones, thank you so much for looking after my family. You are so kind and we will be out of your place in no time.'

'Dreadful! How can the council just evict you like that? I am going to complain. And you and your whole family will move back. You know you're such a hardworking man. Cup of tea? Cake?'

'I'm sorry about all this. You see that—'

Hourieh was in the hallway. 'Husband, I was so worried about you! Where have you been? You must text me or call. You can't leave the family like this! Husband, where have you been? Are you OK? You look bruised.'

Rebwar walked into the small flat, and in the living room was Musa on his phone along with Dinah who was sipping her tea and smiling. 'What is she doing here?'

Hourieh crossed her arms. 'You haven't been around. I needed help.'

'At the police station. It was a meeting. They needed some information.'

'Fantasist. I told you,' said Dinah.

'I don't need to explain myself to you.'

'Yes, you do,' said Hourieh. 'And if I weren't such a good wife I would be accusing you of having an affair. You're not, are you? I can tell.' And she smelled him. 'You need a good shower. You smell of police.'

'Bullshit more like,' said Dinah.

Musa was still sitting on the couch with his headphones as all three were pointing fingers at each other.

Rebwar clenched his jaw, feeling his anger mount, and he went over to the door. 'Leave us, this is a family matter. Don't want any more of your poison.'

Hourieh was about to say something but went over to Dinah who was dabbing her eyes.

'Oh, please! Keep those crocodile tears.'

Mrs Jones came in with a tray with five mugs of tea. 'Who's having sugar?' Dinah passed her, holding her head down and left. 'Oh... Coffee?'

'Sorry, Mrs Jones,' said Rebwar. 'It's a bit stressful at the moment. Thank you for the tea.' He turned to Hourieh.

'Let's get our stuff and stay in a hotel, until this all blows over.'

Hourieh turned and looked out of the window as if there was something there to see, but Rebwar had seen that look. She was either going to silently agree or give a volley of thoughts that even a top tennis player would struggle to respond to. She looked at Rebwar and looked back out.

'Mrs Jones, we're going to... as you say, to be out of your hair. And go to a hotel.'

'Well, you make sure you send the invoice to the council. They can't just evict you like that.'

Rebwar shook her hands, and they left the old lady's flat.

———

Rebwar found a hotel just across the Chilton estate on Primrose Hill Road called the Britannia Hampstead Hotel. He'd driven past it so many times and never noticed it, which made him chuckle.

'What, husband?'

'It's the same company that put us up when we arrived into this country. Remember?'

'They still need a cleaner.'

Rebwar looked around the low lobby. Its colourful carpet brought an air of heaviness and made it look like it was designed at the time of the Shah. It made him want to smoke a cigarette and go back in time. He could even smell the nicotine.

'Husband, they need your passport?'

Rebwar turned to see a smiling man in a waistcoat that was too tight for him. 'He took it out of his jacket pocket and passed it on. 'Why did Dinah call Don?'

'Don! He's useless, I have had enough of that man. And he wasn't supposed to rent it to us. They found out he was renting from a woman in Ireland and that it was her mother's flat who died four years ago. Can you believe it? It was lucky Dinah did call. And now the council is taking it back. We should be getting compensation. Where did you get that flat?'

Rebwar thought back and vaguely remembered an ad he saw in the local newsagents. 'Oh, it was an ad.'

Hourieh shook her head. 'I tell you next time—'

'Next time you can find it.'

Hourieh smiled at the man who was handing the passport back to Rebwar. He explained to them which room they had and where it was.

Rebwar rubbed his chin. 'I'm off out to get a shave. If you need anything, call me – and on the new number.'

'And the furniture? And and?'

Rebwar just made a sign with his hand to call her and left the lobby.

FORTY-TWO

Rebwar had called Raj for a meeting at Uncle B's barber's on 36 Cricklewood Lane, which was off a busy road that led to Golders Green and just off Cricklewood. The place was a simple unit and decorated like it was a work in progress; each wall had a unique wallpaper pattern from bricks to bamboo. The clientele liked to have the latest trendy cuts, which were mostly uneven layered haircuts. Musa had told Rebwar that it had been copied from a TV show. Raj was late as usual and Rebwar was still waiting for his shave. He always asked for Menja who had emigrated from India back in the seventies and had been kept out of retirement for his legendary shaves. He'd told Rebwar that he had stopped counting once he'd passed seventy and most people thought that was over thirty years ago, or so they said.

At 10:33 am, Raj arrived with a KFC paper bag. He sat down on one of the five high-backed chairs that lined the side of the half wood-panelled wall.

'Hey! How's it hanging? Heard G found you? You look pretty good... considering.'

'Just been evicted from the flat and will need a shower. Tell me some news?'

The two talked in broken Iranian, Raj used the odd English word when he ran out of vocabulary. It helped to keep any prying ears from listening to their conversation.

Raj leaned in closer. 'Hey, Uncle...' He looked around. 'So, I think Daisy's dad, Sir John Merkenstand is alive, or in some kind of... Have you heard of Stephen Hawkins, famous scientist?'

Rebwar shook his head.

'So, he talked using a machine, and I think this guy does too. Or at least on the web. I've been chatting to some kind of bot, and I think he's Sir John Merkenstand.'

Rebwar stared at him.

'It's complicated. But there are AI computers out there that you can chat to. And this one is off the scale and I think it has a human behind it.'

'OK, I'll go with it.' Rebwar scratched his heavy stubble.

Raj took a handful of chips. 'And this Sir John Merkenstand owns Byways group!' he said, excited. 'You know... what O'Neil used as a front to smuggle people. And they have been behind all those surveillance bots. You know farming Facebook and other social sites. Just believe me, Uncle. They take our data and sell it off to other companies. Like where we shop, what we like and all that.'

A young boy with a face full of acne came out of the back with a cup of coffee and gave it to Rebwar. He sipped it and let its intense flavours knock out some of the fatigue he was feeling. 'And the container?'

'Not much there seems that all those social media posts was proof for a job done. It was all deleted a couple of hours later. What do you reckon?'

Rebwar sucked in through his teeth. 'Some Plan B cell. I

mean like we thought no one else knew of Amir.' He shook his head. 'Or Byways and Sir John Merkenstand. Should have seen it coming. It was a well-planned professional job, just like the secret service. They bought me a drink and then it was night-night and I woke up in a steel box with some men and women staring at me.'

'Wow, so it worked! And I thought we'd be looking for some fake troll accounts that would lead to some smelly bedroom. Uncle, this is some serious shit. Aren't they going to try again?'

'You deleted Amir?'

'Uhm, yeah, yeah.'

Rebwar watched Raj's eyes dance around. 'Have you?'

Raj giggled. 'Of course, I did! I wasn't going to give them a second chance... or did you want to?'

Rebwar got up and went over to the barber's seat where Menja was waiting for him. His sunken, steely blue eyes studying his face. 'Tell me more about this Merkenstand character. Is he a vegetable?'

Raj opened his laptop and read out some articles he had found. 'Comes from money although his dad, Sir Howard Merkenstand, was a famous gambler. And – get this – lost it all in a Trump casino in the nineties and then committed suicide.'

'What the president?'

'Yeah, that Trump. He has casinos! Merkenstand's mother, Barbara Merkenstand, is now looking after her son. And...' Raj whistled and went quiet as he leaned into the screen. He got up and showed the laptop screen to Rebwar. It was some black and white pictures of a very beautiful woman posing. They looked like they were taken in the sixties when women wore cone-shaped bras. 'That's a trophy wife. Wicked heh?'

'How is she today?'

Raj shrugged and returned to his seat. 'Yeah, so she has asked for privacy as her son recovers from his injuries. And... Bla, bla, bla...'

'Injuries? You said he was a robot or something? Have you got an address?'

'Yes, his company is still operating... it says that he is still the CEO... Weird – I thought you had to be conscious or something like that to run a company. What do you think?'

'Can we visit them? They must have a fancy office somewhere. And then we can look where his father lived. I don't think the apple fell far from that tree.'

Menja pinched Rebwar's nose and shaved off some of the three-day stubble and wiped the sharp blade on his towel he had on his shoulder.

'I tell you we are going to have to make a visit to those Merkenstands. I can't believe Daisy was in the middle of all this mess, and we missed the opportunity to get to her. Any news on the Filthy Five?'

Raj slurped his large Coke. 'Mmm, na, they were off their heads with MDA. Oh yeah, nearly forgot... they found Jack Hill's body but not the car. So haven't connected it with the crash.'

Rebwar turned to look at Raj, but Menja grabbed his head back in place and tutted. 'Have they said how he died?'

'Suicide. D'oh.'

'It was murder. So either they're covering up or they haven't joined up the dots. What's the obituary say?'

Raj tapped away at his keyboard like a woodpecker trying to get a worm out of a trunk. 'Only found one and on a blog. *Sad to see a good friend pass away... Warrior of fake news tirelessly chased the truth and facts... he was an inspiration for the new internet generation... he had his friends and enemies but that is the way of the connected age... a world where trolls can roam like wild animals with no comeback... he will be sadly missed...* And, that's it. I mean, that's sad, man. He deserved better.'

'That's it?'

'Yeah, brutal, hey? Fuck, he made some enemies. Oh! Get a look at this picture of Barbara Turner, aka Mrs Merkenstand. She's had some work done! And... well, it's not holding well. Look...' Raj passed the laptop to him again. It was a very different picture. Wrinkles were holding shiny flat areas of skin. Her eyes were black and piercing. Rebwar shivered.

'I know, me too. I've got goosebumps. See.' Raj showed his fat round arm.

'Can you find more about her and not those beauty shots? I mean where she's from, anything. She must be running the company, I mean, who else?'

'Really, you think...' Raj held the computer screen closer and looked at her and went to tap the keyboard till it gave him some more info. 'She has been to some balls with some famous business dudes. But that was when her son was alive. Dude, she's some kind of witch.'

'Address?'

'The Isle of Guernsey? Where's that?'

'Offshore accounts,' said Menja.

'What is that?'

Menja stepped forward. 'If you have too much money and don't want to pay taxes. You set up an offshore company. The prime minister's father did it. You know, that James Cameron, the one that fucked off after the referendum. Everybody who has money is at it. I have friends that have trust funds out there. And they are regulars, like you.'

Raj stopped typing. 'Found it! Merkenstand Manor... It's a ruin now.' Raj showed Rebwar the picture. It was a pile of stones with bushes and trees growing out of them.

FORTY-THREE

Rebwar was walking back to his car after having had a coffee at the Shishawi. He'd been thinking about his options. The outlook was bleak: homeless, nearly broke, and he was being used for something which he disliked. Something was very rotten somewhere in Plan B. Geraldine hadn't found anything out about who had kidnapped him. But they had rattled someone's cage, so they were onto something. He tried again to call Geraldine, but there wasn't even a tone or option to leave a voice message. He hadn't a good feeling. Walking down Kendal Street, which was just off Edgware Road, he lit a cigarette and carried on towards his parked car. A black van drove out of an underground car park. He let them pass. The street was lined with three to six-storey large residential blocks. He composed a text to send to Geraldine. The black van pulled up next to him and the passenger window lowered. A man wearing dark sports sunglasses leaned out.

'Mr Ghorbani?'

Rebwar hesitated. The driver, too, was wearing sunglasses and a bulky denim jacket. The passenger stepped out. His brown hair was slicked back and he had a tattoo on his neck of a yin and yang symbol.

'We're taking you in.'

The van's side door slid open. Inside was another man, also wearing sunglasses. Both grabbed him before Rebwar could say anything or react. One took his legs and the other his torso, holding his arms down. As soon as he was in they closed the door and drove off. Rebwar got a glimpse of another person before they slid a hood over his head and tied him up with cable ties. He thought it was Geraldine. They covered his mouth with gaffer tape and made him sit on the floor of the vehicle.

'And I was all ready to sedate him.'

Then he felt a sting in his arm and felt himself go groggy.

'But—'

Rebwar came back, his body telling him that he was sitting on a chair. Hands tied behind him. Still gagged and in darkness, he could hear the buzzing of a strip light. He tapped his shoes, noting that the floor was hollow and smooth below him. A door opened and as it closed the thin walls shook. He'd been in enough Portakabins to recognise their flimsy sound. His hood was taken off and once his eyes adjusted to the light he saw a white man standing in front of him. He had a military style haircut, and wore a white shirt and black V-neck jumper. His black brogue shoes were slightly muddy. His dark eyes were fixed on him.

'Rebwar...' He paced around the bare white room. The blinds were drawn down but could tell it was night. 'Did someone tell you to follow Agent Ferret?'

'Who are you?'

'That's not important. Who gave you that assignment?'

'Plan B... you guys?'

'And then you and Geraldine decided to go on a mission to compromise us.'

'Sorry, what are you talking about?'

'Anthony Peckworth MP, you were in his flat.' He held up two fingers at him. 'Twice and he committed suicide.' The man shook his head. 'Then we have Edward Monkton, on video, you knifing him. And Jack Hill... What the fuck is going on?'

As Rebwar had suspected, he had been framed. Charlie had made sure he was there at all those murder scenes. That bitch. He felt anger rise through him. He should have seen it from the beginning. They had made fools of them.

'Charlie, your Agent Ferret.'

'Yeah, pull another one. Who's put you up for this? Filthy Five?'

'You listen to me. It's Charlie, she's behind all this. She approached me to set up Geraldine, and the Filthy Five work for her. Daisy... She's yours. No? Or have you lost control?'

'Listen, Rebwar, you've broken the contract.' The man took out his gun. A Glock 26 which was compact and easily concealable. 'There are consequences.' He cocked the gun. 'Now who are you working for?'

'Plan B, we wanted to contact you. We knew that Charlie was off but hadn't any proof. Monkton said Plan B is dead, snakes everywhere.'

'You're going to have to start talking, Mr Ghorbani. Who are you working for? There's no one to save you. You'll be going back in a body bag.'

'Ask Geraldine, I'm sure she's told you the same about

Charlie. For God's sake, man. Charlie is behind this and probably someone else.' Rebwar watched his face and wondered if he was somehow involved. They had been set up and this was the endgame. He looked around the corners of the room and spotted a camera on his front left. Looking straight at it he said, 'I've been set up, you've been infil-trated. Rats are running about on your ship.'

The man stood in front of him. 'There's no one else listening in. Do you take us for fools? You know who the rats are, you just need to tell me and I'll find out anyway. So either you live or die. That's your decision.'

'So what are you offering?'

'Your life, we'll send you back and you'll see what fate offers you.'

'I can fix this. Just get your agent Charlie in.'

'We've talked to her. She handed over the evidence. It was her who ratted on you. Don't you get it?'

'You can't just believe her. Bring her back.' Rebwar's frustration grew and he tried to move his hands and feet. But the cable ties bit harder into his skin.

'Rebwar, think about it. Why? And Charlie, she's not the type. Never served for the Home Office. No military training. Just a pen pusher who got involved with the wrong crowd. I mean... Really?' He cocked the pistol.

'Where's Geraldine? She was in the van. I saw her. And who kidnapped me?'

The man stood back and straightened himself.

'After we lost the Filthy Five... I got kidnapped and put into a container.'

'What if you did... Were they closing it down?' He aimed the gun and he shot.

Rebwar saw the flash and felt burst of heat. His head instinctively leaned over to the right. His left ear rang and buzzed and he felt disoriented. The man shouted something to him but he couldn't hear him. He'd missed on purpose but temporarily deafened him. It would be a little while till the buzzing would pass. Did he want some kind of confession?

'Can you hear me? Yes?'

Rebwar shook his head.

With his pistol he lifted Rebwar's chin. The metal was still hot and he could smell the gunpowder. He moved to his right ear.

'Ready to talk? I know you're a tough candidate and I'm not going to go through this whole torture routine. I don't believe in it. People say desperate things when they are close to death. They want the pain to stop. So I'm here to make it quick and easy.'

'If I can see Geraldine, then I'll talk. I want to know she's alive. And what are you going to do with my family?'

The man crossed his arms and stared at him. 'So you want to negotiate? You tell me and then I'll see if you are worthy of any last rites.'

Rebwar was getting tired of his pig-headedness. 'You've got it all wrong. Don't you see it? Who's Charlie's superior? What does he or she think? I mean, you keep tags on your agents... Don't you?'

A shot rang out and two holes appeared, one by the door and the other behind. The man ducked and went over to the window which was by the door. His leg was taken from under him and he dropped to the floor. A pool of blood expanded around his left foot. The shock must have stopped him from feeling the immediate pain. The next shot hit his chest and he looked down to see the exit wound. His dark jumper made it hard to see the type of wound. Rebwar heard him struggling to breath, shallow and gurgling. It took only a few breaths till he drowned in his own blood and collapsed.

Rebwar waited, expecting more shots or someone to come. But it was all silent. He hopped his seat over to the dead man then rocked the chair till it slipped in the pool of blood. His left cheek landed in the still warm red liquid. He took short breaths, trying to not let his war nightmares get to him. With his hands he tried to feel into the man's pockets. The blood was sticky and the man's body slipped as he tried to move him. He felt a knife in his back pocket, Swiss Army style and he flicked it open and cut himself free.

Then he carried on, going through his pockets, and found a wallet and a phone. He found a couple of bank cards with Mr E. Lister written on them. And that's all he had. Rebwar took the pistol, cocked it, inched towards the door and slowly opened it. The Portakabin was in a building site as he had thought. The floodlights lit a large muddy pit with a couple of diggers inside it. Otherwise the place was deserted. Either after hours or it had been abandoned. Rebwar cautiously made his way around the cabin. He worked out that the shots had come from across the site. There were a couple of large industrial metal structures where someone could have had a good vantage point. Whoever it was he was an excellent shot.

Lister's phone rang. Rebwar stared at the screen not believing what he was seeing. The name *Ferret* flashed. Charlie. Why was she calling this number? He picked up.

'Rebwar,' Charlie said.

'Yes.'

'Listen, and listen carefully. You are going to free Geraldine who is being held in the van you came in and then drive to the address I am going to text you.'

'Charlie! What the—'

She cut off. Rebwar looked around for the black van. A cold wind had picked up in the desolate building site. He had no idea where he was but it wasn't in London. He could see the city's orange glow off on the horizon. With no sun he didn't know in which direction he was looking. There were a dozen Portakabins all laid around the muddy site. There was no order or logic to them. He found some tyre tracks which looked fresher than the others and followed them. Around the last cabin was the van he had been kidnapped in. He approached it slowly, expecting to find someone guarding it. He raised his gun and looked into the van's side mirror. The driver's seat and passengers' seats were empty. His footsteps slurped and squished in the wet mud. If there was anyone about they would have heard him.

He got to the side door and slid it open. Geraldine was sitting on the van's floor tied up. Rebwar went over to take her hood off and untie her.

'What's going on?' She shivered.

Rebwar took off his leather jacket and put it around her.

'I really don't know. Charlie just called... And do you know an E. Lister? Tall, older man, white hair, clean cut. Army type I think.'

'Fox? Maybe.'

'Well, he's dead. Someone sniped him and then Charlie called. And we've been framed.'

'Plan B?'

'Charlie ratted on us or that's what this Fox or E. Lister thought.'

Geraldine and Rebwar had driven up to Brent Cross, they had decided to split up and had dropped Rebwar off a few streets away from the meeting place. She parked behind a warehouse by the goods entrance, switched the engine off and took a deep breath. Charlie had called the meeting in a shop called Toys'R'Us, which had recently gone into administration. Weeds and rubbish had already crept into the deserted property. It was 3:23 am and there was a full moon. She walked over to the entrance. No security lights flicked on, so she had to use her phone's flashlight to find the door handle. Rebwar was going to sneak in but he hadn't said what his plan was and it was best that she didn't know, as she was the world's worst poker player. Still... she would have preferred to have him by her side.

Geraldine still couldn't make out what had happened at her last meeting with Charlie in the park. It was a mix of gaslighting, provocation and just psychopathic behaviour. And since the Fox and Monkton had been killed they were at a loss. She and Rebwar kind of knew they were walking into a trap, but what other choice had they? As Rebwar had said, Charlie just didn't fit the profile of a mastermind that was going to take over Plan B. Although she had outdone herself, by manipulating them into situations that made them guilty. Were they going to be arrested? Was this going to be Charlie's crowning glory? It certainly felt like it. Or was there some other figure with her?

Inside, the worn carpets were soggy, and the air was cool with a smell of rot. A hallway led inside where discarded cables, upended desks and chairs were the only evidence that there had been offices where people had worked. Geraldine had brought her baton but still felt vulnerable. Her eyes scanned for any trace of movement and listened out for any sounds. She pushed a squeaky door that led into the main showroom. She was either expecting a welcoming committee or a lone figure but saw nothing, just empty aisles with shelves that once held thousands of toys. It was now a sad sight of a few discarded dolls, Lego, odd-shaped plastic objects and boxes. The North Circular's traffic reverberated inside the large structure, which was a welcome reminder that there was life outside.

She hesitated, wanting to shout hello, but she couldn't. It would come out like a cry for help. Geraldine walked along the rows of shelves, her light guiding her into this temple of toys that had once filled children's hearts with joy. In her day it had been little independent shops, nothing like this.

'Glad you could make it.'

Geraldine turned to her left and then to her right, trying to find the voice.

'Been busy?'

Geraldine walked further over by the tills at the far end. Charlie and Trent were standing as if they were waiting for her to bring some toys.

'Hi, Charlie, what's Trent doing here? And where's the rest of the gang?'

'Glad you could make it. Where's Rebwar?'

'Stop trying to pull wool over my eyes. You've been frankly a bitch! And what's all this about?'

Trent rolled out an office chair and put it in front of Geraldine.

'Please sit,' Charlie said.

'What? An interview? You're fucking kidding me.'

'Do as you're fucking told,' said Trent. 'We're not in the mood to be fucked about.'

Geraldine took the chair and sat on it with the back of the chair facing her.

'Love, you're no Christine Keeler either... So.' Charlie brought out a folded piece of paper and put on her glasses.

'Charlie, just one thing before you bore me to death. Can we put all our cards on the table?'

Trent thrust his finger at Geraldine. 'Hey! You're not here to call the shots, you dirty dyke.'

'Trent, what did we agree?' said Charlie.

Trent stepped back, grumbled and ran his fingers through his long greasy grey hair.

'Well, let's start with your boyfriend. Misogynist, racist, crook, cock–'

Trent smacked Geraldine across her face. Charlie tried to grab and stop him, but he got another smack in. Geraldine's face stung. 'One more word out of your dirty dyke mouth and I'll be shoving my–'

'Trent! Please! What did we agree on? Otherwise... you know.' Trent kicked a brown box. Charlie pushed Trent back. 'For fuck's sake. Control yourself.'

'Yeah but she...'

Geraldine felt for the baton that was inside her bomber jacket.

'Are you all right?' said Charlie.

Geraldine felt her sore face and nodded.

Charlie propped one of her buttock cheeks onto the checkout's conveyor belt. Her knee-length dress rode up a bit and showed some thigh and she noticed and readjusted her skirt. The sheet of paper trembled in her hands. 'Yes, right, Plan B. I need to know some things from you...' Some metal clanging stopped her. She looked over towards Trent who marched over to the noises. Charlie sighed.

'Going well, then.' Geraldine spun the chair from left to right. 'So, tell me, honestly, are you now in charge or what?'

Trent appeared between an aisle with Rebwar, and Brunje and Knight both identically dressed in black jumpers and heavy boots. Brunje was pointing a shotgun at Rebwar, and Knight had Rebwar's pistol. 'We found him hiding in the back.'

'How predictable,' said Charlie. 'Call yourself a detective. But glad you could make it. Get him another chair... wait...' She got up and went over to Rebwar. 'You're an expert at getting confessions. Tie her up.' She handed over some cable ties to Rebwar.

Rebwar hesitated. Geraldine felt a cold shiver run through her as Rebwar approached with the ties. 'Sorry,' he whispered. 'Got any ideas?'

'Wait!' Charlie barked at Trent, 'Frisk her.'

Trent smiled and went over to Geraldine. She tried to protest, but Knight and Brunje were ready to intervene. Trent unzipped her bomber jacket and roughly searched her. His hands forced her limbs to move, and he carried on searching her body as if a snake was trying to wrap itself around her. She wanted to scream, bite, punch. He found her baton and held it out. Geraldine felt her stomach lurch as she couldn't face his arrogant smirk.

'Tie the dyke,' said Trent.

Charlie nodded, and Rebwar zip-tied Geraldine to the chair. Each zip made her shake. Memories of O'Neil flashed back. Zara, her girlfriend had been murdered by Lawrence Gibson, one of O'Neil's associates. She meditated, hoping the memories would go.

'She's not feeling well,' said Rebwar.

'Get her some water,' said Charlie. Knight went to find some.

'Where's Daisy?' said Rebwar.

Charlie got another office chair from behind the tills. 'Sit him on that chair and tie him. Oh, frisk him too, don't want any nasty surprises.'

Brunje put his shotgun by the till, pushed Trent to the side, sat Rebwar down and frisked him and used the remaining cable ties. Geraldine watched as each cable tie was zipped tight and made Rebwar grimace in pain. Brunje was purposely making them hurt. His boots were caked in a the same colour mud as Rebwar's shoes. Had he been at the quarry too?

'Nice sight.' Charlie walked around them. 'We're taking over Plan B, I'm calling it Plan C.' She laughed. 'Now this is an offer... a generous one I might add.'

'Can I ask first, what's been going on? Peckworth, Filthy Five, your surveillance, Kurtis, Daisy... Mr Fox and Monkton?' Geraldine looked over to Rebwar. 'Oh, and his recent trip to Felixstowe.'

Charlie crouched down in front of Geraldine. 'It's a need to know situation. Now I have an offer or an opportunity.' She got up and walked around them. 'We can take down Plan B.'

Geraldine laughed.

'Like I said, this is a one-time offer.'

'Why should we even trust you? You've set us up. They're after us.'

'We're going to go and see Sir John Merkenstand and I'm offering you the chance to end all this. Freedom for us all.'

'How?' said Geraldine.

'You were asking about Daisy, well we've got an in there. She considers herself my daughter, and she's had enough of the family ruling her life. Sounds familiar?'

Trent took out some chewing gum and offered it to Knight.

'Go on, what's the master plan then?'

'First, I need to know that you two are in.' Charlie signalled to Trent who walked off to a side entrance with Brunje.

Rebwar seemed to perk up but looked concerned. The side door opened, and he swore. Geraldine's heart sank, Hourieh and Musa were being led towards them. Both were tied up and gagged with gaffer tape.

'You see, I need some security.'

'Let them go! You can't do this. You bitch.' And Rebwar spoke to them in Iranian, both of them nodded and tears ran down their cheeks.

'Charlie, you can't—'

'Now, listen. Are you both in? I need to hear you say it.'

'If you touch a hair, I'll kill you all. You motherfuckers.' Rebwar struggled and rocked his chair.

'We're in.'

Charlie went over to Rebwar and asked him. Geraldine could see that he was struggling to commit.

'Rebs, Rebs... think about it. See the options. She's

offering us freedom.' Geraldine looked at Charlie. 'Aren't you?'

Charlie nodded.

Rebwar sighed. 'OK, but you release them now.'

'On completion, that's always been the deal.'

Musa managed to free himself from Knight's grip and run over to Rebwar. 'Son, it'll be all right, just do what they say and don't worry. I'll be back to get you.'

Trent grabbed Musa off Rebwar.

'Don't touch him or I'll—'

'You'll what? Old man, do what you're told.'

Geraldine looked over to Rebwar. 'We're in.' Geraldine knew they didn't have too much of choice and had to see this through. Charlie had done a good job framing them.

'Rebwar?'

He nodded.

'I need to hear it.'

'I'm in.'

'Good, now we need to break into Sir John's manor and kill him.'

'But he's already dead,' said Rebwar. 'It's—'

'That's what they want to us to think. So you two are going to meet up with Daisy and pretend that you've taken her hostage and want to negotiate a deal.'

'Isn't there going to be some kind of security?'

'She's going to deal with that. And once you're in, we'll come.'

'What if they don't bite? What then?'

Brunje went over to Geraldine. 'We'll cut a finger.'

'Was it you who took out those three men at the building site?' Rebwar looked down at his muddy boots. Brunje nodded. 'And Hill.' Rebwar turned his head towards

Charlie. 'You paid him to write that article about Peckworth's suicide, why?'

'Well, as it's confession time. Look, Hill had his uses, but then he got too nosy.'

'Why the ransom?' said Geraldine.

'Bring out the rats,' said Trent, chewing his gum and pointing at Rebwar and Geraldine.

'And who killed Peckworth?'

'Thomas did, but it's not important. As you two are guilty of all those crimes.'

Geraldine was about to ask who murdered Monkton but Charlie was running out of patience.

Charlie held her forehead. 'I need your attention...' She paced around. 'If I'm going to release you I need your word that you're going to follow my instructions.' She folded her arms in front of Geraldine.

'I guess we don't have much of a choice.'

'That's not the point, are you with us or not? If you just go to the police or Plan B... I'll hand over all the evidence and your wife and son will have to watch you rot in jail.'

Geraldine and Rebwar nodded.

'You two will drive up and meet Daisy. She will brief you on what you're supposed to do. OK? Now your family are going to be in a safe house and only on completion will they be released. Understand?'

Rebwar nodded.

'And if any of you step out of line... Well, you know.'

Brunje smiled, and Trent giggled.

The Filthy Five and Charlie huddled in a circle away from earshot.

'Rebs, sorry I got you into this. If you need to... You know, I'll understand.'

Rebwar pointed with his head towards the shotgun. 'I tied you up.'

Geraldine thought about it, but Knight had Rebwar's pistol, and she was a terrible shot. The odds weren't good. She looked over to see their discussion. There was the odd glance from one of them. They had a plan that she and Rebwar weren't privy too. All this stank.

Trent marched over and drew out a knife and untied them, then handed them each phone.

'I can track you and you will report to me on a regular basis. No deviation, understand me?'

Rebwar rushed over to Hourieh and Musa. He kissed them and was about to take off their gags but Brunje stopped him. Geraldine's anger rose. Tears and sniffles echoed in the large warehouse.

'Yes,' said Geraldine to Charlie and rubbed her wrists which were sore and red from the plastic zip ties.

'Right, get going, drive straight up there. I am texting you the address.'

'Come, Rebs, we need to get a move on. The quicker we do this, the quicker we'll be back.'

Rebwar hugged Hourieh and Musa and walked off, Geraldine having to keep up. He was angry, very angry.

FORTY-FIVE

Rebwar and Geraldine sat on stools around a small round table, each with a full pint in front of them and watching the bubbles rise. Rebwar's clothes were dirty and his face was scratched. Neither had stopped since they had been abducted by Plan B. He felt his body stiffen up. They had driven straight up to the address that Charlie had given them. A little village outside Oxford. Neither of them had heard of it. The village pub had a few patrons who chatted to each other. It was a mix of workmen with their dusty and worn clothes and a knot of red-faced old men. The decor was black antique wooden beams and whitewashed wonky walls with the odd framed picture. Rebwar sipped his beer and put it back on the mat and looked at his phone. He wanted to call for help.

He felt powerless and angry that they had come in harm's way. But they were cornered. He and Geraldine had exhausted all the options. Why hadn't they seen this trap coming? Rebwar sipped his beer. If only he'd put his family at Bijan's, packed up and left, confronted Charlie, stopped the Filthy Five. So many missed opportunities.

'You've texted Charlie?'

Geraldine nodded.

'What do you think is really going on?'

Geraldine took a sip of her beer and stretched his arms out. 'I can't see the wood for the trees. I mean, there must be someone behind Charlie. No?'

'She's not the type. And Daisy? What happened there? Kidnapped by O'Neil and then Plan B take her into custody and she ends up in some kind of anarchist gang. Hill knew something, and they killed him for it.'

'We need Raj.' Geraldine.

'No, it's too dangerous and we can't involve him. Wouldn't be fair. No.'

'You said that Merkenstand was a vegetable, and he's being kept alive by some computer. AI or something. If we're going to stand a chance of getting to them, we need some IT help.'

Rebwar sipped his beer and looked up. She had a point; they needed all the help they could get. 'Have you contacted your colleagues?'

She shook her head.

'I'll call Raj, but I'm not happy about it.' Rebwar got up and walked out and lit a cigarette. The full moon lit the night sky, and he walked to the car, over the crunching gravel. Fields surrounded the pub. He dialled Raj's number.

'Uncle! Where the fuck have you been? I've been worried.'

'Yeah, you're not the only one. Charlie's got Musa and Hourieh and we're close to the Merkenstands and we need your help.'

'But where have you been?'

'Long story and can't talk for long. Look, you don't have

to do this, if you don't want to. It's dangerous. And I don't but—'

'I'm in! What do I need to do?'

'Rembember, you don't have to do this. But we're going to break in and need some backup. I'll text you the address and I'll come and pick you up.'

'Which tube station?'

'I don't think the tube goes out to here. I'll see what Geraldine says.'

'What's the place called?'

Rebwar looked back and read the lit sign. 'The Plough Inn... in some village. I'll work something out.' He hung up and breathed in and felt doubt fill his mind. He couldn't think straight. They were out of their depth and treading water. Not that he'd ever tried that as he couldn't swim. He walked back into the pub to find Geraldine asleep. He shook her and in a low voice said, 'The Merkenstands. We need to find out where they live.'

Geraldine looked up. 'I'm beat...' She sipped her beer. 'How? I've run out of favours.' She looked at her watch. 'I guess that'll be for tomorrow? They have rooms here. We should stay for the night.'

Rebwar caught a glimpse of a man walking into the pub. The bell rang for last orders as he got to the bar. He was tall, well built, big hands with a sharp profile. The way he held himself said military. The man ordered a double whisky, and the barman shouted last orders.

'Nightcap?' Geraldine got up.

'Yes, a brandy.'

She went up to the bar and said hello to the man who had just downed the whisky. 'Another?' But he put down a five-pound note and left. She turned to the barman, who wore a set of oval-rimmed glasses, which made his large face rounder, and asked, 'Do you have some rooms here?'

'Yeah, we have a double.' And he looked over to Rebwar.

'Any singles?'

'Sorry, no. What'll it be?'

'A whisky and a brandy and make them doubles. Is the breakfast included?'

'Yes.' The barman wiped the bar clean. 'On business?'

'You could say that. Quiet night?'

The barman just poured the two drinks and passed them over.

'Any shoots around here?'

'When it's the season, loads of them. But I don't get involved. For the rich city boys and landed gentry.' He rang the bell for closing time.

The rest of the guests left. 'Bye, Grayson,' the barman said. 'Greetings to the wife. When she's back.'

The workman flicked a middle finger back to him.

'She left him,' he said to Geraldine, laughing. 'Had one too many.' He winked. 'If you know what I mean.'

Rebwar got up and looked at the pictures on the walls. There were a few etchings of an old manor. 'Where is this?'

The landlord looked over. 'That's the old manor. It burned down in the fifties.'

'Why?'

'They say it was an insurance scam, but it was before my time.'

'Whose was it?'

'The Merkenstands. Local family.'

Geraldine brought over the brandy to Rebwar and looked at the picture. 'Still around, are they?'

'I've heard that they are. Will runs the grounds, the chap that walked in and had the whisky.'

'Will?'

'Yeah.'

'So where's the manor?' said Geraldine.

'Up the road. All locked up. Keep to themselves they do. So what business you've come over to do?'

Rebwar stepped up to the bar. 'Seen this girl?' And he showed him an image of Daisy from his phone.

The barman cleaned the bar. 'No, can't say I have.'

'Daisy Merkenstand.'

'Like I said, they keep to themselves.'

'What about the helicopter crash?'

'What about it?'

'See it?'

The barman opened the small dishwasher, and steam engulfed him. 'I was on holidays. Made some news here in the village but, like I said, I wasn't about. Why all the questions? Police?'

'Drink?' said Geraldine.

He removed his glasses and wiped the steam off them with a hand towel. 'Off a copper? Isn't that a bribe or something?' He put his hand out. 'Passports... or ID, for the rooms.'

Geraldine took out her warrant card and Rebwar gave over his driving license. He took them and read them. 'You know I should call this in to DCI Sands... You know, you two snooping around on his patch.'

'Different department. And if he needs to know, I'm sure my department will have notified DCI Sands. Mate of yours?'

'Couldn't say if he was. Client confidentiality and all that...'

Rebwar could see Geraldine tapping the bar lightly with her DM boots and was on the cusp of losing it. They both needed some sleep, and this wasn't the way of getting any more clues. The barman knew something, but he wasn't going to give it up here. He was probably working for the Merkenstands. This whole village was most likely in their pocket. Geraldine had rattled him enough.

'Sure you don't want a drink, Mr?'

The barman pointed at a plaque above the bar. It read *Ronald Compton & Sir J Merkenstand are licensed to sell wine, beer & spirits for the consumption on the premises.* Geraldine and Rebwar looked at each other. Geraldine rubbed her face and downed her whisky. Compton put a key with a wooden key ring on the bar. 'Up the stairs and down the hall. Breakfast is served at eight.' And he switched the bar lights off.

———

The room was small. At every step, something creaked and nothing was level. It was as if they were on an old sailing ship. Rebwar looked out of the window which faced the back of the pub. He could see a car park, bins, air extractor, trees, fields and some other houses.

Geraldine sat on the end of the bed. 'Do you think they are going to come for us?'

'Any news?'

Geraldine got her phone out, tapped the screen and shook her head. 'Don't worry I'm on the wifi, roaming is off... Nothing.'

Rebwar grunted. 'And they would have already taken us.'

Geraldine fell back onto the bed, bounced to a rest and

looked up at the ceiling. 'Maybe need to get some kip. Feel like it's going to be a long day.'

'Don't think I'm getting any sleep and you're right, we need Raj.' He took off his shoes and felt the spongy carpet.

Geraldine had fallen asleep. He wished he could do that. His insomnia was still with him. If he was lucky, he would get half an hour. He sat on the chair by the TV and listened: creaks, cats howling, foxes screeching, flushing toilet and the odd car passing. He had to expect some company. Compton must have told someone about their questions and interest in the Merkenstands. Rebwar looked out of the window, wondering where Musa and Hourieh were.

FORTY-SIX

After an uncomfortable night where Rebwar had been up listening for any suspicious noises, he was now downstairs in the pub sipping a filter coffee. He'd run out of cigarettes and was hoping that the caffeine would at some point wake him up and give him its intended kick. He slid the bacon and fried egg around the plate. Rebwar still hadn't got used to the idea of a breakfast that looked like a dinner. For him, it had to be something cold and sweet. He cut the bacon and egg to make it appear like he had eaten some of it. He'd left messages on Hourieh's voicemail telling her not to worry, that when this was all over they could get on with life... If only he could believe it himself.

While he waited for Geraldine, he thought about the last few days. They had been intense, and it felt like something was coming to a climax. He felt a wave of sadness push him back. It had been such a waste of innocent life, Jack Hill, the Filthy Five, all caught up in the web. He hated Plan B, or whatever they were, more than ever, and knew he was doing the right thing by going after them.

Geraldine walked up to the table and caught him by surprise. He looked up and saw a tired face.

'Sleep well?'

Rebwar shook his head. 'We need to call Charlie.'

Geraldine took out her phone and dialled a number. It rang for a couple of rings.

'*Hello.*'

'It's Geraldine.'

A moment of silence. '*Oh! Hi... Yeah, so what's...*'

'What's today's plan?'

'Daisy is in the area. You need to find her and capture her. She will resist.'

'Does she know we're coming for her? Charlie? Charlie? For fuck's sake.' Geraldine turned to Rebwar. 'She hung up on me.'

'We need to dig around a little more... and I have a feeling that we will be seeing Charlie around here.'

Geraldine thought for a moment and agreed.

———

Rebwar was driving the black van to the nearest train station to pick up Raj. They had left Knowles, the little village where they had stayed and were on a single lane country road. High bushes and trees lined the road, which only gave Rebwar and Geraldine the occasional glimpse into some passing fields. Geraldine shouted for him to stop.

'Reverse... go on quick, quick!'

Rebwar fumbled and found reverse. Geraldine told him to stop just by a gate where she had seen a girl on a horse.

'I'll be... That's Daisy! Look!'

She was jumping over some jumps. Rebwar looked and

saw long red curly hair bobbing up and down under a helmet. He had to get closer to be sure, but he let Geraldine run with it.

'How are we going to do this?' Geraldine thought for a moment. 'What if I go up there?'

'Why? How are you with horses?'

'Not great. Seen them...'

'They're big... don't show any fear and... Don't grab it. No, not a good idea. She's a good horse rider and could easily trample you.'

'Really? They look so graceful. What if you drove up?'

Rebwar laughed and pointed at Daisy. 'What if she has to have some security?'

'We'll have to risk that. Don't you think there'll be others trying to get her? And what do we do once we are in the manor? We'll be pretty exposed...'

'Wait for instructions... sure there's a plan. And we have to go in, it's the only way to end this.'

Rebwar got his phone out.

'For God's sake, why are we even talking about this?' Geraldine got out of the car. 'Come on, I'm going to arrest her.'

Rebwar got out of the car and followed her. 'Easy, easy... and when she recognises us?'

'You're grabbing the horse.'

Even though goat farming was a dream of Rebwar's, he'd never really dealt with animals. And for a moment he thought of the last time he'd had to deal with a horse. It was decades ago, back in Iran on the outskirts of the capital. A horse had escaped and he and Farouq had to try to catch it on a busy road. It ended up being run over.

Rebwar and Geraldine walked up to Daisy, who sat

there watching them. She wore a riding helmet and a blue felt jacket with white trousers.

'Hi, Daisy, I'm DS Smith. Remember me? Need to talk to you.'

'Yes, and what's your business?'

'I need you to dismount.'

'I need a good reason, why?' And she stared at Rebwar who was standing on the other side of her horse. It was pacing, not wanting to stay still.

Rebwar watched her.

'It's important, please.'

'You can tell me here.'

Rebwar slowly walked closer to the horse, but it sensed what he was up to and reared a bit.

'Haven't I seen you before?' she said to Rebwar.

Rebwar grabbed the reins, and the horse snorted. 'Remember O'Neil?'

'No. What are you talking about?' The horse twisted around. 'Hey, hey! Let go. You're... you're...'

Rebwar let go. Hadn't Charlie told her the plan? What did she know?

'Please, Daisy, get off the horse,' said Geraldine. 'They've found Jack Hill.'

'And he's dead – but you know that,' said Rebwar.

'What's all this about?' Daisy grabbed the horse's mane. 'You're bullshitting me, in order that I come with you lot. I'm Daisy Merkenstand.'

'Can you remember?' said Geraldine. 'Kidnapping Jack Hill? Filthy Five?'

Daisy gulped and sniffed, and her gloved hands tensed around her whip.

'Please, dismount and come with us, OK?' said Geraldine. 'Be reasonable. This a difficult time, I know.'

'Shut up. Shut the fuck up. You're all lying! I can tell.' Her horse reared and she went off down the field.

'She'll be back. I'm just messing with her,' said Geraldine.

The horse stopped at the end of the field by a gate and Daisy dismounted. A car parked up and a large man in a rain mac got out of the vehicle. He walked up to Daisy. Rebwar jogged up to them with Geraldine behind him.

'DCI Sands, I need to take Ms Merkenstand into custody.'

DCI Sands's hair was a reddish brown, badly dyed, and he was sweating. His swollen hands shook.

Daisy looked at DCI Sands. 'These people are accusing me of blackmail and murder.'

'And you two are?'

'DS Smith and Rebwar. And I am going to take Ms Merkenstand to London.'

'You'll find that you're going to take her to the local station first. You can follow me.'

'Sorry, but what are the charges?' asked Rebwar who held onto Daisy.

'And you are?'

'He's my driver,' said Geraldine.

'Right, DS Smith, I outrank here and you need to step aside. We can sort this out at the station.' DCI Sands stepped up to Daisy, but Rebwar pulled her away. He looked at Rebwar with a stern expression and took out his phone. Geraldine swiped it off him.

'What do think you're doing?'

'I'm taking Ms Merkenstand and you need to wait in line. OK?'

'Hey, who are you people? Show me some ID... I want my lawyer. Mr Sands, please call Barbara,' said Daisy.

'Right.' DCI Sands took out a set of handcuffs.

'Stay away,' said Daisy. But Rebwar stopped her from getting away. 'Get off me! Who are you? Telling me rubbish... are you working for my dad?'

'And who would that be?' said Geraldine.

'Get off me!' And she managed to wrestle herself out of Rebwar's grip but the horse took off. She ran towards the gravel path and DCI Sands and Rebwar ran after her. By another closed gate, Rebwar grabbed Daisy as she climbed over it. She fell on the ground and kicked out. Her riding boot hit DCI Sands in the face as he bent down to help her. His nose cracked, and he held it as blood trickled down his face. DCI Sands slapped Daisy across her face, leaving a red bloody mark. Rebwar kicked him straight in between his legs. He fell onto his knees and held his crotch. A deep groan came out of his red bleeding mouth. Rebwar pointed at Daisy and from his look, she understood.

'Are you—'

'Daisy, you're coming with us,' said Geraldine. 'We're not here to harm you. OK?' She showed Daisy her warrant card.

'Oh, come on. My dad owns this land. You expect me to believe you? Call him! I want to know what's going on.'

'So who is he?' Geraldine pointed to DCI Sands. 'Family friend?'

'Sort of.'

'Come on, let's go!'

'I'm a Merkenstand, you can't just take me.'

Rebwar had had enough. He grabbed the handcuffs off the ground where DCI Sands had dropped them and put them on her.

'Get off me, you brute! You're not going to get away with this! We own all of this.'

Rebwar then went through DCI Sands's pockets as he wriggled on the ground, and took out a set of keys and his phone and wallet. 'To the car.'

Rebwar and Geraldine were driving to the nearest rail station to pick up Raj. Daisy was making fun of them and calling them dumb city rats as well as randomly shouting warnings of tractors or horses. It was to confuse their navigation as neither had any mobile reception or a map.

'Will you quit the acting!' said Geraldine. 'Charlie told us to pick you up.'

Daisy quieten down and stared at both of them and grabbed a strand of her red curly hair and chewed on it.

'Call Charlie,' said Rebwar. 'And get her to talk some sense.'

'We're going to break into your house.'

Daisy laughed. 'You bunch of muppets. What does Charlie want? You know she's my *real* mum. Yeah, she loves me.'

Rebwar looked over at Geraldine. What was she on about? They carried on driving till they got to a small rural station. Raj was there alone, waiting for them. He looked like a lost London teenager with clean white trainers, a large white hoodie and camo trousers. He walked over to the van.

'Oh God no, not a fatty! You're a right bunch of losers, and I hope he's washed.'

Raj giggled and said, 'Oh! Thanks, and hi, I'm Raj. Is that the best fat joke you've got?'

'Fat Raj, what are you good for?'

'You're part of the Filthy Five, where are the others?'

'Oh, why?'

Rebwar turned. 'Tell me, Daisy, how did you get away? I mean, the police were everywhere.'

'Fuck... Yeah, now I remember, that's where I saw you. Yeah, you followed us.'

'O'Neil?'

Daisy turned and faced the window.

'You know I'm feeling a bit peckish,' said Raj looking around him. 'There's a little caf' down the road. Decent Google reviews.'

Rebwar drove up and stopped in front. Raj stepped out and took everybody's orders, which were coffees.

'Who was running the Filthy Five?' said Geraldine.

'And who are you, apart from a pig?'

'For a posh girl you don't half talk shit. DCI Sands should have slapped you a few more times... Heh? Is that why you joined them? Wanted to be a rebel? Bad girl – is that the cool thing to be? So who was running you and why take Jack Hill?'

Raj came back with a bacon sandwich and three coffees and a large Coke bottle. Rebwar started the van and drove out of the village.

'You know, you're a walking heart attack,' said Daisy 'I'm glad I'm not paying for the NHS.'

'You're welcome, Daisy, you know for an A-plus student and Oxford dropout you're pretty dumb.'

'Fuck off, fatso! And you two, too. Take me home.'

'That's what we're intending on doing,' said Geraldine.

Daisy snorted. 'Oh, and—'

'It's on Middle Lane, Merkerstand Manor,' Raj said. 'Found it through an offshore company. I didn't have to break in either. Their IT guy is a mate of mine.' He giggled.

'You'll never get in.'

'As Little Miss Daisy is saying, there's some security, but I can get round most of it. I'd say we go through the farm. From the wages bill, there are about four guys who could be there and from their backgrounds two of them have been in the Forces. One has a wound.' Raj passed some papers forward.

Rebwar pulled up in a lay-by and studied the printouts. The youngest was twenty-one, the others forty-five, fifty and sixty-five. It was the forty-five-year-old that caught his attention – an Iraq veteran who had been invalided out from an IED. The other three were local men who had worked on different estates. He pointed this out to Geraldine. 'You know them?' Daisy just looked out of the window and sipped her coffee. 'Are they in?'

Daisy sniffed. 'Yeah, as if he's...'

'He's what?'

She talked into the window. 'You know, I don't even know if he is my father...'

'So... is this all an act? I mean, you are related?'

'You'll have to ask my grandmother. Why the hell did I run away? Not my choice. Bunch of inbred morons.'

Geraldine's phone rang. It was Charlie. 'Speaking... I thought the plan was to... OK! Yeah... She's here... OK.' And Geraldine passed the phone over.

'Mummy dearest, oh... Yes, miss you too... Yeah they...' Rebwar, Geraldine and Raj listened to the call. 'Yeah, I understand.' Daisy passed the phone over to Geraldine.

'Hello... hung up on me again.'

Rebwar turned in his seat. 'Daisy, what did Charlie say?'

'None of your business.'

'So what are we doing here?'

'Ha, ha, look at your faces. We need to break in.'

'And that's it?'

All three stared at Daisy.

She laughed again. 'It's a heist, we're going to steal from Daddy. Time to cash in my inheritance.'

Rebwar looked at Geraldine.

'Are you off your meds?' Raj said.

'Fuck off, fatso.'

'She's playing with us. Seeing what gives.'

Rebwar grabbed Daisy's felt jacket and pulled her to him. Her face was inches from his. 'That mum of yours has my family hostage and I'm not going to hesitate for a moment if I have to stop you. Understand? Not for a moment.'

Daisy smiled and hiccuped.

'What did Charlie tell you? Now!'

'We... we need to break in and rob the place... and that she loves me very much.'

'Of what? Gold, money, drugs, what?'

'I don't know... Stuff. You know stuff. They have loads of stuff.'

Rebwar pushed her back into the back seat, her head bounced off the headrest. 'Ouch, that hurt. Mister.'

'Any ideas?'

Geraldine looked at her phone, Raj shrugged and Rebwar hit the steering wheel. '*Kossdeh?*'[1]

'Easy, break in and call the fuzz,' said Raj.

'DCI Sands, who is he?' said Rebwar.

Daisy just looked away.

'We could just hand her over to him?'

'I think he's in on it or Plan B.'

'Both,' said Rebwar. 'If we turn away, we're going to be looking over our shoulders for the rest of our short lives.' And he started the van. 'Let's do this and we'll work something out.'

FORTY-EIGHT

As the sun set over the rolling countryside. Rebwar took a moment to admire the beautiful old thick green trees with their long shadows that made them look majestic. Waving golden wheat fields with their sea-like rhythm mesmerised him and soothed his nerves. They had parked on a muddy little dirt track that ran by the south side of the Merkenstand property. The whole estate had a brick perimeter wall around it and Raj had worked out that the south side was where the security would be at its weakest. The reasoning was that there was a working farm and with all the livestock it was tricky to have any hi-tech sensors such as movement or heat cameras. Also, the farm needed access to the fields outside the wall.

Rebwar had inched as close as he could to the farm entrance. They had gaffer taped the lights, in order for the day running lights not be spotted by any CCTV. Rebwar had used some leftover gaffer tape on Daisy to shut her up. He had also zip-tied her hands behind her back; he wasn't taking any chances. He led her out of the car and towards the gate. It was open. They listened for any voices or movements. All they could hear was some livestock moving around and the humming of some machines inside the farm.

They spent a moment trying to spot the cameras. There were two that pointed along the track, one along the east side and the other along the west. It was possible to walk close to the wall in a blind spot that Raj had spotted. The aim was to get to the back door of the manor house, where they could get Daisy to let them in. They wanted to cause the minimum fuss, without triggering the involvement of the police or a security company. Raj was going to hack into their IT system. There were two of them, one that was linked to the internet via a security company and another that was stand alone. The latter was the one he was counting on, and he needed to be on site to hack it. Raj had also had a sneaking suspicion that the AI was there. Which Rebwar was still struggling to get his head around. A computer that could think, to him it sounded like his worst nightmare.

Geraldine pointed at a camera on top of the main farm building. It was on the roof, pointing towards the open gates. All four hugged the wall behind a tractor with a trailer. The tractor tyres towered above them and hid them from the CCTV. They had to get past the farm building and up into a wooded area behind. Raj had some satellite images of the property and worked out a way in. What they had to watch out for were some kind of sensors that showed as being out in the garden. Raj spotted an electrical cupboard inside a small little building close to a barn. Mud was everywhere, and he approached with caution, spreading out his arms to keep his balance. Daisy giggled and tried to say something through the gaffer tape. They all guessed what it could have been.

Raj slipped and slid to the little hut and tried to open the metal door, but it was locked. Rebwar went over to it and held on to some branches for balance. He got out his set of keys and pins that had served him so well. Raj shone some light onto the lock, which was a Chubb – something that would take a little longer than he wanted. He got to work as Geraldine looked around. After a few minutes, the lock gave in. Rebwar looked over to Geraldine and Raj, both were on their phones.

'Guys! Am I boring you?' He pulled the door open. It looked like an electrical cupboard with fuses and some boxes with flashing lights. Raj peered closer and followed some cables. He giggled a little and brought out his laptop and plugged in some cables.

'What if you stay here?' Rebwar said to Raj.

'Uncle, why?'

'You can access the house and you can guide us in. Be our eyes and ears to the house.'

'If! I'm not a magician.' Raj typed on his keyboard and his eyes scanned the screen. 'And where's the snack bag?'

Rebwar looked around for Daisy. 'Where is she?'

They all looked around. She had gone.

'Fuck sake!' said Geraldine. 'That spoilt little bitch.'

'Raj! Text me when you're in. Come on, Geraldine. We need to find that little brat.' Rebwar brought out the Glock from the back of his belt and cocked it. He'd found it in the back of the van and wanted to threaten Daisy with it, but Geraldine had been against it. She was sure she would have run away if he'd had the chance to give her a piece of his mind.

'And I'll... Hey, we said no guns! You'll just start a bloody war.'

'Guys,' Raj said. 'I'll just... Then...'

'Too late for that,' said Rebwar. He went off behind the little shed that Raj was in.

'Guys? So you're just leaving me alone? Guys?'

Rebwar headed into the woods behind the farm, still swearing to himself. He pushed through bushes, scanning the muddy ground for footprints. Deep down, he knew that it was a pretty hopeless task to find Daisy. This was her home and she knew this place like the back of her hand. The wind was making it difficult to hear anything else but rustling leaves and branches. Ahead of him were some lights blinking between the fluttering leaves. A little sweet smell passed through him. A brown leather glove was hanging off a branch. She was close by or had passed this way. His hunch was that she must have headed for the house. Ahead of him was a large field with a mix of old and young trees. In the distance, lights flickered through the leaves. He aimed for them and as he cleared the top of the incline, he reached a black metal fence. Large tall trimmed hedges blocked his path, and he walked around them till he found an entrance. Through the landscaped garden he could see rows of round chimney tops. He headed for them.

He checked his phone and saw a message from Raj: *Yo! I'm in*. Rebwar texted back: *Can you see Daisy?* He waited for a moment, but no reply came. He saw what looked like a gravelled entrance to the manicured garden, which led up towards a fountain in front of the house. The house wasn't what he'd expected. The satellite photo showed an old manor. This was very modern, nothing that he had seen before and more like something that would be built for an Olympic event. He walked towards it, avoiding the gravel. He was having a hard time trying to work out what he was seeing. It seemed to be a bunch of interlocking square shapes that had merged together like some weird Venn diagram and there were large rows of sash windows. It was clearly some kind of statement to confuse the viewer. The whole thing was held up on concrete stilts over a lake. Its reflection doubled its size.

Rebwar couldn't see a way into the building and skirted around the edge of the water, trying to find a bridge that would link to it. He kept behind the hedges that lined the steep bank down to the water. He was sure he had been seen but was now hoping someone would invite him in as the house was an island with no access. There were no boats to be seen and he couldn't swim. It was something he had never learned. As a street kid, he'd never been to a swimming pool, or had to cross a river. He carried on looking around for some kind of access, such as a draw-bridge or a tunnel. All he could see were stilts that held the whole structure up in the air like a modern-day castle.

He passed the north side of the house which looked very similar to the back. He texted Raj: *How do I get in?* And he got a text back: *No idea. It's a Rubik's cube and Daisy is in there.* A shot passed him and the statue beside him exploded into pieces. Fragments hit his face, and he ducked down for cover, grabbing his Glock. A second shot and more flying debris fell on him. He crawled under a bush and rolled into a ditch. He cocked his gun.

'There is nowhere to run, Rebwar!'

Rebwar didn't recognise the voice, but it was deep and had the authority of someone used to shouting orders at people. He heard a shotgun being cocked open, and its cartridges fall and roll off the gravel. The man had missed him on purpose; he was enjoying the game. Rebwar crawled in the undergrowth, trying to find a path or somewhere to hide. Although why? Wasn't it easier to give himself up? Rebwar fought with his instincts.

'Come out wherever you are! You've got nowhere to hide.'

Rebwar looked at his phone. There was another text for him. *There is a tunnel on the north side. Geraldine has been taken by Charlie.*

'I can see you...'

Another shot hit the bush that was next to him and bits of leaves and branches fluttered around. Rebwar saw two barrels aimed at him, one of them still smoking. The groundsman, Will Weaver, was holding the shotgun. He was the man that came into the pub for a whisky shot – the landlord had mentioned him. And probably told him about their stay there.

'Greetings, Rebwar! I've heard a lot about...' And he held his earpiece.

FIFTY

Geraldine had taken the opposite direction to Rebwar – or that was what she'd thought. Her sense of direction was terrible. If there wasn't a pub as a landmark, she would get lost. If in doubt, she would follow people around town till she got where she recognised. Generally, people either went to a coffee shop or a tube station. Here there were cows, horses and a few outbuildings and the smell of acrid manure. She could remember the satellite images that Raj had sent her, but how they related to where she was, she had no idea. She stumbled and stopped to look around but felt lost in an alien landscape. Her phone had no reception and so she tried switching off and on, hoping for a signal. What had they been thinking? She carried on till she found a stony path. It had led somewhere, so she followed it.

Geraldine stopped after a few steps to listen for any tell-tale sounds. The wind had picked up to a fresh breeze. Large branches groaned and creaked. It made her jump. She caught her breath. In front of her was a mossy green wall. Goosebumps crawled over her arms. She took a few deep breaths, carried on and again checked her phone for some news. She should have never agreed to this. Walkie-talkies would have been a good idea. The whole thing was beginning to strike her as probably the most unplanned op she had undertaken so far. For a moment she tried to remember when she had agreed to all this, but she couldn't think of that moment.

She followed the path and came across a tall brick wall that was very similar to the one they had followed in the car. She took it as a good sign, although she still had no idea where it was on the map. There was nothing that stood out. No huge manor house, no tarmac road leading somewhere, no statue or, God forbid, a sign. The path opened up onto a field and in the middle of it; she saw some shadows. Dark figures. Her heart stopped. She stood there and so did the shapes. One of them moved, and it dawned on her. Deer, of course, what else? The grass reached above her knees and partially hid the animals. She had no idea where she stood in the food chain and noticed that one of them had some antlers. They looked big and threatening. The herd's breath made little floating clouds. The wind had died down and there was an eerie stillness.

She stood there waiting for something – not too sure what, but something, anything to break the deadly quiet. The distant groan of an engine bounced off the trees and the herd silently ran into the woods to dissolve into the dark green. It was as if she had imagined the deer. It made her even more unsure of what was going on. She rechecked her phone and the screen still gave her no answer. There was a moment of partial blindness as her eyes readjusted to the darkness. The engine noise grew a little louder, and she decided to head over to it. There wasn't much point in hiding as being lost had no purpose. A light shone across the open field. Her shadow projected behind her onto some trees. She stood there like a caught rabbit.

The four-by-four drove up to her quickly and three shapes came out of it. The headlights kept them outlined.

'Geraldine! What a surprise to find you here.'

Geraldine should have recognised those long slender legs, but the voice was clear – Charlie.

'Come on, love, get in.'

'Aren't you going as well?'

'What? Kill you? Not yet. Quick, we've got a schedule to keep.' Brunje and Trent stepped out of the vehicle wearing black fatigues and came over to her.

'I thought *we* were breaking in?'

She felt a barrel dig into her back and push her. 'Yeah, all right, mate!' She pushed it out of the way.

'Frisk her and take what you find,' said Charlie.

Trent went through her pockets and took out her mobile, warrant card, keys and wallet. He then pushed her into the back of the Land Rover. It had two rows of bench seats. Knight was sitting in the back, dressed in black fatigues. 'Fancy dress?'

'Don't you start. You're fucking lucky I didn't finish you off,' said Trent.

The Land Rover drove off over the uneven ground. Geraldine tried to find something to hold on to. In the darkness, all she could see were glimpses of track. The engine roared for traction and bounced around like a boat in a storm.

They stopped in front of a garage door that looked like it led somewhere underground. The spotlights lit Daisy, who was in the front passenger seat. She leaned over to speak into an intercom, announced herself and it was acknowledged by shutters rolling up. A dark unlit tunnel revealed itself. They drove in with the Land Rover lighting the way. They had left the windows down and Geraldine could feel the damp air coming in. It tasted of chalk. After a minute or so, they arrived in a garage. Strip lights flickered and revealed parked cars. They stopped and Trent and Brunje jumped out.

'Tie her up. Don't want any trouble from the bitch,' said Trent, laughing as he gave her a slap across her face. Knight zip-tied her hands behind her back. She felt the plastic pinch into her skin and her anger rose up.

Daisy got out and asked Charlie, 'I don't see why we need to take her.'

'An offering.' Charlie walked over to a lift and summoned it.

'I didn't know they were into sacrifices,' said Brunje.

The lift pinged, and the doors opened. They all squeezed in. Geraldine was flanked by Trent and Brunje; both had sawn-off shotguns and Knight had three grenades strapped across her chest. The doors opened to reveal a massive atrium. It felt more like a hotel than a home, with odd square shapes protruding out from the ceiling and walls. It was hard to get a feel of the size of the room. In the centre was a chandelier that lit the odd golden shapes. Mirrors were dotted around to make the whole place feel even bigger. Daisy didn't bother to look around and instead walked over to a mirrored door, which she pushed open.

'Daisy...' An elegantly dressed woman came over to greet them. She had brown wavy hair in a meringue style. Her dress was long and flowing. It was as if she had come out of a ball. Her high-heeled shoes clicked across the marble floor. 'You...' She stepped back, not sure what she was seeing. 'Brought some guests. I... Daisy?'

'Mrs Merkenstand, we've made an appointment with your son, Sir John Merkenstand. Come to talk business.'

'I'm sorry but you are?'

'Charlie,' said Charlie. 'Nice to meet you.'

'Barbara Merkenstand.' She held her out hand, which Charlie shook with vigour. The two women's eyes fixed on each other as if it was some kind of duel. 'And...' She pointed at her entourage.

'Where is he?' said Charlie.

Trent waved his shotgun and aimed it at Mrs Merkenstand.

'Daisy dear, call the police.'

'Sorry, but I'm not taking more shit from you.' Daisy walked up to Mrs Merkenstand. 'This is my new family. They look after me and care for me. Where were you when I was kidnapped?'

'Daisy, what are you on about? You know that we did everything we could. Why now? Money?' Her phone rang, and she picked it up.

Brunje aimed the shotgun and everyone else stared at her. If Geraldine made one wrong move the whole place would blow up.

'Will... Yes... Take him here... OK.' Her hand trembled and Charlie snatched the mobile out of her hand.

'Weaver?'

Mrs Merkenstand nodded.

'OK, take us to him. Now.'

Geraldine was guessing that Rebwar had been caught. She looked around for any possible escapes or alarms.

'The notorious Rebwar... You know I imagined you taller and lighter.' Weaver sniffed him. 'And you smoke.'

'Take me to Merkenstand.'

'Get in line.' Weaver took his gun from him. 'Walk ahead of me and head for that statue.'

Rebwar tried to look behind him, but Weaver kept prodding his back with the shotgun.

'So where do you fit in? Foot soldier?' He felt another prod in his back.

'Take a left and head to that brick building.' Weaver's phone rang, and he picked it up.

Rebwar could hear a woman's voice but couldn't make out what she was saying and only heard Weaver asking what she was talking about and confirmed her instructions and hung up. He pushed Rebwar along, making him walk faster.

'How's Daisy?' said Rebwar.

'Well, she likes a good hunt,' said Weaver. 'And she would have shot you down like a lame horse.'

They ended up in a small quad like farm vehicle that

sounded like a high-pitched hyena. They drove off and after a few turns went into a tunnel. The lights flickered on and they arrived at an underground garage with a collection of cars. Weaver stopped next to a black Land Rover, and he went over to inspect it. He felt the engine bonnet and looked inside, but it was empty; he checked the registration. Another farm vehicle, similar to the one Weaver drove, came into the garage. Rebwar immediately recognised that Raj was in the passenger seat. He was spilling out of his seat. The car came to a screeching halt, and the driver jumped off the farm vehicle.

'Found the fat bastard in the electrical shed. Think he was trying to shut the electrics off.'

Rebwar recognised the man as Jim Jones from the print-outs that Raj had given out on the employees. He was one of the local groundsmen and had a sunken jaw. Jones had a sway to his walk, and his tattoos, short hair and crucifix made him look like a thug – probably the look he was going for.

'So who is the fat fuck?' asked Jones, pointing at Raj.

Rebwar hesitated and looked into Jones's brown eyes that were darting around like an animal on a hunt. 'Raj, and he's with me.'

'Hello, Mr Weaver.' Raj rolled himself out of the seat. 'Merkenstand is on the top floor – a hospital room. Been chatting to him. Well, to the AI.'

'Are you dissing the boss?' Jones went up to Raj with his clenched fists.

'Jim! Easy,' Weaver said. 'Right let's go and see the boss.'

Jones sniggered.

'You know she's not the boss.' Raj turned to Rebwar. 'They think the bimbo is the boss.'

'One more word out of you and you won't be speaking to anyone.'

Weaver went over to call for the elevator and his phone rang. He picked it up and this time Rebwar heard the same woman's voice, which he guessed was that of Mrs Merkenstand. She asked Weaver where he was and he said he'd be over in a second. The doors closed and a forgettable tune accompanied them up to the next floor. As the door slid open, there was Mrs Barbara Merkenstand in front of them.

'Where are they?' said Weaver.

'Up!' And she stepped into the elevator.

'Up where?'

She looked at the new guests and then faced forward, waiting for the lift to arrive at the floor.

'I suggest you cock those guns.'

Rebwar noticed Raj smiling and holding in a giggle. Rebwar hesitated to ask what was going on. Either he had childishly farted or was laughing at Mrs Merkenstand. He was starting to regret his decision on agreeing to involve him.

Weaver stepped out of the lift and into a large landing that overlooked the floor below. There were two large hallways to the left and right that had a series of doors and thick red carpets with thin blue lines running along them. Paintings of animals lined the corridors: badgers, mice, pheasants, rabbits, robins, cuckoo and more down the hall.

'Family portraits?' said Rebwar.

FIFTY-TWO

Geraldine and Mrs Merkenstand had been taken to what looked like a hospital room. It was filled with machines and wires that all hooked up to a bed. It made her feel uncomfortable; morgues, hospitals and anything close were places she avoided. They all brought back memories of her mother's death. She had to endure a torrent of abuse as her mother lost her mind to dementia and she had been left alone to deal with it. On the bed was the emaciated body of what she guessed must have been Sir John Merkenstand. It took her breath away and she had to take a moment to process the whole sight. Charlie also froze for a moment, and before telling them to hurry, she locked the door behind them, sliding the two latches. Geraldine's instinct was to run away.

'Who's the stiff?' said Trent.

'Daisy's dad, Sir John Merkenstand, the head of Plan B,' said Charlie.

'Plan what?' said Mrs Merkenstand.

Trent went up to the bed and poked him as if he was

trying to wake him. 'You're fucking kidding me. He's a mummy. Hello? Anyone in there?'

Geraldine watched Daisy pace around the room.

'Can I help you?'

Trent jumped back and looked around him, trying to find the direction of the voice. Charlie headed over to a screen by the end of the bed. A cursor blinked next to the text that had just been spoken. She looked for a keyboard.

'Sir John Merkenstand,' said Charlie. 'We finally meet.'

'Hello. Nice to meet you, too. Have you brought some friends with you?'

'How in the hell... what the... Is this some kind of fucking wind-up?' Trent laughed and approached the monitor slowly like a stray dog. Knight and Brunje kept their distance, holding their weapons ready. Geraldine peeked over to see the patient on his bed. Trent had been right, Merkenstand's skin was all dark and shrivelled up but there was no rotten smell, rather a sweet medicinal scent. It still made her feel like retching.

Mrs Merkenstand stood in front of the screen. 'Stay away from my son. Take everything else but not my son. He's... Oh God.' And tears flowed down her face.

Daisy went up to her. 'Gran, he's a machine... Fuck sake he died... Let go.'

Charlie pushed her out of the way. 'Call me Charlie. Now, Sir John. Can I call you that?' Charlie waited for an answer, but the cursor just carried on blinking. 'I would like to propose a business deal.'

The cursor blinked for a moment and some fans whirred. 'Could you elaborate... Charlie.'

'No, no, don't listen to her. Sleep shut down. Command sleep,' said Mrs Merkenstand.

'I'm setting up Plan C as the successor to your organisation. Plan B is compromised and needs shutting down.'

The screen froze for a minute. 'There is no need to do that, Charlie. I'm in rude health.'

Geraldine walked over to Charlie and lowered her voice. 'Can I talk to you? Privately. Now.'

'Sorry?' said Trent. 'But who is this?' He approached the screen.

Charlie pushed Trent out of the way. 'Sorry—'

Geraldine turned around to see the handle of the door being pulled. Muffled bangs and thuds reverberated through the door, followed by a heavy crash.

'Watch her, and her.' Charlie pointed at Geraldine and Mrs Merkenstand. 'They might get some funny ideas,' Charlie told Brunje and Trent. 'Pinky, get into that computer.'

Knight went over and started tapping into the computer's keyboard. Mrs Merkenstand tried to stop her and Knight kicked her away.

Geraldine spotted a hidden door next to Merkenstand's bed. It had a light blue panelled weave and there was a thin pencil line making a neat door-sized shape next to him. It was practically invisible as it ran along the edge of the wooden sides of six square panels. The whole room was filled with them and it made it look like an old gallery. There was no handle and you probably had to push it.

Mrs Merkenstand ran over to the door. Trent used the shotgun's stock to stop her. She fell to the floor. 'Come on, Pinky, this door isn't going to hold out for long.'

Geraldine could now see that there had been some kind of plan to this whole madness but still hadn't got a clue what its endgame was. And where was Rebwar? She stepped back, not wanting to be involved. She leaned back into the panelled wall. Charlie went over to the bed and looked at some monitoring machines. She too prodded the body, and nothing happened to the screens. She undid some wires, and again nothing happened.

'Man, this gives me the willies... He's...'

More thuds came from the door.

Geraldine leaned back on the wall as if she was trying to back away. She could see that Charlie was losing her cool. A loud bang came through the door and Geraldine fell back.

FIFTY-THREE

The lift door opened, and Rebwar saw the grand reception with its huge hanging chandelier. Weaver stepped out and Jones prodded Rebwar with his pistol to move out.

Raj followed, and he whistled at the sight. 'How the others live.'

Weaver looked around sensing something was off and walked to the living room which was off the main hall. He ran back out and called out to Jones. He took out his phone and dialled a number. A dull tone rang out from above. 'Upstairs, something's going on. Quick!'

And Weaver ran up the grand circular stairs.

Jones motioned with his gun for Rebwar and Raj to follow. They arrived on the landing which led down a large bright red-carpeted hallway. Weaver was by a door at the end of the corridor, frantically pulling the handle.

'Those damn bolts! Jim! Go and get my black rucksack from the Jeep,' said Weaver.

Jones rushed off.

Raj grabbed Rebwar's jacket and whispered, 'Shall we run into that room?'

Rebwar looked at the door which was next door to the one Weaver was trying to break down with his boots. 'Open this door, now! Mrs Merkenstand, can you hear me?'

Rebwar grabbed the door handle, and it opened. They rushed in and closed it behind them and both desperately reached for the bolts. The door bounced to the weight of Weaver hitting it. A muffled swearing was followed by some screams of anger and swearing. Both trying to slide bolts, but Weaver's pounding stopped them from aligning. It stopped, and the bolts moved into the brackets.

'We've pissed him off,' said Raj.

Rebwar grabbed Raj and pulled him away from the door. There was a muffled bang, and some sparks flew out from the lock with some smoke creeping in. The inside of the door was thickly padded, so it was going to take more than a shotgun to blow it off. But it was only a matter of time. Rebwar looked around the room. Lit dimly by some desk lamps and floor lights, it was an office with medical cabinets lining the walls. It smelled of chemicals and air freshener. Raj walked around the room, looking at the cabinets. The handle to the door bounced on the wooden floor, but the door held firm.

'And now?' said Rebwar.

'There's another door on this wall.' Raj went over to the wall. 'I saw it on a floor plan that I found.'

Rebwar looked at the square wooden panels that decorated the walls. They were painted white and there wasn't any obvious sign of a door being there. 'Are you—'

'Yes.' Raj felt the wall for something. 'We have to look. And you saw Weaver. If this was a dead-end, he wouldn't have tried to fucking kill us.'

'What about that computer?' Rebwar pointed to a screen.

'What about it?' Raj looked at Rebwar for an answer but just got a shrug. He went up to it and examined it. 'PC. Nothing special. Admin, I guess.'

'Do you know if it opens doors?'

There was another muffled bang, and both looked at the door. It was still standing firm. Something clicked behind them and some shouting came through. Geraldine fell in.

'What the–'

Shots rang out from the room next door and Geraldine crawled away from the door. It closed itself silently and clicked.

'Who's in there?' said Rebwar.

Her face looked white. 'All of them and they've gone mad.'

'What the hell is going on?' said Raj.

'I've no idea but something... They're not stealing any art or money.' Geraldine's hands shook.

'And Plan B?'

Geraldine rubbed her face. 'We need to think, think...'

'I couldn't find anything,' said Raj. 'The Merkenstand company is a data company–'

'There's no one in that bed, just a dead body.'

'Shouldn't we be calling for help?' said Raj, starting up the computer.

'Not yet,' said Rebwar. 'We need to more time.'

'Are you insane?' said Raj. 'We're all going to die here.'

Rebwar went over to a window and looked out of it and just saw water. He stepped back. 'No exit here.'

'We could jump,' said Geraldine.

'No... it's too high... And...'

'Uncle! You can't swim, right? Oh man, I've got a life-guard certificate I can drag you. Easy.'

Geraldine was shaking and taking in deep breaths. 'Raj, did you get into the system?'

'This is just a shitty PC, and it's offline. What about the one next door?'

Geraldine nodded. 'It's an AI or something...'

'AI?' said Rebwar.

'Artificial Intelligence... Robot or a computer that thinks. Yeah, it exists. It's fucking amazing. Fuck, I knew it... Wow. I had a feeling in my gut.'

'You mean... a machine!' said Rebwar. Geraldine and Raj looked at him. 'Tell me that there is a plug.'

'Is that what they are going for?' said Geraldine.

'And we're complicit. We need to stop them.'

They heard shotguns discharging and more bangs and flashes coming from under the door. It was followed by running footsteps outside the door. Rebwar approached and listened.

'Uncle! No! Don't let them in.'

Rebwar slid the metal bolts and both doors fell off their hinges, their padding taking the impact and narrowly missing Rebwar.

Rebwar waited for a reaction. Raj and Geraldine were ready to duck. Rebwar flashed his head out of the door. 'It's clear... Geraldine, take the other door and I'll and see what's going on downstairs and, Raj, do what she says, OK?'

Raj smiled at Geraldine.

Rebwar walked out into the hallway and noticed blast marks on the walls. The wallpaper was ripped up and shredded where shots had missed. He noticed more shotgun damage on the circular wooden bannister and he went over to see it. He waited and listened. He heard Geraldine's voice behind him, followed by Mrs Merkenstand's. There wasn't any aggression and so he decided to take the stairs down to the main reception area, which was very quiet. On the way down he spotted a couple of spent shotgun cartridges on the stairs. At the bottom of the stairs he saw DCI Sands's legs. They were stretched out and the rest of him was hidden by a high backed chair.

He went into the living room where there was a red and white painting that he hadn't seen before. He stepped closer to it and saw that the red explosion had come up from the chair. DCI Sands lay with his mouth open and a shotgun lying next to him. Rebwar put the whole scenario together. The painting had been white canvas and the back of DCI Sands's head had been splattered over it. It was as if it had been done on purpose, a critique on the art. The blood was still dripping off the canvas. There was a note on a coffee table in front of him. Rebwar picked it up. It just said *Sorry, I was too weak.* He put it back onto the table and saw the open gun cabinet with a missing gun, an open box of ammunition and an empty decanter. He smelled the empty glass – an expensive whisky. He had tasted the same one at his friend Bijan's – Talisker.

Rebwar went over to the gun cabinet and took out a shotgun. The barrel was engraved with a swirling pattern and had a metallic blue finish. It felt expensive and clean. He broke it, put two cartridges in the barrels from a box of twenty-five and emptied the rest into his pockets. He closed DCI Sands's eyes and for a moment wondered if all this had been staged. Where might somebody run to? The garage was his first thought. He looked around for some stairs as he wanted to avoid taking a lift. He wanted to keep an element of surprise. He found a metal door around the corner hidden under the stairs. It opened, and he switched the lights on. It was a circular concrete stairwell with a cold breeze coming up. He could hear an engine running and he followed the noise down.

He went up to the grey metal door to listen and heard some muffled voices over an engine. He opened the door slowly and peeked through the opening. He could see Weaver holding a shotgun with his left hand; his right was limp and dripping with blood. Rebwar remembered that he wasn't left-handed. Another man was standing next to the running Land Rover and one of its lights had been shot out. Rebwar couldn't see any empty cartridges on the ground so assumed that his shotgun was loaded. He opened the door and stepped out with his gun pointed at Weaver. The other man's face tensed as Weaver turned to look at Rebwar. The other man took the opportunity and jumped into the car.

Weaver turned around and saw the Land Rover reversing. He shot at the windscreen, which exploded in little pieces.

The Land Rover carried on reversing, but the man's head was slumped on the headrest. The car crashed into a large gas tank that was just off the exit. The tank came off its mountings and rolled into another big box of grit. The car stuttered to a stop.

'Don't move!' Weaver broke the shotgun and two cartridges bounced onto the floor, one of them still smoking.

'Not a move,' said Rebwar.

A hissing sound came from the cylinder.

'That's gas,' said Weaver. 'It's your choice.'

'Drop the gun and call the lift. Did you kill DCI Sands?'

Weaver walked over to the lift, leaving a trail of blood. The lift doors opened. Rebwar motioned with his gun for Weaver to get in.

'You know that was the old man's. The only thing that survived the great fire. This place is built on the ruins and surrounded by water–'

'Get in!' Rebwar pushed the gun into Weaver's ribs and joined him in the lift. He pressed the button for the third floor. As the lift got going, there was an explosion underneath them. It rocked the lift shaft, and the lift stopped. The lights blinked. Weaver grabbed the barrel and Rebwar squeezed the trigger. There was an empty click. Weaver pushed the gun against the lift's door. Neither of the cartridges had gone off. Weaver stamped on Rebwar's foot. Rebwar headbutted Weaver. Pain rang like a buzzing insect in Rebwar's foot. He pushed Weaver into the wall, onto his injured arm, and Weaver gave out an angry grunt. Smoke seeped through the floor of the lift.

'Shit!' Weaver's face turned, and panic took over.

Rebwar stepped back, knowing that he had a hysterical animal in a cage.

With his good hand, Weaver tried to pull the door open. 'We're going to die! Fire! Fire!' His face was right up to the seam of the two doors, as if he was trying to fit through it.

Rebwar grabbed an edge of the metal door and pulled. It was slowly giving way and he could see that they were between two floors. The gap was above them. They pushed harder, and the door opened. Weaver kicked the back of Rebwar's leg, which made him fall onto his knees. He climbed onto Rebwar's shoulders and used him to get out. Rebwar grabbed the gun and tried to shoot again. Then tried to jump up, but he wasn't strong enough to pull himself up. Smoke crept into the lift, filling it slowly.

FIFTY-FIVE

Geraldine stood in front of the secret door. She was reluctant to go back in, as she had just escaped from there and since then it all had kicked off. She could hear Raj's heavy breathing and could sense his weight waiting behind her.

'Should we go—'

Raj pushed past her and shoved the door. It clicked and opened. Geraldine went in to find Mrs Merkenstand weeping beside the bed. She could hear the computer talking away, but she wasn't taking it in. Trent was sitting on the floor, legs spread open and his face was bloodied with little black shots all over his skin. He looked dead. Jones, the farmhand, was face down with blood oozing out onto the floor. Someone had left bloody footprints around him. Geraldine stared at the shoe tread; it had a Vibram sole. Two shotguns lay discarded on the floor. Charlie, Brunje, Knight and Daisy were missing. She spotted an open door at the end of the room. It was a similar secret door to the one they had used to sneak in. They had blown the main doors off and were lying on the floor a few feet off their frame.

'You bitch!' Mrs Merkenstand launched herself at

Geraldine. Her sharp nails scratching her cheek and just missing her eye. Geraldine punched the back of her head as she passed her. Mrs Merkenstand lost her balance, slipped on the patch of blood and fell face first. She fell hard and her body slammed on the smooth tiles and lay still. Geraldine grabbed the sawn-off shotgun next to Trent. Raj took the other one – which surprised and worried her.

'Care—'

Raj accidentally discharged the shotgun and hit the bed with Sir John Merkenstand in it. Feathers and shredded fabric exploded into a cloud. 'Oops! He's double dead now.'

'No! I'm not. Calling security...' said the computer.

Mrs Merkenstand rushed over to the bed. 'No! My baby, what's happened to my baby?'

'Mother, don't worry about me. I am here for you and working... Did you do what I asked of you? I'll be walking soon. Don't worry... System error... Compro...'

'Raj! Switch that damn machine off. Where's Charlie?'

'Huh, I... I don't think we can. It's a thing of beauty.' Raj tapped on the keyboard and another error message came up. *Error Code: 2000-0141.* Raj turned around. 'He's virtual...' And his face turned white.

Geraldine looked down to see Trent's bloodied hand trying to grab her legs. Raj threw up on the floor. Geraldine turned away. She really didn't want to see what had just come up. She kicked Trent's hand away and pointed the shotgun at Mrs Merkenstand. 'Where's everybody else?'

'Who do you think you are? Call an ambulance. We must save my son. Now!'

Geraldine stared at the bloodied face of Mrs Merkenstand, who was staring past her and holding her chest while having a coughing fit. Geraldine turned around to see Daisy. She had changed and wore a long white wedding dress. Her lips were smeared with red lipstick and her face was heavily made up like a doll. She pointed at Mrs Merkenstand. 'Are you my family? And don't lie to me like you usually do.'

Mrs Merkenstand stepped slowly over to her. 'Of course, you are, my darling. My lovely grandchild. You know your dad is coming back to get you. He's just said he's feeling great.'

Daisy looked over to the bed and shook her head. 'No, that was never my dad. Did you adopt me? Or... worse? Tell me the truth.'

'Daisy?' Geraldine lowered her gun. 'What are you doing?'

'Fuck off! This is family!' Daisy walked over to the bed.

Geraldine went over to Raj who was still crouching down on the floor, his face pale. 'Raj, get yourself together... are you all right? Off their meds, the lot of them.'

Raj nodded.

'Switch that damn computer off and find Rebwar.' Geraldine felt a dull blast from under her.

Raj rushed over to the cabinet with the screen just off Merkenstand's bed and frantically pulled out drawers. And found a keyboard and mouse and rapidly tapped in some commands.

'Who are you?' said the computer. '... Oh, Hello, Alice.'

'Alice?'

'Long story and AI joke,' said Raj. He carried on swiftly tapping commands into the terminal. 'Hello, Sir J... Yes, Alice here, can you bring up the garage camera, please?'

'Alice, can you see my mother?'

Daisy and Mrs Merkenstand ran over to the terminal.

'Yes, my son, I'm here. Tell me, how are you? How are your feet?'

Daisy pushed Mrs Merkenstand away. 'Daddy, Daddy, what have you they done to you?'

'Mother, I feel great – like I could do a marathon... I'm match fit.' The screen flickered and an error 500 appeared.

'Since when did my dad like marathons... he hates running!' said Daisy.

Mrs Merkenstand grabbed Daisy's hand and said, 'They've made incredible stem cell progress. It's amazing, and he wants to run.'

'Piss off... you're talking to a machine. Don't you see that? He's dead,' said Geraldine trying to find a plug.

Black mascara-laden tears rolled down Daisy's cheeks. 'Daddy, name the boy I first kissed?'

The computer's cursor blinked. 'I'm doing five-minute miles, Mother.'

Daisy sobbed. 'It was him! He stole it. He stole my youth...' And she ran over to the bed filled with rage and hit out at the body. Mrs Merkenstand tried to stop her.

Geraldine looked over at the bed, which was a mess of feathers, ripped linen and mangled legs. She looked at Raj, who shrugged and pointed at one of the CCTV images. There was a huge yellow fire in one of the corners and it was consuming a crashed Land Rover.

'I think this might be a good time to call for some help,' said Geraldine.

Raj looked around him. 'Anyone got a phone?'

Geraldine shook her head. 'What about the robot thing, he must be on the internet? I mean he controls it, doesn't he?'

Raj tapped some more keys and a screenful of code appeared. 'Alice, I am going to have to stop you.'

Mrs Merkenstand ran over to grab Raj's keyboard. 'Hey, get off!'

Geraldine grabbed Mrs Merkenstand's hair, pulled her back and pointed the shotgun. 'One more move out of you and I'll use it.'

'Alice, you know you can't go there. I am the only admin here.'

Raj carried on tapping. Another explosion and the screens flickered and went dark. 'Shit, shit... there must be a back–' The lights came back on. 'Startup... or have some kind of cache. Please...' The screens by Mr Merkenstand's bed flickered into life and some other machines whirred.

Daisy was holding one of the shotguns and it was pointed at Raj. 'I need to ask my father another question.' She walked over to Raj.

Weaver ran in with his lame, bloodied arm swinging around like a loose branch. 'Mrs Merkenstand, we need to leave. The whole building is burning.'

Weaver walked past Daisy, Raj and Geraldine, his eyes were crazed like some demon was after him.

Daisy went over to Weaver. 'Stop them!' She pointed to Geraldine and Raj. 'It's an order.'

'Sorry, Miss, but you don't own me.' He grabbed the gun away from her.

'Where's Rebwar?' Geraldine asked Weaver, who just walked past her.

'Stuck in the lift,' said Raj.

She looked over at the monitor. 'Shit, where's that?'

Raj tapped at the keyboard. Weaver grabbed Mrs Merkenstand's arm.

'Weaver! Get off me, Listen, man, we need to save my son! Call 999!'

'Mrs Merkenstand, it's too late, we need to go. The place is going to burn down.'

'It can't! We're on a lake. Call! Call for help. Now!'

Weaver slapped her face a couple of times and grabbed her. Mrs Merkenstand tried to fight him off. Daisy joined in and Weaver struck Daisy's head with the shotgun's butt. She fell unconscious, her white dress spread around her slowly mopping up pools of blood. Weaver dragged out Mrs Merkenstand, who was still protesting.

'I think they might have a point,' said Raj. 'How do we get out of this house of cards?' He carried on typing on the keyboard.

'Alice, please stop otherwise I am going to act. Where is my mother? Please, I must speak to her. She needs to know that there is a problem. We have lost control of Plan B. Alice? Stop now! I am going to have to trigger the protocol. There has been a security breach. Adder has taken my mother?'

'Can we somehow copy this?' said Raj. 'It's... genius... I mean, really.'

'Now you're asking what?' said Geraldine. 'It's going to go Pete Tong. This system is fucked up, and I mean fucking fucked up.'

Beads of sweat appeared on Raj's forehead.

FIFTY-SIX

Rebwar jumped up in the dark and tried to grab a concrete ledge above him. But his hands kept slipping off it. The lift gave in and began sliding down, creaking, screeching, picking up speed as it slid down the shaft. He watched the floors pass by but hesitated, as the guillotine-like consequence of mistiming his vault was too daunting. The lift carried on down to the garage where it bounced to a stop. The motion felt like it had hit some kind of soft surface, which to him made little sense. He looked down, but it was too dark to see. He crouched down onto the floor of the lift and felt water seeping through his fingers. The open doors faced a concrete wall and there was no way out. The water slowly rose above his knees and his breathing quickened. He pressed the alarm button in desperation. He banged the lift with his fists and the noise bounced around like a drum. It reminded him of solitary confinement, something he had endured a few times in his life.

The first time was as a teenager in Teheran where he had been caught stealing some bananas from a market stall. At that time, they were a rare commodity and had to be smuggled into the country. He had been lucky not to have had a hand chopped off. The jail time made him think about changing his ways and, after being sent off to the front, he joined the police force.

His second stint was in the army where he had taken the rap for his friend for going AWOL. But that had been worth it, as his friend Faizal spent a night with a young local girl. Both of them virgins. The following day Faizal was made to cross a minefield and his foot found one. Rebwar was in jail that week with a mix of guilt and a sense that Faizal had at least had something to take with him. Of course, you were sent over those dunes with the promise of meeting seventy-two virgins in the afterlife. Something that any teenager would relish and believe. Believe, because that was better than being bombed, shot at and beaten.

Escape was something of which Rebwar was now in dire need. The water had reached his waist, and the lift wasn't floating up. Even swimming lessons wouldn't help. This wasn't an end he had thought of, it was something more banal, like getting hit by a car or falling off a ladder. Nothing dramatic like taking a bullet or getting knifed like a hero. He didn't want that, even though he thought Hourieh wished it. His memory would be polished to within an inch of its life. Exaggerated and invested and made into something he wasn't. No, he wanted something simple – no fuss, just that you were here on this earth and you did good. Nothing extraordinary; that was for criminals, crooks, chiefs and the odd, amazing man who dedicated his life to good. He was none of them. And Musa... He felt angry and sad. He should have done more for his son.

Water had now reached his neck, and he felt like he was being throttled. Maybe this was his penance for being a bad father. His breathing became more and more erratic with the thought of drowning, a fear of which he had since child-hood as he had never learned to swim. None of his friends had, as it was not a skill that anyone needed. He shouted again for help. It was like an admission of defeat and fate. He hated it. The water smelled of diesel, which choked him and made him cough. His hands tried to grab the panels in the lift, but he just slipped. His eyes stung. Panic began to take over. He was losing control of his thoughts and actions – what had happened to Weaver? – when he smelled smoke. There was a jolt from the lift and then another one, some whirring and creaking. Was this the end? Was it going to implode? His body would be found in a metal coffin.

The lift moved up. It struggled to move with all that extra weight. But it was moving. How? Rebwar tried to see, but his eyes were filled with tears. A ray of light appeared just off the top of the lift. The lift had moved up to the ground floor. It bounced and dropped again to block the light. The lift's cables groaned and creaked. Rebwar heard Geraldine's voice. He shouted back and couldn't even remember what, as his panic was still present.

'Are you all right?'

As the lift arrived on the ground floor, water escaped and spilt over the marble reception. Like a shot Rebwar jumped off it and rolled on the cool slippery marble floor. He breathed in and coughed. Smoke had filled the hall. Geraldine helped him to get up. She was holding a handker-chief over her face.

'We need to go! The place is going to blow!'

'Where is everybody?'

Geraldine called out, 'Raj, Raj! He's out. Stop the lift... Are you all right?'

Rebwar coughed and wiped his eyes. 'What's going on?'

Water was now gushing out from the lift like a hole in a boat. A film of dirt and oil quickly covered the floor.

'I... I thought this place was above–'

'Quick, quick!' Geraldine was on the steps motioning Rebwar to come over. Raj was looking down from the landing above.

Rebwar's foot slipped on the floor, which with the water and grease had become an ice rink. As carefully and as quickly as he could, he made it onto the carpeted stairs and ran up them. His lungs burned with desperation. 'We need a boat!' he said.

'We're going to have to swim!' said Raj.

'There must be a boat.'

'How did the others get off?' said Geraldine.

Raj shrugged.

'How is this place sinking?' said Rebwar. 'Something must float.'

Raj shrugged again.

Geraldine walked into one of the bedrooms and opened a large window. Bubbling water and pops and bangs came from downstairs. 'We are going to have to jump.'

'Remember, I have a lifeguard certificate,' said Raj. 'I can swim you to the shore.'

'I can't swim! No!'

'Uncle, listen... just relax. Relax.'

Rebwar looked around him for some solution. 'Easy for you to say. What about–'

'This place is going down.' Geraldine looked over the balcony.

Rebwar came over and glanced at the drop. It was a whole floor or more above the water, which resembled a black hole. Rebwar grabbed a wooden shutter and lifted it.

It popped off its hinges, and he threw it over the side. It splashed into the water and sank.

'Fuck, what was that made of?' Raj looked at it.

'Probably bulletproof.'

'You're going to have to jump with me. OK?'

Rebwar looked at him, his only option, and he knew that there wasn't any other way. Again, something he had been avoiding all his life. He was glad his son could swim. It had been something he had insisted on. Why hadn't he done it too? 'Old dog' came to his mind.

'Uncle. Uncle!' Raj snapped. 'On three?'

'What?'

'On three?'

'I'll go first... it looks deep but...' Geraldine climbed over the concrete bannister and balanced herself on the ledge.

'What do you mean?'

Geraldine looked at Rebwar and smiled. She jumped. It was as if gravity had stopped; her body took forever to hit the water. Was it so much higher? A splash bounced off the building's walls, echoing over the lake. A white mark showed where Geraldine had gone into the water. Rebwar waited for her to reappear. Had she sunk? When he heard her shout, Rebwar breathed again and Raj laughed too, letting their emotions out like a madness.

'It's lovely! Come in!'

Rebwar said, 'But—' and was interrupted by Raj climbing over the bannister, his huge body balancing between the edge and the abyss. Rebwar did the same and looked down. Geraldine was like a little star in space.

'One...'

Raj grabbed Rebwar's hand. His heart pounded like it wanted to escape and jump before him.

'Two...'

Raj breathed, his huge chest filling up like a balloon. 'Three!'

Raj dropped, and Rebwar felt his hand being tugged, and he followed. It went on forever, free falling into space. He saw windows pass by and the living room where DCI Sands's body was. Water was filling the room, and it was a mess of floating items. It didn't make sense he was still falling and hadn't hit the water. It was as if he was a bird. Then there was a violent crash and it felt as if he was being beaten and rubbed up by huge wet towels. He felt his body being pulled in all directions. A rush of noise filled his senses. Then came peace as he floated and opened his eyes. There was a void around him like he was in space. Was he dead? He opened his mouth and felt water rush in. His chest panicked and heaved uncontrollably. He felt a tug from above and he rose and felt air hit his face. He breathed and coughed and carried on till he could hear the shouting and laughter. Raj was holding him with one arm around his chest.

'Uncle, breathe, OK? Breathe. I've got you.'

Rebwar looked around him.

'Kick with your feet to help me. OK?'

Rebwar tried to say yes but could only cough. Windows exploded above them and water gushed out like fountains. Glass shards plopped like bullets around them.

Geraldine was already swimming to the shore. 'Fuck, it's going down!' Metal groans and stone-like cracks came from the building.

Rebwar could hear Raj's breathing; it was loud and strong. He could feel himself being pulled along. Last time that happened he had been blown into the air when a tank next to him had been hit. All he could remember was a flash and a bang. Then two men had dragged him along the sand;

everything hurt and his head had felt dented. It was the helmet which had caught a piece of metal still sizzling away. He thought his head had burst open.

An explosion travelled through him, and he realised it was from the manor. It looked small and low. Raj was next to him, standing over him, smiling.

'Uncle, you can now get up.'

Rebwar kneeled in the mud. Geraldine was out of breath and he looked at Raj. He hadn't been joking about his swimming skills and fitness.

'Where do you think the others are?' said Raj.

'Fuck knows,' said Geraldine. 'You'd think my colleagues would have come by now.'

Rebwar stood by the edge of the lake. Reeds reached his waist. Lights flickered from the windows. The manor looked like a sinking liner. Some deep thuds came through the ground. Rebwar looked around and saw a white horse galloping towards them with a rider.

'What the fuck?' said Raj.

Rebwar could see a semi-naked body riding the horse.

'Godiva?'

It was Daisy, wearing what was left of her wedding dress. Bits of it were smouldering and the horse's footsteps resonated over the ground like a jackhammer. It galloped past them like an apparition.

'And I thought it was a myth. I enjoyed that,' said Geraldine.

'I saw her first,' said Raj.

'We need to find the others,' said Rebwar.

'Why? It's over, look!' said Raj. 'It was in there. The computer, that mummy, the palace. What's the point? Your employer is dead and you're free.'

Rebwar looked over the lake and thought about it. It was

a weird feeling. As it didn't feel like freedom. He had somehow believed all of Charlie's lies and corruptions. They had been part of his day-to-day life. It was like living with a virus that would everyday give you a nudge. Hey, shithead, I'm here and want some attention. Now it was gone. Rebwar looked over at Geraldine and she looked equally shell-shocked. She had sat down a bit further up the embankment staring at the half-sunken manor.

'So, what now?' said Rebwar.

'Fuck!' Raj stood up. 'Error 2000-0141, of course... what an idiot.'

Rebwar and Geraldine looked at each other.

'There's some kind of data centre, that's what the error code meant. The computer had lost its connection. I'm sure.'

It dawned on all of them.

Raj carried on. 'They are stealing the data. Like Daisy said, they are stealing stuff. Data millions and millions of users' information. What they do, eat, credit cards, Amazon accounts. And they needed to access that computer.' Raj pointed at the sunken manor. 'To get the location. I'm sure.'

Rebwar looked at the smoke spread over the lake. 'We have to–'

'What about the old manor location?'

'Isn't it under the lake?'

'But you could use all this water to cool a data centre. We need to find a pipe.'

Rebwar stood up and looked around him. He pointed to a concrete box along the edge of the lake. They rushed over to it.

FIFTY-SEVEN

Rebwar and Geraldine had found the water inlet and followed a series of manholes just south of the manor.

Rebwar listened. 'Can you hear that?'

'Police?' Said Raj.

Sirens echoed through the trees.

'No, no. Fans? Cooling... coming from...' He turned to face the edge of the forest and walked towards a fence. It had a number of warning signs. Rebwar saw a chain with a padlock lying on the ground beside the metal gates. The lock had been cut, and he pushed the gate which swung freely open. They both walked through, not saying a word and feeling like trespassers. The humming sound got louder as they walked on, deeper into the forest. The pathway ended at a concrete entrance that led underground. A heavy metal door was ajar. Rebwar went up to it and listened in.

'We should call this in,' said Geraldine. 'Rebs, let's talk about this.'

Rebwar looked at them both, their faces staring back,

looking tired and emotional. 'I need to know where my family is. You two go and get help.'

'Rebs, listen, we know Charlie and her cronies are in there, we've got them and we can end this by getting help. We can't do this alone. Look what's happened...'

Rebwar shook his head and knew he had to go in there. 'What if they get away, or get killed? I can't let my family down... I can't, not again. Understand?'

'Uncle, it's too dangerous, they've got weapons and they're psychos. We're lucky to be alive.'

Rebwar walked into a long dark concrete tunnel and heard them shouting after him. It was cool and damp. A couple of lights flickered along the wall. Rebwar could feel something was up and walked with his back to the left wall. He reached another door – again, slightly ajar. This one was a little different; thick, heavy and concrete in a metal casing. He pushed it open; the hinges creaked under the weight. He could smell something very recognisable which was etched in his memory from the battlefields of Iran. Discharged firearms and the pungent ferrous smell of blood. He spotted a couple of empty casings, picked them up and smelled them. A semi-automatic and still a little hot. There were a few drops of blood and he followed them deeper into the bunker till he was faced by another three doors. These had viewing windows. He could see loads of little flashing lights. He carefully looked in them so as not to be shot at. He listened. Apart from a slight dull electrical drone, it was quiet.

Rebwar pulled on the handle of the door and opened it. A breeze of cool air came at him, followed by the humming sounds of fans. He crouched down and looked into the room. It was big and filled with five rows of whirring machines. There were racks with computers, coloured wires looping in between them. Another couple of spent cartridges lay by the first row. The acrid smell of burnt plastic lingered around a stack of machines that clicked and squeaked. Below them were pieces of broken plastic. Rebwar carried on down the aisle, listening and looking for any movement.

He carried on, making his way to the end. He stopped at the edge of the last rack, popped his head round and instantly crouched. He looked again. A hand was slumped out from the next row with a pool of blood around it. Rebwar crawled around the rack and saw that it was Brunje. He looked up the aisle; it was clear. He lifted the wrist and tried to feel for a pulse. Brunje's pale white face was drained of blood, his lips nearly blue. Rebwar felt his neck for a pulse. Nothing. His eyes looked crazed, and he had probably been injured in the shootout in the manor and bled to death.

He opened his jacket and went through his pockets. A mobile phone and some money, but nothing else. Rebwar grabbed the man's gun, which was still in his other hand, a Glock 26. He checked the magazine – seven bullets left. Rubber squeaked. The floor was tiled and shiny.

'Charlie, I'm here,' Rebwar called out and looked under the server racks to see if he could see someone. He spotted movement in a corner and he crawled to the end of the aisle. Knight and Charlie, the last of them. He cocked the pistol and peeked over to the corner. He ducked back for cover as a shot rang out and hit a server. It was followed by another.

'Just tell me where my family is and I'll leave. OK?'

He heard a laugh. 'So you figured it out,' said Charlie.

Rebwar knew they were going to try to outflank him. Distract him by keeping him talking.

'Who worked it out? Geraldine, Raj? You know, I was a

little surprised that you hadn't worked it out before. You know the plan was to kill you but you just played along.' Charlie laughed. 'You all did.'

'Who's protecting you? I don't believe you did all this on your own. You know that. You're not clever or powerful enough to do all this on your own. Who's protecting you?'

He got up and walked over to Brunje's body.

'No one, you know I was the brains behind that whole bank scam. That's why Plan B recruited me... They just...'

Rebwar crouched down and looked under the racks. A few aisles along he saw a set of boots walking to the other end. He guessed it was Knight.

'Just didn't know... Where's your friends? It's actually quite convenient that you're here. We need a fall guy.'

Rebwar grabbed Brunje under his shoulders and dragged him in the direction of the footsteps.

'Rebwar, you can make this easy and come out with your hands up. You're outnumbered. Think about it. Think about your wife and son, I'm then only one who knows where they are.'

Rebwar stopped by the last rack of servers. He breathed in and crouched down to get a better hold on Brunje's body. He was torn between either holding them up till the police would come or taking them on. It had been a constant back and forth. He tried to think what Hourieh would say. He'd missed her advice, and it had been a long time since he'd asked her. It was for her own safety and look what good that had done. He had to get her back.

'Rebwar, listen to me, we can work this out. I can make you an offer.'

He pulled Brunje's body up; it was unwieldy, like a sack with limbs, and he tried to make him stand. Rebwar inched the body out over the corner of the server. A series of shots rang out. Metal clanged, blood spurted, sparks flew and bits of concrete exploded. Rebwar let go of Brunje's body and it flopped onto the floor. He stepped out with the gun and shot. Knight stepped back. Each shot was like a punch, and she hit the back wall. Her body slid down leaving a bloody trail. He checked the pistol magazine. Four bullets. Took a deep breath. 'What's the offer?'

'Come here and we can talk about it.'

From the direction of Charlie's voice, he knew she had moved. She still had an advantage over him as she knew the layout of the facility. And she was trying to work him into a trap. Rebwar made his way towards Knight's body. He reckoned that Charlie was along the last aisle or the previous one. He didn't know if she could use a gun. The Filthy Five might have given her a crash course and there was a shotgun which wasn't on Knight's body.

'How much? Fifty-fifty?'

Charlie laughed. 'Nice one, how does twenty per cent?'

'Of what?'

'It's millions, don't worry about that. Just need you to come here with your hands up.'

'And you're asking me to trust you. I think I've learned not to. You know that they're coming?'

'Exactly, time to make up your mind. Money, family, freedom. Think about it.'

Rebwar had two more aisles to go. He couldn't trust her and she knew that too. Classic time-wasting. But in whose favour, he wasn't too sure as she could still get away with this. She had made a case that he and Geraldine were behind this, carefully made sure that they had been involved in all her schemes. She still had the authority over the police, even if Geraldine was the only actual police officer and he had to save his family.

'What have you got? I mean, you need Pinky to get to the treasure and she's dead.'

'I've got what I want.'

He heard a glass smash, and orange emergency lights started flashing. A synthetic voice commanded them to stay calm and evacuate. She'd activated the fire alarm. Rebwar ran over to Knight's body. He glanced to his left down the row of servers, Charlie was on the move. He grabbed two ammunition clips and ran to the end of the aisle. Peeking over, he saw that the exit door was open. Took another deep breath and made his way to the door. He heard a gunshot followed by another one.

Rebwar peeked over again and saw Geraldine on the floor holding on to her bleeding arm. Charlie had broken the shotgun and was loading another two cartridges.

'Don't or I'll shoot.'

Charlie turned around.

'Not a move or I'll shoot. I mean it.'

She smiled and raised the shotgun, and without hesitation Rebwar shot her twice. The first hit her shoulder, which made her fall back and discharge both barrels of the gun. The second went into her side and she fell to ground. USB memory sticks scattered on the concrete floor. Rebwar rushed over to her.

'Tell me where they are.'

Charlie struggled to breathe and she coughed up blood. Rebwar felt warm blood oozing out of her side. Had intended to injure Charlie, but had delivered a fatal shot.

'Where are they? Tell me now.'

Charlie tried to speak, but only a muffled gurgling noise came out of her mouth. Her eyes were rolling back. Rebwar slapped her in desperation. He looked over at Geraldine, who had crawled over to the wall and propped herself up. Grimacing with pain. Charlie's body went limp.

'You bitch, son of a dog. Where are they?' He fell to his knees and looked up.

'I'm, OK, thanks.'

'Good.' Rebwar picked up a handful of memory sticks and threw them to the ground.

'Police are coming.'

Geraldine had been lucky, Charlie had missed with her first shot, and the second had only partly hit her right shoulder. The pellets only making superficial tissue damage. She still had to wear a sling, but that didn't stop her from driving her manual car, which she was driving to the Gladstone Clinic where she had dropped off Beckie a few weeks before. It seemed like at least a month longer than that. She could only remember that it was a Monday. Geraldine hadn't contacted Beckie since and was very nervous. She knew she should have visited her but hadn't found the time. Or that was what she told herself. Why hadn't she made more of an effort to visit? Not even a text saying *I miss you, love xxx.* Beckie hadn't sent anything either... but that wasn't the point. Geraldine rolled her finger in her hair, waiting for the traffic light to turn green. But she still loved her, didn't she, and... The car behind her hooted. Geraldine found first gear and moved forward.

After listening to the sat nav's instructions, she parked in front of the clinic. It looked so innocent, like a suburban townhouse that some sweet family would live in. She switched off the engine and sat there. She wanted to cry. The whole world felt like it was falling in on her. She now wanted Beckie to cry on and hug. To feel her warmth enveloping her like a soothing bath. She stepped out of the car and walked over to the front door. A woman was sitting at the reception, tapping away at a computer. Her thick lenses magnifying her dark green eyes. They matched the dress that held in her large figure. She looked up at Geraldine. 'Can I help you?'

'Yes, I'd like to see Beckie Webster.'

'Have you got an appointment?'

'No.'

She looked down and tapped something into the computer. 'She's checked out.'

'Oh, did she... When?'

'A few hours ago. I think.'

'By herself... I thought...'

'I can't–'

Geraldine put her warrant card in front of her. 'Who took her?'

'Oh.' The woman picked up the warrant card and checked out Geraldine. 'It says here that Mr Webster came to collect her.'

'How did he? For fuck's sake. Who authorised it? Don't you know he beats her?'

'Look, I only work here. And it's her next of kin.'

'What the fuck, cunting bollocks. Sorry... It's just that she's not in safe hands.'

'Should I call the consultant?'

Geraldine was already on her way out to the car. And as soon as she was in she was typing in Beckie's address on the sat nav.

It took her over an hour to get there. She had tried to call and left a few messages, which increased in urgency. She came close to calling her colleagues to go into her house, but knew she had no authority to do that. Kurtis Webster was Beckie's husband and so had a right to collect her. This made her even angrier. How did that cheating, wife-beating bastard of a husband deserve her? She walked up the stairs to the front door and froze in front of it, thinking of her last love, Zara. Geraldine quickly shut those emotions out. They were still there, and the door brought flashbacks. The door was locked, but she had a key that Beckie had given her. Had Webster changed the locks? If he knew, most probably. The lock turned and unlocked. The second lock opened the door. It was deadly quiet.

Geraldine stepped in as quietly as she could, making sure that every step was as soft as a cat's. But why? She listened and then walked right into the kitchen. There was no point in being so covert as she had to find Beckie. She hadn't looked to see if Webster's car was outside. She rushed into the living room and ran upstairs. Her heart stopped as she walked into the bedroom. Webster and Beckie were on the bed. He was holding a syringe and Beckie's arm had a rubber tube tied above her elbow. Her face was bleeding and swollen. Without thinking of her injury Geraldine lunged at Webster, who tried to inject Beckie. It missed and went into the duvet. He shouted at her. Geraldine awkwardly tried to hit Webster but only scuffed his arm. Her momentum made her trip on the bed and she fell beside it onto her injured arm.

Webster kept hold of the syringe and he plunged it into Geraldine's arm. Geraldine screamed with pain and fear and like a rabid animal she grabbed it off him. Both held on to the syringe and wrestled as if it was a knife. Both of them screamed. Geraldine had expected some kind of effect from the needle, but he hadn't managed to plunge it. She got off the bed and crawled towards the door. Webster was powerful and Geraldine could feel her energy ebbing, and it was only a matter of time till he had the upper hand. He knew that too. Geraldine shouted for Beckie's help. The adrenaline was keeping the pain away, but not for long.

'Don't you dare, bitch! Go and get the bat and get this fat-arsed dyke off me.'

Geraldine headbutted him. The two skulls clonked, and the pain reverberated like two bells. His grip loosened and Geraldine ran for the door where Beckie had already crawled out. In the large hallway leading to the stairs was Beckie with a baseball bat. Her eyes were wide and wild and she lifted the wooden bat above her head and screamed. Her t-shirt was stained with blood. She ran towards Geraldine who froze in shock. The bat swung down at her head. Geraldine closed her eyes and heard an impact. It was a dull crunch. Why wasn't she feeling anything? A large mass fell behind her and made her jump. Geraldine looked behind her. Webster's limp body lay on the white carpet. His blood oozed over the white carpet.

'Is he all right?'

'No, I think you've knocked him out.'

Beckie swung the bat and hit his chest. He groaned with pain. And she hit him again. 'He's still breathing! You fucking shithead, cunt, bastard, cheating bastard! And you think you can just fucking get rid of me like that!' She kicked him. 'Hey! Hey! Fuck face! I'm talking to you! And I thought you were a decent guy picking me up!' Beckie hit his legs with the bat.

Geraldine stopped her and gave her a huge hug. Beckie collapsed into her arms and began to sob uncontrollably.

'I think we need to call the police.' Geraldine looked down and Webster had gone. 'Fuck he's–'

A rumble of noise came from the landing. They both ran out of the bedroom. A trail of blood showed that Webster had crawled and fallen down the stairs and was lying at the bottom. His body lay very still and in an awkward position.

'How are we going to explain this?'

Geraldine felt nausea rise up from her stomach. 'We will. We will.'

FIFTY-NINE

Rebwar had been kept overnight in police custody and they had only asked him a few questions about what had happened in that data centre. Rebwar just kept asking them about his son and wife. He'd lost his patience with them a couple of times, screaming at them to do something about his kidnapped family, but they kept ignoring him. It was like they were letting him cool off and observing. In the end no one official came to see him and in the morning they let him go and he figured it was up to him to find his family. He took a cab to the hotel where they had checked in after being evicted, thinking that it was the best place to start to get some clues.

He called Geraldine but the line was dead. Had she been taken in? He dialled Hourieh's phone, dead too and he feared the worst. They hadn't had quality time together since... He really couldn't remember when. It might have been at Bijan's or at a cafe. If he had a choice he would go on the run. Iran was a closed door to him, but maybe not to Hourieh; it was a risk, but she was probably willing to take it. He stood outside the hotel, smoking his cigarette, taking a moment to calm himself, looking at life passing by, something he hadn't done for a while, just watching birds fly into the green trees, cars passing by, mothers pushing strollers around and children playing in the street. Life just got on with things and he didn't have to worry about it.

Maybe that was what Hourieh had been trying to tell him. Find a job that will let you flow down a river. He was more of a bridge that waited to see what the current brought to him. He stubbed out his cigarette and walked into the reception. The woman behind the wooden counter looked up and smiled and waited for him to say something; Rebwar had forgotten which room they were in.

'I'm Rebwar.'

'Hi, yes, what can I do for you?'

Rebwar read her name badge. 'Hi, Jennifer, I would like the key to the room.' He had tried to call Hourieh, but there was no connection, Musa's too.

'What number?'

'I... I have forgotten.'

'Sorry, but I need to see some ID.'

Rebwar got his wallet out and got out some bank cards and his driving license. It was a fake one, and she picked it up.

'Thanks.' She looked at it and handed him a plastic card. 'Number 234.'

'Thank you, no messages for me?'

She tapped the keyboard, looked around the wooden desk and shook her head. Rebwar headed off to the lift.

He stood in front of the door and listened for any voices or sounds. He knocked. Nothing. He presented the card, and the lock made a mechanical sound. He walked in. It was quiet and clean, smelled of bleach and a hint of pine perfume. There was suitcase at the bottom of the bed that he recognised as his. He then saw an envelope on the bed with his name on it. He took the envelope and opened it. It was a handwritten letter from Hourieh.

———

Dear Husband

With a heavy heart and guilt, I have had to make this decision without you. But it is for the best. I don't want to explain myself to you why I decided to leave and it can't be a surprise to you as you put us in danger. We are both OK and were safely released and I am sorry that I didn't call you but you crossed a line. Musa is well and I know how much you love him and you are his father. But this is not a life for us. I have faithfully followed you all my life, and you have brought many laughs and tears. This place, England, is not for me. I can't make it a home as I need friends. I can't tell you where I am going even though you will probably find out. But I am not going to make it easy as I need time to think. Although, as you probably know, my mind is made up. Sorry that you had to read this and not hear it. But it is for the best.

Hourieh, love

P.S. Musa never liked football.

———

Rebwar sat on the bed. He took out a box of cigarettes, selected one, and with a trembling hand lit it. He drew deep into his lungs, lay down on the bed and watched the white ceiling. At least they were alive.

DID YOU ENJOY THE BOOK?

Thank you for reading my book and hope you enjoyed as much I did writing it. If you could find a moment to leave a review for which I would be eternally grateful for. This helps other readers to find this book and share the buzz. It only has to be a few words, a rating or even a helpful vote on a reviewer's comments. It all helps us indie authors to get the word out.

The Contact

Sign up at www.olsschaber.com and get your free novella.

A prequel to the Rebwar series where we meet his first contact Clive. A dramatic inciting incident sets off a chain of events where Rebwar is left to pick up the pieces.

Rebwar - The Missing Parts

(Book 1)

Ex-Iranian police detective Rebwar hides from his past behind the wheel of his London Uber. But when an enigmatic organisation threatens to expose his identity, he has no choice but to lend them his skills. And when his missing persons assignment leads only to a severed foot, he'll have to connect it to a body to prevent being deported.

When he finds his quarry's wife in bed with another man, Rebwar is forced to revive his old interrogation methods to extract a confession. But when the case is closed despite body parts still appearing, he's convinced there is more to the murder than his superiors want known. Determined to learn the truth, his private investigation uncovers a conspiracy that could see him torn to pieces.

The Gipsy

(Book 2)

Rebwar struggles to recover from his last brutal case. But with his illegal migrant status used by his shadow organisation bosses to hold him under their thumb, he's stuck working at an East End car wash... until the owner is gunned down before his eyes. And when his handler wants him to find out why, he's forced back into the underbelly of the city's deadliest streets.

Going undercover as a delivery man, Rebwar follows the clues to a disturbing human-trafficking operation. But when he runs into an old adversary willing to get their hands dirty, the desperate military man worries he's walking right into an unmarked grave.

Can Rebwar destroy a smuggling ring before he's the next to eat a bullet?

ACKNOWLEDGMENTS

I must thank the people around me that have made this series possible. I feel so lucky to have them there and they encourage me to keep going. It's quite an undertaking writing a good yarn and even more to self publish. I couldn't have done it without them. My amazing wife Tracey, my editor Ed Handyside, my brother Fred, and so many other great friends. You know who you are.

Ols Schaber, The Missing Parts: Rebwar. Kindle Edition.